HUSTLE

OWEN MULLEN

Boldwood

First published in Great Britain in 2022 by Boldwood Books Ltd.

Copyright © Owen Mullen, 2022

Cover Photography: depositphotos

A CIP catalogue record for this book is available from the British Library.

Paperback ISBN 978-1-80048-435-1

Large Print ISBN 978-1-80048-434-4

Hardback ISBN 978-1-80415-498-4

Ebook ISBN 978-1-80048-436-8

Kindle ISBN 978-1-80048-437-5

Audio CD ISBN 978-1-80048-429-0

MP3 CD ISBN 978-1-80048-430-6

Digital audio download ISBN 978-1-80048-431-3

Boldwood Books Ltd
23 Bowerdean Street
London SW6 3TN
www.boldwoodbooks.com

For Devon and Harrison Carney

One of you told me real monsters don't wear shoes.
Very soon you'll read this and know that isn't true.

Three people can keep a secret if two of them are dead.

— DANNY GLASS

THE PLAYERS:

Luke Glass... Head of London's most powerful crime family
Nina Glass... Luke's sister and front woman of Glass Houses Real Estate
Charley Glass... Luke's sister and face of LBC nightclub
George Ritchie... Front man/enforcer for all illegal activities south of the River Thames
Mark Douglas... Head of security north of the river
Oliver Stanford... Once Danny Glass' pet poodle, now a high-ranking officer in the Metropolitan Police Service and still on The Family payroll
Felix Corrigan... Gang boss in east London and George Ritchie's second in command

Posh Boys (the Toffee gang):
Rafe ... Henry's elder brother and leader of the gang
Henry... Rafe's younger brother and reluctant member
Julian... Rafe's partner in crime
Coco... Rafe's lover and thrill seeker

Street Gang:
Thomas Timpson, aka TT ...Gang leader
Jethro/Jet...Gang member
Boz... Gang member

POLAND STREET, SOHO, LONDON

It had been a cold day in the capital, the coldest of the year, and with the temperature dropping snowflakes fluttered and fell on the crowds hurrying about their business on Shaftesbury Avenue. A guy in a Santa beard and jeans torn at the knees knocked seven bells out of the Wizzard classic 'I Wish It Could Be Christmas Everyday', loud and raw, his breath condensing in the chilly air. He wore a red and white woolly hat, and gloves with the fingers cut off so he could play. On the ground in front of him a collection of coins, mostly silver, lay in his open guitar case. The woman in a cashmere coat rushing by had gone for a walk to kill time before her appointment. Now, she was late and didn't give the busker a second glance. In Wardour Street, she passed St Anne's churchyard and kept going. Across from The Ship public house, once a watering hole of John Lennon and Jimi Hendrix, she made a left, then a right into Poland Street where her car was parked, walking purposefully, in no doubt where she was going.

The entrance to the building was lit by a single bulb hanging from the ceiling inside the doorway. She hesitated, drew her expensive coat around her and climbed the stairs. Behind her, a car pulled to a stop near the green and gold façade of the Star and Garter. Like the busker with the guitar, she didn't notice the three people in black reefer jackets who got out, or the good-looking guy with the stylish blond hair leading them.

In his office on the second landing, Jan Stuka was waiting. With more than sixty years in the trade, the old jeweller had no need to advertise his talents. He'd owned the room in Poland Street for decades, though only came here when he had a client to meet. Stuka was a craftsman, an artist, a stout little man with a goatee and spectacles, who could've set up shop in Hatton Garden like so many others and guaranteed himself a comfortable living. Instead, he'd gone a different route, fashioning bespoke pieces using only top-quality gems, singular creations for those interested in the best.

When she'd explained she wanted a bracelet for a man with the inscription *From N to M – all my love,* he'd stared balefully over his wire-rimmed spectacles; romantic messages on an item she could've bought from any high-street shop left him unmoved, and for a second the woman was convinced coming to him had been a mistake. The necklace had brought a different reaction. As she'd described what she imagined, he'd mellowed, making notes in a small dog-eared book, asking questions in a guttural accent, even finding the enthusiasm to suggest the male jewellery might be a classic design, eighteen-carat gold cuff – simple and stylish.

Perfect; she was delighted: someone was going to be very pleased.

During her second visit he'd shown detailed charcoal sketches based on their previous conversation, including the otherwise plain bracelet and its inscription. Stuka was an old-school artisan crafts-man; he didn't understand high-tech computer-modelling software and made everything by hand. The third time he'd proudly unveiled wax replicas of what he intended to produce, subject to her approval. This evening, they'd select the stones to make the necklace a reality – FL diamonds, flawless and clear, and pure blue sapphires, AAA quality. Finally, he'd tell her how much it was going to cost.

Not that she gave a damn about that.

On the landing, a bodyguard stood to attention, steroid-induced man-breasts pressing against the fabric of his shirt, thick arms folded. He didn't turn his expressionless face towards her until she reached him. When he did, there was no recognition in his dull eyes and she realised the guy was on more than hormones. Swollen fingers tapped the door, the electronic lock buzzed and released. Before he could react, the three figures she hadn't seen on her way in rushed from the shadows wearing balaclavas and pushed her through the door; the butt of a revolver crashed against the side of the guard's head and they dragged him into the room, screaming threats at the old man.

'Open the safe! Don't fuck me about or I'll blow you away!'

Rafe Purefoy's well-modulated voice was at odds with the jargon. The jeweller didn't blink. 'Do this the easy way, granddad, and nobody gets hurt. Don't be afraid.'

'I'm not afraid.'

'Good for you. Just don't be a hero.'

Stuka was telling the truth: by the time the Soviet army arrived, Jan was ten kilos underweight, suffering from tuberculosis and barely able to stand, yet he'd survived in a place where more than a million had perished, his parents and grandparents among them. After that, what was there to fear?

He pulled up his sleeve to reveal the tattoo – 6613145 – faded into the mottled skin.

Defiance burned in the old Jew's eyes. Anger thickened his accent. 'What would trash like you know about heroes?'

The slight didn't faze the robber. He said, 'On another day, I'd buy you a drink and you could tell me what it was like. We'd have an interesting conversation. Except, that isn't where we are, is it? And respecting what you've been through won't stop me putting a bullet in you. Whatever you believe, believe that. Now, open the fucking safe.'

Stuka spat on the bare floorboards at his feet. 'Nie.'

Behind his mask the thief smiled. 'I'm guessing that's Polish for no.'

He grabbed the woman by the arm, pulled her towards him and held the gun to her temple. She stiffened but didn't cry out. Rafe spoke to the jeweller. 'You should've died a long time ago. Somehow, you got lucky and didn't. Eighty years down the line you're fine about it. I understand.' He dug the muzzle into the female's smooth skin. 'Take a look at her. She's what? Thirty-five, thirty-six, maybe? How does she feel about it being all over? Ask her.' His finger closed round the gentle sweep of the trigger. 'In thirty seconds, we'll be leaving empty-handed and you'll both be dead. What I'd call a lose-lose situation. Imagine making it out of a Nazi camp for it to finish in a grubby little cubbyhole in Soho because of a few stones. What would the poor bastards in Auschwitz, Buchenwald and the rest of those hellholes say?' He shook his head at the irony. 'Do what I'm telling you or she gets it. Right here. Right now.'

On the floor the bodyguard groaned, regaining consciousness.

'The old fucker thinks we're bluffing. Let's show him we're not.'

Under the reefer jacket and the balaclava, the speaker was indistinguishable from the other two. The words were hard despite the soft tone. Coco went to the helpless man on the ground and straddled him, arms straight, pointing down, both hands on the revolver. staring into his terrified face, savouring his fear. The bodyguard realised what was coming and held his palms up impotently against it. 'No! No! Don't! It was me who told you.'

'And we're grateful.'

The silenced shots popped like balloons. Nobody would hear

them outside the room. She stepped over the limp body and took up position at the only window as though nothing had happened.

Through the frosted glass, snow was falling on Soho. Stuka said, 'I've met your kind all my life. You're animals.'

The gun barrel carved a perfect circle on the hostage's neck. Tomorrow – if there was a tomorrow – there would be a bruise.

Rafe said, 'We're serious people – you saw what we did to the guard. Tell this old fool you don't want to die. Tell prisoner 6613145 to open the bloody safe before I blow your pretty head off.'

The jeweller's resistance was admirable but it was fading – he *was* afraid, though not for himself. For her. She took a deep breath. 'Don't open it. They're going to kill us, anyway.'

Stuka had seen unbearable inhumanity, yet he couldn't allow himself to believe what she was saying. He shook his grey head. 'No, no, they won't. Not if I give them what they came for.'

'We've just watched them murder an unarmed man. They can't leave us alive. We're witnesses.'

Stuka shook his head. 'Witnesses to what? Masks and jackets? No, we'll be okay if they get what they want.' He turned to the safe embedded in the wall behind him and knelt in front of it. In the silence, the tumblers falling was the only sound. With the last click, the door swung open. Stuka lifted out a grey metal box, set it on the desk and raised the lid. The robbers edged closer: this was why they were here. Inside were four small purple velvet purses with drawstring tops. The jeweller spilled the contents of each one onto the desk in neat piles. Even in the poorly lit office, the gems sparkled and shimmered.

Rafe had to know. 'Why four? Why four pouches?'

'Diamonds and sapphires. Two pouches each: the very good and the very best. I only work with quality.'

'How much are they worth?'

Stuka eyed his captor with contempt. 'Anyone who looks at

these and thinks only of money is a cretin. Sapphires take millions of years to form. A blink of an eye compared with diamonds.' He rolled a perfectly clear stone away from the others with his finger. 'The process that created this beautiful thing began more than a billion years ago. Perhaps even as much as three billion.'

He gave them a second to take in the enormity of what he'd told them, then tilted the desk; a small fortune in stones cascaded in a drumroll on the wooden floor and scattered – after the old man's history lesson, it was the last thing the thieves had expected. The jeweller seized his opportunity, reached for the mask nearest him and clawed it away. 'Now we can identify these cowards.'

Coco screamed, 'Shoot him! Shoot him!'

Rafe hesitated, blinking rapidly, as though he couldn't take in what had happened, and fired. Mr Stuka fell over, his white shirt instantly turning red: shot through the heart, the man who'd survived the horror of a concentration camp died instantly.

Rafe shouted, 'Get the stones! Move, we need out of here!'

The third robber twisted the woman's arm up her back. 'What'll we do with this bitch?'

Coco had no doubts. 'She's seen Rafe's face. Put her down.'

Rafe disagreed. 'No, we'll take her with us in case there's a problem.'

'Don't be stupid. She's seen you, heard your name.'

The leader stood his ground. 'Don't argue, she's coming.'

* * *

Out on the street, the car was waiting with the engine turning over. Behind the wheel, Henry couldn't hide his nervousness; he was still in his teens, younger than the others, and only here because he was Rafe's brother.

'Did something go wrong?' He saw the stranger and realised his question had been answered. 'Who's she?'

'Drive! Just drive!'

'With her? Where?'

'Stick to the plan. Hampstead. Julian's aunt's place like we agreed.'

The wheels spun on the icy road. In the back seat, the woman sitting between Coco and Julian hadn't spoken since telling Mr Stuka not to open the safe. Jan Stuka hadn't listened and it had gone badly for him. The thieves, murderers now, took off their balaclavas. The guy in the front was handsome: perfect white teeth, piercing blue eyes set in smooth boyish skin, and blond hair expensively styled so it fell to one side of his face at the front. Beneath his jacket he wore a midnight-blue silk scarf casually tied at the neck. The girl was slim, twenty-two or -three, with crimson streaks in her black bob matching her painted nails. Two minutes earlier she'd ended a life; no one would guess. Her breathing was steady and calm, detached from the callous crime that had left two dead in the upstairs office.

The third man pulled off the mask and let it drop from his slender fingers to the floor. His face was white, unnaturally pale, the lean jaw covered in designer stubble. Above it, a receding hairline made him look older than his years. Intensity surrounded him like an aura. At its core, an anger that curled the bloodless line of his lips at the edges. He spoke quietly, his tone sharp and crisp, each word heavy with foreboding.

'This is a mistake, Rafe. A huge fucking mistake. We ought to have finished her when we had the chance. She's dangerous.'

Rafe airily dismissed his objection. 'Be a good chap and put a sock in it, Julian. She's fine.' He turned in his seat and smiled at the woman. 'You're not going to be a problem, are you, darling?'

Julian Greyland lowered his grey eyes and resisted the urge to argue. The exchange revealed the pecking order in the group and the tensions between them. The driver didn't count – an immature boy out of his depth on a good day. The other three were very different people with one thing in common – the absolute certainty they were superior.

It wasn't just the plummy accents or the assured way they held themselves; it was everything, and it rolled off them. Killing the jeweller and the guard had cost them nothing because they believed them to be nothing.

Outside the world went about its pre-Christmas business, unaware of the drama. On Wardour Street, heading north, Coco had never felt more alive. She snatched the woman's bag, emptied it onto her lap and sifted through the contents. The soft-leather Hermes purse inside held cash and credit cards, lipstick, a comb and a compact. Nothing unusual. Until she read the cardholder's name.

'Well, well, well.'

Rafe saw the excitement on her face. 'What is it?'

'Guess who we've got here. Guess who this bitch is.'

'Stop fucking about, Coco, who?'

'Nina Glass. We've only kidnapped Luke Glass' sister. Christ Almighty.'

PART I

1

The car crossed Marylebone Road and skirted the black void of Regent's Park on Albany Street. By the time they reached Haverstock Hill, it was snowing heavily and they were forced to slow down. Nobody spoke – not a word – the unnatural silence broken only by the rhythmic slap-slap of the wipers. The young driver's frantic questions about what had gone wrong and why they'd brought the stranger with them had failed to get an answer. Henry didn't ask again and concentrated on following the wet tracks left by the vehicles that had gone before them, glancing wide-eyed across at his brother, seeking reassurance. It didn't come. Rafe stared unblinking through the windscreen and offered him nothing. In the back seat, pressed between the woman who'd shot the bodyguard in cold blood and the third robber, Nina felt the strange mix of tension and elation: whoever these people were, they weren't pros. That brought no comfort; amateurs were unpredictable, likely to panic if they were cornered and do something that couldn't be undone. Robbing the jeweller wasn't supposed to end this way – taking a hostage, especially Luke Glass' sister, hadn't been part of the plan. The driver and the man beside her were spooked – she could smell their fear on them. And frightened people were dangerous people.

The reaction of the leader in the front seat was very different.

'Ye-e-e-sss!!! Yes! Yes! Yes!' He drummed on the dashboard with his fists and turned, grinning, to the three in the back. 'Fucking hell, people! Coco, that was...'

Coco beamed. 'Amazing, just amazing.'

Rafe took her face in his hands and kissed her. For half a minute they locked together. Nina watched until they pulled apart, eyes glazed, cheeks flushed.

'Can't you feel it, Julian? Unbelievable.'

Julian's reply was delivered through gritted teeth, like the warning hiss of a serpent, the intensity behind it unmistakable. 'You and your crazy girlfriend are barking mad.'

'Shut up, you're spoiling it.'

Julian's face was tight with rage. 'I told you she was bad news, you wouldn't listen.'

'And I'm telling you to put a sock in it.'

Julian's fingers dug into the seat. 'Understand me, Rafe, you're responsible for this fiasco.'

Rafe dismissed the accusation. 'You wanted excitement, didn't you? Well, you can't say you didn't get it. Don't be a poor sport.'

'Excitement, yes, absolutely. Not murder.'

'Oh, please, spare me the guilty conscience. This is the best high you've ever had in your dull little life. The blood rushing through your veins, the tingling in your hands – that's adrenaline. What being alive feels like.'

'I'm not going down because you're off your head.'

Rafe didn't rise to it. 'Nobody's going down for anything. We've got away, haven't we?'

'Have we? Let's hope so. If you want to stay out of prison, put a bullet in Glass' sister and toss her out of the car.'

'Are you volunteering?'

Julian's lips pressed in a line; he'd known from the beginning getting mixed up with Rafe Purefoy wasn't one of his better ideas.

Rafe said, 'That's what I thought. Now, be a good little chap and shut your stupid mouth.'

They passed the Stag Belsize Park pub with snow coming down heavier than ever. Henry took a left and edged the car into Fleet Road, gripping the steering wheel in his hands, trying to blot out what was going on.

Coco's tone lacked malice – she might've been offering to make everybody a cup of tea. She said, 'I'll shoot her, if you like.'

Nina heard the detachment in her voice and blanched.

Julian grunted and shook his head. 'Barking fucking psycho bonkers.'

Rafe reached into the back and grabbed him by the lapels. 'Don't push it or you can have the bullet instead of her.'

Coco didn't understand what the fuss was about. 'I'm only trying to be helpful.'

Rafe tightened his grip and pulled Julian closer. 'Are you listening? Coco's only trying to be helpful. Show the girl some appreciation.'

* * *

The disagreement flared and faded, heightening the already toxic atmosphere in the car, but the menacing exchange laid bare the unstable dynamic between them. Rafe went back to staring out of the window, distant and aloof. Henry drove, no longer curious, just scared; Julian restricted his objections to muttering under his breath.

Coco's statement had been chilling. Nina realised all it would need was Rafe to say yes and her life would be over. Rafe had won the power struggle. This time. So long as he was in charge, she was safe. But the female was still dangerous: in the room on the second floor in Poland Street, Coco had taken the lead and murdered the guard, eyes blazing from her balaclava's sockets, on fire with the thrill of ending the helpless man's existence before the others could stop her.

They approached the junction of Pond Road and Elm Terrace at a crawl, wipers working overtime, visibility down to yards, no other vehicle in sight. Through the snowstorm, the lights of the Royal Free Hospital glinted like the amber eyes of wild beasts waiting to attack. Wedged between two of her captors, Nina knew the chances of getting hold of her mobile were nil. Even if she could, they'd take it from her before she could call Luke.

From the moment they'd killed the guard, Nina had understood they couldn't afford to let the old concentration-camp survivor, or her, live. Knowing Luke would hunt them down, drag them to the derelict factory and torture them like the vermin they were was no consolation. She'd only been to Fulton Street once and never wanted to go there again: sometimes, even now, she'd come awake with the sound of wings beating in the rafters of the collapsed ceiling in her ears, and images of the ground stained dark with the blood of those who'd dared cross Danny Glass in her head.

Danny was gone – Nina didn't miss him; he'd been insane. Although the mad bastard would've known how to deal with anybody foolish enough to kidnap his sister – tied to a pillar, screaming in anguish, for them, leaving the world would be agonisingly slow. Luke would do what had to be done without relishing it the way Danny would have, she had no doubt. The result would be the same: long before the end they'd beg to be put out of their misery.

Sweet music Nina regretted she wouldn't hear.

Henry dropped to first gear and edged up South End Road, wheels spinning, losing traction and finding it again. Julian panicked. 'For Christ's sake, don't let it stall. In this weather it might not start again.'

Rafe said, 'My brother knows more about motor cars than you and I put together. While you were cheating your way to a 2:1 at Cambridge, paying people to sit the exams for you, he was taking engines apart and putting them back together. He rebuilt a 1966 Triumph Spitfire all by himself when he was fifteen. Red, wasn't it, Henry?'

'Green.'

'Green, of course. So, fuck off, Julian. Leave him alone.'

'But if it dies on us, we're goosed.'

Rafe didn't hide his irritation, the warning note in his voice clear. 'Keep your nose out.'

The car slewed and slipped back as the tyres polished the surface beneath them to ice. Henry lifted his foot off the accelerator to stop the wheels spinning and steered into the skid. Ten yards further down, the pavement ended the slide with a bump. He voiced what they already knew. 'It can't handle it. We'll have to push.'

'Push?'

Julian's reaction defined him. Rafe's patience had worn thin. 'Yes, push. Get those lily-white hands of yours dirty for the first time in your idle life. Unless you'd rather walk? Everybody out.'

The twin beams of the headlights cut through the falling snow and were lost. Nina's coat, stylish and expensive, was warmer than wool but still useless. She closed it round her and bent her head into the blizzard. Rafe pressed his back against the car's rear end. On the other wing, Julian's snarling complaint was ripped from his lips and tossed into the night by a wind that had arrived from nowhere.

Henry rolled the window down. 'When I say push give it everything you've got. Okay, push!'

The engine roared, the wheels spun impotently, churning up grey slush without gaining an inch.

He shouted. 'Again!'

Blue smoke poured from the exhaust. The car moved a foot, then lost ground.

Running was a poor choice – but it was the only one open to her. Nina palmed her mobile, shrugged out of her coat and handed it to Rafe. 'Put this under the wheel before we all get hypothermia.'

He took it from her, a flicker of something that might've been admiration passing behind his eyes. 'Clever girl. Except, one isn't enough.' He snapped his fingers. 'Coco, give me yours.'

'But, Rafe, it's a Bottega Veneta. Mummy gave—'

'Don't argue. If we don't get out of here, your fucking coat will be the least of your worries. This weather won't last. When it stops, we need to be gone.'

Coco glared at him and did what she was told. Rafe threw the garments under the wheels.

'One more time! Call it, Henry!'

At first, nothing happened, then the tyres gripped the fabric – the car shot forward, Rafe and Julian fell to the ground and Nina ran. Rafe jumped to his feet and started after her.

The options were limited; a hedge kept her to the road and stopped her escaping onto the heath. Snow dragged at her feet, sapping her energy; freezing air burned her throat and chest. Nina heard footsteps behind her, tried to go faster and didn't see the tree stump sticking out of the ground. The heel of her shoe snapped and she sprawled full length, grazing her temple, losing her grip on the mobile. When she raised her head, Rafe was standing over her the way Coco had straddled the bodyguard, his breath clouding in front of him, holding the phone so she could see it.

'Thank you for reminding me about this. We're going to need it.'

Nina brushed snow off her legs and sat up. 'You've no idea what you've got yourself into. My brother's going to take you apart.'

Rafe said, 'You're a spunky lady, Nina Glass. I like your style. But it won't save you.'

2

Beyond the frosted window, Hampstead Heath could've been a dead star a million light years from the sun. In the icy spider's web etched on the pane, Coco saw her reflection splintered like shards of a broken mirror – the short dark hair with its red streaks, the full lips, the self-assured eyes still sparkling from the kill. Her kill. Christ, she'd never felt anything like it.

Behind her, the argument that had been going since they'd left central London raged on, Julian angrily blaming her for what she'd done – a sleaze with an axe to grind.

Rafe had introduced him as a colleague from Sangster-Devlin Global Securities – they both worked in a specialist department known as equity arbitrage – and boasted they were one of the most successful trading teams in the City. Julian had shaken her hand, smiled politely, and pretended they were strangers. They weren't. Far from it: he'd tried to fuck her at a party in a flat in Flood Street. All over her, his hands everywhere. He'd been drunk and got bloody stroppy when she'd rejected his advances. Not something his fragile ego would allow him to forget.

That night in Chelsea, Coco had made an enemy.

With his dark hair and designer stubble, he wasn't unattractive – a lot of women would fancy him. In fact, if he hadn't been a such an insufferable prick he would've been in with a chance. But he *was* a prick. Worse, he didn't know it.

He lifted the brandy to his lips and stabbed an accusing finger in the air. 'Girlfriend or no girlfriend, Rafe, you must've realised she's a headcase! You bring her in, she goes over the top and the whole bloody show turns to shit!'

Julian glared his frustration at the carpet and played with the empty cut-glass tumbler between his palms. 'Killing the jeweller, killing anybody, wasn't supposed to happen.'

Rafe rolled a coin over the backs of his fingers, absently following its progress. He said, 'But it has. You really need to learn to adapt. "Go with the flow" as they say. Poland Street was, on some levels... unfortunate... but the old man gave me no choice. On the other hand—'

The dismissive explanation fired Julian to new heights. 'Gave you no choice. For Christ's sake, listen to yourself, Rafe!' He paced the floor. 'You're starting to believe your own bullshit. We didn't do this for money. Before Toby Lennox at Sangster-Devlin caught on to us messing with the share price—'

'Caught *you*, Julian. Toby caught *you*. I had nothing to do with it.'

The interruption took the heat out of the argument. 'All right, before he caught me, the Jolly Boys were making a ton of the stuff. This was supposed to be a high, a fucking laugh. We're not career criminals. We're not murderers.'

Rafe stopped short of reminding him that, after an eighteen-month-long investigation, both of them had been judged to lack the integrity to work in the Square Mile and been expelled from the register all City professionals were required to be on. Prosecution was still being considered. Jumping out of the bushes and scaring the little people was an exciting distraction and a way of keeping the coffers filled. But Julian was right – it wasn't about money. It was the last hurrah of the disgraced Jolly Boys, the name they'd given themselves, pushing back against the judgement of their peers.

Julian took a step towards Coco. She thought he was going to attack her. He said, 'The jeweller's dead because this bitch told you to shoot him after she'd finished the bodyguard. That wasn't in the plan either. He was on our bloody side.'

'Oh, grow up. He could identify you.'

He shook his head. 'I can't believe what I'm hearing.'

Rafe said, 'Leave her alone.'

Julian turned on him. 'Or what? Or fucking what, Rafe? You two have some weird Bonnie and Clyde thing going on? Is that it? Well, count me out. I've seen that movie. I remember how it ends.'

Rafe lit one of his Gauloises, leaned back in his chair and let him speak; it wouldn't change anything. Julian was rattled and needed to get it out.

'You're overreacting. And you're insulting Coco. She isn't the problem here.'

'You're not serious? Of course, she's the problem. You saw how she stood over him. Saw the look in her eyes. She enjoyed it. Have you any notion what that makes her? I'd put her down like the mad dog she is.'

Rafe went on as if Julian hadn't spoken. 'I realised the plan might go off the rails. Assumed you would, too.'

'Really? This is the first you've mentioned it.'

Rafe sighed. 'You know, you really aren't as bright as you think you are, Julian. Tonight was inevitable.'

Julian let the insult pass; the time would come. His reply fell like a heavy weight. 'Was it?'

'Yes, actually, it was. The moment you bagged us those guns, old chap.'

'Then, why go through with it?'

'You've forgotten why we started. At Sangster-Devlin we were pushing it. We understood that. Didn't stop us, did it? Didn't stop the Jolly Boys.'

'And in case you've forgotten, Rafe, we got caught. Our reputations are in tatters. If we live to be a hundred, we won't get another job in the City.'

'Fuck reputations. As for another job, would you want one? I wouldn't. The same as in Soho tonight, the money had sod all to do with it. Out on the ledge, afraid to look down. Scared shitless and going for it anyway. Admit it to yourself even if you won't admit it to me. It's the best feeling in the world.' He held out his arms. 'What's done is done. The bodyguard was a weak link – look how easily he blabbed about the jeweller when you met him in the gym. For sure, he would've talked and we'd be on the run, instead of in your aunt's house on East Heath Road, helping ourselves to her very nice brandy.'

Julian's opinion didn't change. 'I don't intend to spend twenty years in prison just so you can impress some tart. You're making excuses. I told you bringing her was a terrible idea. Thanks to you and your slapper, we're well and truly in it.' He added a final rebuke. 'When you insisted on involving Henry, I wasn't happy – he's too young – but he was your brother, so, yeah, okay.' He glared at Coco again. 'Being somebody's squeeze doesn't merit a place on the team. The guard was a mistake. Her mistake.' Julian nodded towards the room above. 'Bringing the woman with us instead of finishing what she'd started was yours. What in hell difference would one more dead body have made?'

Mention of his young brother reminded Rafe Henry wasn't in the room; he hadn't noticed him leave. He said, 'It was a spur-of-the-moment decision.'

'Fine, except as soon as we discovered who she was, we should've got rid of her.'

Rafe had listened to as much as he was going to. 'For fuck's sake, grow a pair. You're missing the upside.'

Julian's mouth twisted in a humourless grin. 'Two people are dead and you see an upside? Perhaps I am thick after all, Rafe, because you're right, I *am* missing it.'

Rafe spoke as though he were explaining a universal truth to a backward child, outwardly calm, unaffected by the tirade. In reality, he wanted to smash his tumbler on the table and stick it in Julian's eye. 'Taking Luke Glass' sister is as exciting as your bloody empty existence is ever going to get.'

The veins in Julian's neck bulged like cords underneath the skin. 'We're stuffed and you can't see it. And the phoney tough-guy act won't wash when we come up against the real thing.'

'No, we're not. We're about to have more fun than we've ever had in our boring entitled lives. That's what you wanted, isn't it?'

Coco moved behind her lover, put her arms round his neck, kissed his ear and whispered something that made him smile. He let her lead him to the door. 'The bodyguard was on borrowed time from the moment he opened his mouth in the gym and tried to impress you with how important he was. You recognised that opportunity quickly enough, but you're missing this: the big one.'

'Shove the flattery. Either she goes or I do. Make up your mind, Rafe.'

'Go where, exactly? You were there. That puts you in it up to your neck, old sport.' He lifted the brandy bottle and tucked it under his arm. 'It's December. Your aunt's in South Africa until the end of March. Nobody knows we're here. My advice would be to chill out and enjoy the trip.'

Julian wasn't done. 'Keep her away from me. I'm serious. She's bad news.'

The smile died in Rafe's eyes. 'One more word against Coco and I'll show you what bad news feels like.'

Julian had seen Rafe Purefoy lose it – definitely not recommended; he backed down before it went too far. 'This conversation isn't over.'

'For now, it is.' Rafe slipped his hand round Coco's waist; she smiled up at him. 'Better things to do and all that.'

'What about Nina Glass?'

'That depends entirely on her brother, doesn't it?'

3

This is what I know: it's a great game when you're winning, and at the moment, I could honestly say I was. London, at least the parts of the city that mattered, belonged to the Glass family. My business was high-risk. I made enemies in my sleep – no surprise some of them would fancy their chances. Bring it on: to take what I'd built away from me, they'd need steel balls and an awful lot of luck.

LBC – the Lucky Bastards Club – in Margaret Street, the hottest nightspot in the capital, was a year old and it was time to celebrate. Everybody loves a party, especially when it was invitation only, the booze was free, and they could say they'd spent the night rubbing shoulders with Luke Glass.

Out on the dance floor, a middle-aged stockbroker danced with a girl who could've been his daughter. At the bar, a nineties pop idol held court, talking about himself to somebody I paid to listen. Their histories were very different but their need was the same: to relive a time that had gone and wasn't coming back. LBC gave them that chance and we charged them for the pleasure.

Mark Douglas, my head of security, pulled me aside. 'Haven't heard from Nina, have you?'

Nina was my sister – one of them – a lady who went her own way in all things; giving the party a miss wouldn't be out of character. Except, that was the old Nina – the new version was all-loved-up with Douglas. Men didn't usually last around her. Often, she hadn't bothered to introduce them. No point. When the novelty wore off, they'd be gone. Douglas had the field to himself.

Nina had been damaged more than me by our dysfunctional family – a mother who'd abandoned us when we were kids, and the alcoholic father she'd left us with. Douglas had brought whatever it was she'd lacked: she was happy. Ex-cops from Glasgow weren't the kind of people I'd normally hire; he was different. His career north of Hadrian's Wall had come to a shuddering halt when they'd caught him stealing more than the tea money. To put the outcome beyond doubt, on his way out of the door he'd given his boss a slap.

At his interview, he'd told me the story himself. Just as well, because I already knew. I'd given him the job and, so far, hadn't regretted it. In fact, I'd come to rely on him.

Better than that, I liked him.

Douglas scanned the crowd. 'She isn't answering her phone.'

'It's still early.'

He checked his watch. 'Nah, she should've been here by now. Something must've happened.'

'Something like what?'

'She's been a bit secretive lately.'

I put my hand on his shoulder. 'Think she's found another man?'

Douglas snapped at me; he was jealous. 'That's not what I'm saying.'

'So what?'

'I'm not sure.'

'Relax, she'll be here. You two haven't had a falling out, have you?'

He ran a worried finger down his cheek. 'No, everything's fine.'

'Look, this is Nina we're talking about. Any minute she'll waltz in like a model off the front cover of *Vogue*, fashionably late. The whole place will notice her – exactly the reaction she's looking for. If you're really worried, ask George to send a couple of his guys over to her flat.'

He rejected the suggestion. I'd known he would. George Ritchie ran the operation south of the Thames. Mark Douglas handled the top end of the business. Professional rivalry meant their relationship hadn't flourished. More than once, I'd knocked their heads together to remind them they both worked for me. Added to that, Nina had held a resentment against Ritchie long before her boyfriend arrived on the scene and wouldn't welcome him interfering in her life.

Through the crowd, on the other side of the room, a woman eyed me over her champagne glass. I took in the long hair, the ebony face beneath, and returned her stare. She smiled into her drink; her work was done. So was mine – the wealth of the people in LBC right at this minute would equal the gross national product of a small country. The club had been a gamble, but the money I'd spent on it had paid off and, after the last six months, I was ready for some serious R & R.

As I crossed the floor a figure cut in front of me and threw her arms round my neck.

Charley said, 'Don't worry, she'll wait.'

I disentangled myself. 'Certain about that, are you?'

'Absolutely.' She mimed an apology at the woman and turned back to me. 'She'll forgive you when you tell her we're related.'

Sister No. 2 was enjoying herself. She'd exploded into my life, a blast from the past I wasn't aware existed, determined to be part of the family she'd never known. Long-lost siblings coming out of the woodwork set off alarm bells, though she'd proved it was Glass blood in her veins, eventually, even convincing Nina. So far, the truce I'd brokered between my siblings was holding. How long it would last was anybody's guess.

Charley was a stunning redhead who ran front of house and the girls on offer to the platinum card members. She'd earned her seat at the table. Thanks to her, LBC had the best-looking hookers in London. And the most expensive.

'Who is she?'

'That's what I was about to find out. Probably blown my big chance.'

Charley shot me a withering look. 'Oh, please, Luke, don't go all modest on me. Tonight, of all nights. These people think this party is about the club. You and I know it's about you. LBC is your success.' She shouted in my ear above the music. 'You can be proud of what you've achieved, brother. The place is rocking. Got more applications for membership than we can handle. Could be time to put the prices up.'

'Again?'

'Yes, again.'

'Isn't it expensive enough?'

'Obviously not or we'd have the floor to ourselves. Exclusivity isn't part of the attraction – it is the attraction. Look around you, brother. These people have made it; they can go anywhere. They come to LBC to be seen coming to LBC.' She paused. 'Speaking of being seen, where's Nina?'

'No idea. Mark's worried she's got another man.'

Charley shook her head. 'She'd have to be mad to mess him about. And, anyway, he's wrong. Her and him are solid. She's probably had a big entrance planned for months.'

'Yeah, that's what I thought. Now, if you'll excuse me, I'm wanted elsewhere. Thanks for the dance.'

* * *

Her name was Shani; apparently, it meant 'wonderful'. Not many men would disagree. Charley had called it right: she'd waited. Her eyes were warm enough to take a bath in and I had a feeling this was the start of something. The music was loud. Too loud for what I had in mind. I ordered champagne and we went upstairs to the door away from the noise. Margaret Street was white; snow was still falling. Shani sipped her bubbles. 'This is my first visit to your club. I like it. LBC. What does it mean?'

'It's a reference to something my brother used to say. Danny hated people who'd had everything handed to them so he invented this imaginary place: the lucky bastards club. A lot of our members fit the bill.'

Shani laughed. 'That's a great story. I'd like to meet him.'

No, she wouldn't.

'Unfortunately, he isn't in London now.'

'Where does he live?'

Asked with the slightest trace of accent. My reply was tinged with regret I didn't feel and wasn't an answer to her question. 'I haven't heard from him in a long time.'

'What a pity. He sounds charming.'

She shivered in the cold air. I took my jacket off and put it round her shoulders. She smiled and drew closer. 'Your brother isn't the only one who's charming. Thank you. We don't get this kind of weather in my country.'

'Where are you from?'

'Egypt. From Zamalek in West Cairo. Do you know it?'

'I can't say I do.'

Shani gazed past me into the bitter night. 'It's an island of quiet leafy streets surrounded by the Nile. My sister and I were born there.'

'You mean there's another one at home as beautiful as you?'

The smile faded and I realised I'd said the wrong thing. 'I'm sorry, I didn't mean...'

'No need to apologise, how could you know? She died three and a half years ago.'

'Sorry to hear that. What was her name?'

'Zahra. It means flower. Losing her so early was hard. It still is. I don't think I'll ever get over it.' She touched a locket hanging round her slender neck on a sliver of silver chain. 'I carry her with me always. She's here now.'

'Is she?'

She lowered her forehead and looked up. 'You're making fun of me but the bond between us can never be broken.' Shani opened the delicate clasp and held it in her palm. 'Do you want to see her?'

Inside, a girl smiled for the camera, the resemblance so striking it could've been the lady in front of me. Suddenly, I felt uncomfortable. On my way to the door with this beautiful creature, the last thing I'd imagined was a conversation about a missing brother and a dead sister. Danny had been many things; charming wasn't one of them.

She stood under the statue of Fortuna, the Roman goddess of good fortune, her long dark hair falling to the smooth skin of her shoulders and the black and gold dress plunging between her breasts. Green eyes observed me beneath the soft arch of her brows, assessing me as thoroughly as I was her. When she spoke, her parted lips revealed straight white teeth.

'Are you shocked I keep my sister's picture with me?'

'Not at all.'

Shani pursed her lips. 'Somehow, I don't believe you, Luke Glass.' She ran a finger over the figure of Fortuna, carved from a single block of alabaster. 'The ancient Egyptians saw death as a temporary interruption, rather than the cessation of life. When they died, they were mummified so the soul would return to the body, giving it breath and life.'

'Is that what you think?'

'Of course not. I love her, there's no more to it than that.'

Her use of the present tense was interesting.

We talked for a few more minutes, even shared a laugh, but the mood had gone and wasn't coming back. Not tonight. She told me she was in town with her father to buy property. Good news. It meant it wasn't my money she was after.

'My sister Nina runs an agency. Perhaps she could help him with his search?'

She nodded, distracted, toying with the locket. 'I'll mention it to him.'

Before I got into my wonder-of-me spiel, a black Merc glided out of the snow and drew up at the kerb. Shani shook my hand. 'I have to go.'

'Go where? It's still early.'

'We're flying home tomorrow. It was nice meeting you, Luke.'

'When will you be back?'

She smiled. 'Soon, very soon.'

4

The couple in the next room were fucking for England, their cries rising to frantic crescendos, dying, and starting again. Imagining the scene wasn't difficult – whether they knew it or not the lovers were feeding on each other, physically and emotionally. Nina had known the God-like superiority of watching the light fade in another human being's eyes, the shattering intensity of the power: she'd been there; she remembered. Compared with it, even the best sex was nothing. The woman – Coco – had had a taste of it tonight, extinguishing a life as casually as blowing out a guttering candle. Relishing the kill. Inevitably, she'd hunger for more.

Doing it again would be easy.

Nina's shoulder and chest hurt from the fall in the snow, a dull ache threatening to become something more. Having her hands tied didn't help. The bitch, Coco, had deliberately pulled the rope too tight so it chafed her wrists; Nina cursed and wiggled her fingers to keep the circulation going. The chair was hard and might've been comfortable thirty years ago; it wasn't now. Behind the door, a pink dressing gown hanging on a peg suggested this was someone's room, but the carpet, the matching cabinets, and the bronzed lamps on either side of the elevated bed were old enough to have been part of the original furnishings. If this house came on the market, she'd buy it and burn it to the ground.

With shadows for company, fear slithered through her and, for the first time, she thought about Mark. She hadn't told him about her visits to Poland Street – the bracelet and the necklace were Christmas presents to celebrate six months as a couple. He wouldn't realise she was missing, let alone know where to start looking for her once he did. Nina was aware she'd forged something with Mark Douglas, something real. She trusted him even more than she trusted Luke, and didn't want what they had together to end with these upper-class idiots.

She forced herself to calm down and think clearly: when she didn't show up at the party, Mark would speak to Luke. Luke would call George Ritchie and a search party would be sent to find her. Ritchie would rub his hands together and rehearse the tired lecture she'd listened to so often about enemies everywhere. George could be an old woman – no doubt about that – but an old woman who understood his business and, for once, Nina was grateful for him.

A groan from the next room told her Rafe and Coco were at it again. Rafe believed he was smarter than everybody else. It wasn't true. He should've kept it simple and shot her – he hadn't; in the heat of the moment he'd taken her hostage. Then, when Coco discovered who they had, their fates were sealed.

The door creaked; the heavy handle turned slowly. She saw it and strained against the ties holding her to the chair. On the other side of the wall, Rafe and Coco had finished and were talking in post-coital togetherness. So, it wasn't one of them. Julian had made his intentions clear. Left to him, her body would be discovered at the side of a road somewhere far from here. Nina held her breath, expecting the worst, certain that, with the leader preoccupied, he was taking his chance.

As it opened, the darkness was broken by light from the hall. Rafe's brother was eighteen or nineteen at most. He came closer, his round face glowing with the freshness of youth. Yesterday, he'd had his whole life ahead of him. Thanks to Rafe and his girlfriend, his future wasn't what it used to be. He hunkered down and pressed a cup to her lips. Instinctively, she pulled away. 'It's okay, it's only water.'

He took a cloth from his pocket and wiped the blood Nina had forgotten about from her forehead – an unnecessary act telling her all she needed. In the position these people were in, kindness of any sort was weakness. Nina remembered his name. 'Let me go, Henry.'

Henry gently dabbed her temple and didn't respond. She tried to reach him. 'Henry, listen to me. Let me go. Let me go and it ends here.'

'What about Rafe?'

'No one will be harmed if you do what I say.'

'I can't – you know I can't.'

'Yes, you can, of course, you can. Until now, this is just a big mistake, a mistake everybody can walk away from. I see where your brother's going with it. The minute he makes that phone call, there's no road back. It's over, for you, Rafe, Coco, Julian, all of you.'

Nina let the threat sink in.

Henry said, 'You don't understand. Rafe is... he's not like other people.'

'Then, you need to look out for yourself. Because nobody else will.'

'You're wrong. Rafe will look after me. Rafe always looks after me.'

'I'm not wrong. He's crossed the line. He can't look after anybody. Not even himself.'

'Stop talking or I'll go.'

Nina wasn't going to persuade him: this boy worshipped his brother. In his eyes, Rafe was invincible. He lifted the cup to her lips again; she angrily turned away. 'Don't touch me. Didn't you hear Coco's reaction when she found out who I am? Ask yourself why that was.' She struggled forward in the chair. 'Because I'm Nina Glass. Luke Glass' sister.'

Henry clung to the mantra he'd had drummed into him. Trust, absolute and unshakable, had become dependency, blinding him to the truth of the situation. 'Rafe won't let anything happen to us.'

Nina spat the words into the semi-darkness. 'He already has! For Christ's sake, use your head. Luke will tear him apart with his bare hands. You'll all go the same way. Screaming in agony. Your bodies will never be found. I'm giving you a way out. Take it, Henry. I'll tell Luke what you did – you won't be harmed.'

'What about Rafe?'

Nina was done with lying. 'Oh, for fuck's sake, Henry. Rafe's already a dead man – he just doesn't know it. I wouldn't save him even if I could.'

The candour of the reply had an effect. Henry faltered. 'It's Coco. Since he met her, he's—'

Nina cut him off. 'The jeweller had made it out of a concentration camp, survived the fucking Nazis – his prison number was tattooed on his arm. Your brother shot him in the heart. He's an arrogant fucker who's wandered into a world he thinks he can control. He hasn't a clue. Rafe is going to pay the price for what he's done and so he should. Don't blame anybody else.' She stopped, breathless, then went on. 'Coco's a bitch who'll kill me for the fun of it. And Julian, well, he made it clear what he'd do.'

'Rafe won't let them.'

Nina was having a conversation with a robot. 'Are you hearing me? For fuck's sake, forget him. He's history.'

The voice startled them. 'I admire your certainty, Nina Glass.'

Rafe leaned against the doorframe, his face hidden in the half-light, smoke rising from the cigarette in his hand. Over his shoulder in the hall, Coco was smiling. He said, 'When I make contact with your brother, we'll find out who's history.'

He dropped the laid-back pretence and came towards her. 'Until we do, try turning my brother against me again and I'll personally remodel your pretty face. Better still, Coco will do it for me.'

* * *

Henry nervously bit his lip, while Rafe closed the room door behind them. As it shut he saw Nina Glass staring at him through the shadows, her eyes coal-black and angry. In the hall light, Rafe saw his young brother's brow furrowed with anxiety and realised he'd age badly – forty years from now, though the boyishness would never entirely leave him, the smooth skin would be lined and puckered: Henry was a worrier. And he was worrying now. Rafe glanced at Coco's untroubled face, the contrast inescapable, and for a moment regretted bringing him into this. He rested a hand on his shoulder. 'Have I ever let you down, Henry? Tell the truth.'

'Never.'

'Not even once?'

'Not even once.'

He prompted him. 'The time you ran away? I went after you. What about that?'

'I was a child.'

'But I made you come back with me. You didn't want to and I made you.'

'You knew there was nowhere for me to go. You were looking out for me.'

Rafe nodded. 'Because you were my brother and I loved you.'

'Yes.'

'Then, why would I stop now?'

Henry hesitated. Rafe was smarter than him, smarter than anybody, twisting him in circles with clever words as he'd been doing as long as he could remember. He shook his head. 'You wouldn't. Of course, you wouldn't.'

'So, when I tell you not to go near her again, I want you to listen. She's Luke Glass' sister. Do you understand what that means?'

'She's dangerous.'

Coco sneered. 'She's trash.'

Rafe glared at her. 'The Glass family run half of London.'

Coco said, 'And they're still trash. I can smell the high-rise from here.'

Rafe returned his attention to Henry. 'Dangerous, yes. But only if we give her the upper hand.'

Henry was still waiting for somebody to tell him what had gone on in Poland Street. 'Why not just let her go? She says you shot an old man.'

'Forget what she says.' He looked at Coco for help and got none. 'Okay, the jeweller's got crazy. We can't go back and change it.'

'I understand that, except it doesn't have to go any further. It could stop, couldn't it?'

A light came on behind Rafe's eyes. He'd always been pushing back against the world. Whatever had gone wrong in Poland Street had changed him: this wasn't the brother Henry had known all his life.

Rafe scratched his ear and spoke as if it hadn't occurred to him. 'Yes, I suppose it could, only where's the fun in that? Ask yourself this: do you seriously believe we can't get the better of some ragtags from south of the river?'

'Why would we even try?'

'Because it'll be the most exciting thing you'll ever do.'

'She says you're going to kill her. Are you? Is that what's going to happen?'

'Julian wants to.'

Henry lost patience with him. 'Fuck Julian. Actually, fuck all of you.'

Rafe put his arm round him. 'Relax. Nobody's going to die. Luke Glass will pay what we ask, we'll have won, and his sister can go back to her tawdry existence.'

Coco broke in again. 'Oh, for Christ's sake, tell the boy the truth.'

'Shut up, Coco, I'm handling this.'

She stepped between them. 'Rafe is trying to protect you. He doesn't want his young brother spooked. I don't have his sensitivities.'

'Coco, don't!'

'We left two people dead in Soho. The bitch you were getting cosy with knows who we are, which means we do her now or we do her later. That's the reality, Henry. Accept it, you'll sleep better. I promise.'

5

DAY 2: FRIDAY

Except for the light in an upstairs window, the King of Mesopotamia was blacked out – no surprise at five minutes to six on a freezing December morning, weeks before Christmas. Driving from my flat had been slow, cautiously edging through deserted streets transformed by snow that kept coming down. On another day, I would've given up. Weather or no weather, that wasn't an option.

Women went missing every day in the city.

Other women. Not my sister.

Not Nina.

My mobile ringing on the bedside cabinet hadn't wakened me. I wasn't asleep. Down the line Mark Douglas sounded calm though his insides had to be churning. As he spoke guilt seeped into my bones and, suddenly, I felt cold – in my hurry to get to the Egyptian lady I'd forgotten Nina. When Shani had stepped into the Merc, I'd lost interest in the party and taken a black cab home.

Nina's history was against her. More than once she'd pulled a no-show, usually because it wound Danny up. Since Douglas had come into her life, she'd quit running to every man that caught her eye and become almost domesticated. Almost. Sister No. 1 was still well capable of leading the rest of us a merry dance if she felt like it. Nina had Glass blood in her veins; she could be wild. But putting what she had with Douglas in danger, risking the most solid relationship she'd ever known for a fling with a stranger, would take recklessness to a new level.

I didn't believe it.

The temperature on the dashboard said minus three. When I'd left my flat it had been minus two: the white-out was just getting started. Wherever Nina was, I hoped to God she wasn't out in it.

I let myself in, climbed the stairs and opened the door. This had been Danny's office, then mine. We'd built an empire from behind this desk though my memories weren't fuzzy and warm.

Anything but.

Mark Douglas sat across from George Ritchie; they looked up when I came in. The similarities between them were few. George was an old-school villain who'd been in the game most of his life, a shrewd operator, in his day, the hardest man to come out of Newcastle. Douglas was a disgraced ex-copper from Glasgow, another hard man, who'd proved himself against people who'd fancied taking over what was mine. Good guys, both of them. Unfortunately, working together had been a problem and still was. Before I got here the silences would've been longer than the conversation.

Glasses and a bottle of fifteen-year-old Glenfarclas sat untouched in front of them, liquid amber, shimmering like a mirage. George poured three fingers into a tumbler and pushed it towards me. 'Charley's on her way. Felix won't make it. Driving from the East End in this shit is a big ask.'

'How's he doing?'

'All right. Now Jonas Small isn't around some of the locals have crawled out of the woodwork.'

'Serious?'

Ritchie swirled the whisky in his glass and dismissed my concerns. 'Nuisance value. Don't worry about it.'

'I won't, George, that's what I pay you to do.'

Douglas took no part in the discussion – I doubted he was even aware of it. He was wearing the clothes he'd had on in the club, sitting straight, ignoring the whisky, his expression carved in stone. And I realised my initial assessment of him on the phone had been right: Douglas was in love with Nina. For him more than anybody, this was personal.

I said, 'What do we know?'

He drew a breath from deep inside. 'I spoke to her late on yesterday afternoon. She told me she'd meet me later. She had something she needed to do.'

'Did she say what it was?'

'I didn't ask. Nina does her own thing. But the last few weeks she's been... strange.'

'You mentioned last night that she'd been secretive lately. What did you mean?'

'Hard to describe. I wondered if...'

I repeated the point he'd reluctantly hinted at in the club.

'There was somebody else?'

He nodded, slowly. 'Actually, yes. Nina could have anybody she wanted.'

'And she wanted you.'

We hadn't heard Charley come in. She shook snow off her coat and stamped her feet; hours earlier, she'd hijacked me on the dance floor in LBC. I studied her for tell-tale signs she was hungover and didn't find any. Both Nina and Charley worked hard and played harder. When it came to drinking, they could slug it out with the best. Charley looked as good as she had in the club. Some women are showstoppers – they just are: Sister No. 2 was one of them.

Under the dark-blue coat with its fur-lined collar, she was wearing flared trousers and a black polo neck that highlighted her red hair and I remembered her dramatic entrance the first time I'd met her in this office the day she'd announced who she was and tossed her birth certificate defiantly on the desk to prove it.

A painted nail pointed at the whisky. 'Got one of those for me, George? Hope so, it's like the bloody Arctic out there.'

Ritchie produced a glass and poured. He hadn't forgotten her arrival in our lives any more than I had. With Nina and Mark Douglas, she made it three out of four who didn't want George Ritchie around. I was the boss and I did, so the rest would have to live with it.

Charley watched the liquid climb the inside of the tumbler. 'Any word?'

We didn't reply. She lifted the whisky, swallowed a third of it and finished the statement she'd started at the door. 'You're right, Mark, Nina could have anybody. But it's you she's in love with. Wherever she is, there isn't anybody else involved.'

Ritchie's face said he wasn't certain about that. 'I've already checked the hospitals. I can try them again.'

Douglas said, 'And the police – she might've been in an accident.'

I let them get on with eliminating the obvious possibilities; they might turn up something – a part of me wanted them to. At least we'd know – but I didn't kid myself. If Nina had been in an accident we'd have heard, or, worst-case scenario, had a visit from two awkward uniforms sent to deliver the news to the family.

I said, 'Okay, let's do this. Charley's sure there isn't another man. For what it's worth, I agree. The last six months have been the happiest I've ever seen Nina. That's down to you, Mark. An accident might be a possibility, except we would've been told. What does that leave?'

George understood the question and answered it. 'It's been quiet on our side. I mean, really quiet. There hasn't been a serious move against us in long enough.'

'Nothing at all?'

'Not south of the river.' He fingered the stubble on his chin. 'Now and again some idiot steals something that doesn't belong to him. Maybe he'll be lucky and get away with it. If he pulls the same stunt again, he'll get slapped-up for his trouble. Broken bones keep the peace.'

'What about the East End? You said Felix was getting hassle.'

Ritchie rotated the whisky glass between his fingers, considering his response. Experience had taught George it was prudent to never say more than was necessary. 'Jonas is singing in the heavenly choir but a few locals liked things the way they were.'

'Give me a name.'

He shook his head. 'Foolish people. Nothing Felix can't handle.'

'Some of them might be feeling brave.'

'They'd have to be more than brave to lift one of your sisters. I don't reckon it.'

I turned to Douglas. 'Anything at LBC?'

He dug deep, more for my benefit than his, and managed a wry smile, which couldn't have been easy. 'Our members wouldn't dream of getting their hands dirty. They're already rich. What would be the motive? And Nina hasn't been to the club in months.'

Charley had preferred to listen rather than talk, allowing Ritchie and Douglas to say what they had to. So far, it wasn't anything we could use. She put her drink down, cut through the speculation, and steered the conversation in a different direction. 'She told you she had somewhere to go. Okay, where's her car? Where did she park?' The questions made sense. 'Everybody parks as close as they can to where they're going, don't they?'

Douglas seized on it. 'The police can get that information, we can't.'

I said, 'Not officially. At least not in a timeframe that's any good to us.'

It was the wrong thing to say and set him off. 'Officially or unofficially, I couldn't care less if it helps Nina.'

'I understand how you feel about her, Mark. Give it a couple of hours. If we haven't heard anything I'll contact some people.'

'Why wait?'

'Because we aren't sure what we're dealing with. Bringing in the police is the last resort.'

It wasn't true. A man in my position had secrets – being able to reach into the heart of the Metropolitan Police Force any time I wanted was one of them. As soon as the meeting ended, I'd be getting my tame copper out of his comfortable bed in Hendon. Mark Douglas and Charley weren't in the loop about Oliver Stanford – that was how it was going to stay.

Danny used to say, 'Three people can keep a secret if two of them are dead.' He wasn't wrong. George Ritchie knew about Stanford. So did Nina. Already more than was wise.

I drained the whisky. 'George, put the word out on the streets. Mark, talk to the girls in Glass Houses and check Nina's emails. See if there's anything unusual in them.'

'Such as?'

Douglas was better than that; he was too close to be any use. I buried my reservations. 'Set up traces on yours, mine, and Charley's phones in case...' I let the sentence go and barked instructions. 'And get a look at the CCTV footage at her flat and the office while you're at it.'

'How far back?'

'From when she first started acting differently.'

Charley said, 'What do you want from me?'

'Discreetly ask your girls if they know anything. Hopefully, some time today we'll have word about the car.'

Mark Douglas was cracking; he needed more. 'And until then are we expected to sit on our fucking hands?'

'Until then, we wait, so yeah, get comfortable.'

6

Oliver Stanford cradled the cup of decaf coffee, enjoying the warmth of it against his palms. By habit and inclination, the senior officer was an early riser, normally behind his desk at New Scotland Yard well before his colleagues. Not today. Beyond the kitchen window, under a black sky, the lawn ran to the trees at the bottom covered in snow. The garden, and everything in it, was his wife Elise's domain – she was always busy with some task or other. His contribution could be measured in pound notes. In spring, when the flowers were in bloom, her efforts were spectacularly rewarded; they'd spent many evenings on the patio, a glass of chilled white wine in one hand, a book in the other, enjoying each other's company and the peace a world away from the ugliness and chaos of central London.

This morning, it was unrecognisable.

He considered having a car collect him rather than driving himself and rejected the idea; the main roads into town wouldn't be clear. His dogs were waiting for him, tails wagging, anticipating the walk he took them on every day before he left for the city.

Stanford opened the door and shivered. 'Sorry, boys. It's brass monkeys out there. The garden is the best we can do.'

His mobile vibrated in his pocket. He fished it out, checked caller ID and blanched: Luke Glass only used this phone if it was an emergency. Recently, Stanford had heard nothing from the gangster and wasn't sure if that was good or bad. As long as the money kept showing up in the private account every month, he wasn't complaining. His relationship with the family had begun with Danny – a mad-arse of the first order, vicious and mercurial. He'd dropped out of the picture, thank God. Luke was running things – smarter, less reactive and more ambitious, but, beneath the surface, as ruthless as his brother had ever been.

Glass didn't waste words. 'I'm messaging you a car reg. Find out where it's parked or if it's been involved in an accident.'

'What make?'

'Renault Alpine A110. Blue.'

'Nice. Who's the owner?'

'Nina.'

'An accident's easy. Where it's parked could take a while unless it's been abandoned or impounded. What's going on?'

'Don't ask. All I want to know is where she's left it.'

'Talk sense. She could be parked in somebody's drive. Are you sure she's even in London?'

'Right now, I'm not sure of anything.'

'I'll file it as a stolen vehicle with my name as the contact, though your sister won't like it if she gets pulled over.'

'Doesn't matter. Get on it as soon as you get to the Yard.'

Stanford watched the snow falling relentlessly. 'Have you looked outside? It's like the North Pole out there. I'll be lucky to get to the end of the road, let alone the Embankment.'

Glass growled down the line. 'Don't mess me about, Oliver. I need that information and I need it now. Get there! Even if you have to hire a team of Siberian fucking huskies.'

* * *

Constance Greyland peered over her sunglasses at Florian arguing with one of the houseboys at the side of the pool; when he was bored, he found fault with everything, including her. Last night at dinner he'd got drunk, caused a scene – the latest in a long line – and embarrassed both of them. She recognised the signs. Florian didn't know it but he was heading for the exit: men were like taxis – another one would be along in a minute.

She heard him swear and called to him. 'What's the trouble?'

'It's these damned waiters. I asked for a G & T ten minutes ago and it still hasn't arrived.'

'Perhaps they're busy.'

'Too busy to do their job? Heart lazy more like it. Next time, let's go somewhere else. Somewhere we're appreciated.'

Constance frowned and went back to her book. There was no point in arguing with him in this mood. One of them would be going somewhere else and it wouldn't be her: Florian had outstayed his welcome, forgetting who was paying his drinks bill, starting to believe he deserved the comfortable life he enjoyed. At her expense. Sad in a way – she'd liked him. Not enough to put up with his crap. If he didn't pull his socks up, he'd be back in England and out on the street by Christmas.

* * *

For six years Constance Greyland had been a well-known face on the Chelsea dinner-party scene with her husband, Simon. The perfect couple, until he admitted an affair with Connie's best friend,

Rosamund Symington: in the aftermath, Simon took his own life. An ignominious end for a man who'd inherited a shedload of money from his late father and married Constance Greyland, daughter of Lord Greyland of Tannoch, whose grandmother had been a lady-in-waiting to a prominent member of the aristocracy in 1936. Simon's demise heralded the start of a great adventure for his young widow: born in Scotland and brought up in London, she'd spent the last twenty-five English winters six thousand miles away in South Africa. Over the years, though the country had changed, some things remained – the service at the Belmond Mount Nelson Hotel in Cape Town was one of them.

Constance had been fifty-two and beginning to feel her age when she'd met Florian at the South Kensington home of a mutual friend. The attraction to whatever lay behind his dark eyes had been instant. Fresh-faced and self-assured, hair stylishly louche, he'd immediately caught her eye and she'd known he was lustfully assessing her when he thought she wasn't looking. Florian had been the life and soul of the party, telling a series of self-deprecating stories about his many failed romances, always ending with the line, 'And I'd thought it was all going so well.' Before it broke up, he had her telephone number. As he'd helped her into her coat, she'd asked, 'By the way, what do you do? You didn't say.'

'Didn't I?'

Now, Connie knew.

* * *

Rafe Purefoy was in a good mood. Julian and Henry didn't share it. Julian said, 'Poland Street was fifteen hours ago. There's nothing on the news.'

Rafe wasn't concerned. 'It will be, eventually, though it won't make any difference. The jeweller was a loner. My guess is he kept his business to himself, a couple of clients a month at most. Nobody will miss him.'

'But when they do—'

'You're really starting to bore me, Julian. "When they do"... what? We hold all the aces.' He counted off on his fingers. 'They don't know who we are, they don't know where we are, and they won't realise until we tell them we have a bargaining chip the size of Big Ben. So, for Christ's sake dry your eyes and think positive. Coco's happy, aren't you, darling?' He pulled the drawstrings of one of the velvet bags, poured the contents onto the table and lifted a diamond up to the light. 'A billion years. Hard to get your head round, isn't it?'

Julian asked, 'How much do you think we'll get for them?'

Rafe shot him a disapproving look. 'The old jeweller was right. Anybody who sees this extraordinary creation of nature and thinks about money is a cretin. You're a cretin, Julian. But we knew that – at least, I did. Our biggest problem is there's sod all to eat in this place. Your aunt must've thrown everything out before she left for Africa. And I'm bloody starving. Somebody's going to have to slog to the shops. Aren't they, Henry?'

Julian interrupted, impatiently. 'When do we tell Luke Glass we have his sister?'

Rafe thought smoking French cigarettes made him look cool; he lit a Gauloises and blew smoke into the air. 'No rush. The longer we leave it, the more desperate he'll be to get her back. I'm thinking another two, maybe three days.' He grinned. 'Allow the anxiety to build.'

Henry spoke directly to Julian. 'She says we're all going to die.'

The laugh from Rafe was forced and unconvincing. 'She's fucking with your head, brother. That's why it's important to stay away from her. Nothing will happen unless we want it to happen. Julian would've done her in Soho, wouldn't you?' He slapped Julian on the back and blew smoke in his face. 'And you heard Coco – the girl's ready any time. You're the youngest, the most impressionable. She sees you as the weakest link. Don't make her right.'

Julian said, 'What's the plan?'

'The plan? Henry's going to the shops. When he comes back, Coco will cook lunch.'

Coco responded with the petulance of the privileged. 'I can't cook, Rafe, you know I can't. I've never cooked anything in my life more complicated than toasted cheese.'

Rafe clapped his hands. 'Toasted cheese will be fine, darling. Once you've mastered that, you can move on to toast and jam, French toast – the possibilities are endless. Treat it as an opportunity to learn how ordinary people live.'

Nina could hear them talking downstairs, Rafe holding court, his confident voice rising through the floorboards. She couldn't make out the words though she could guess what the topic under discussion would be: what to do with her. Julian and Coco would urge Rafe to kill her, while Henry slowly realised everything she'd told him about his brother was true. Rafe relished the role of leader. Coco egged him on, encouraging him to match her wildness with his own.

Last night had been the longest of Nina's life; in the chair with the ties digging into her wrists sleep had been impossible. When dawn broke and the shadows thinned, her prison had slowly taken shape around her. Nina was a south London girl; the north was an unknown place. Because the abductors hadn't bothered to keep their destination secret, she knew she was in Hampstead, close to the heath – another reason they couldn't afford to let her go.

Mr Stuka and the jewellery had been her secret; she'd kept it well. Mark had been suspicious – one time she'd sensed he was close to asking her outright where she'd been. He'd stopped himself, almost as if he didn't want to force her to lie to him. Before they'd met, she'd been headstrong and selfish and spoiled, a pain in the arse. Being with the man from Glasgow had changed her. Mark Douglas was everything she'd ever wanted, everything she'd ever dreamed. Her soul mate. Imagining how he must be hurting dragged her to the edge of despair and she resolved to survive the nightmare.

The old jeweller had managed to survive his nightmare, so would she.

As the party in LBC rolled into the small hours, Mark and Luke would've assumed she was pulling some stunt, delaying her entrance to cause a splash. When it didn't happen, they'd start to worry. Now – more than twelve hours later – George Ritchie's men would be scouring the city looking for her. The knowledge didn't reassure Nina – they wouldn't know where to start.

The landing creaked outside the door. It opened and Coco came in wearing the black polo neck she'd had on the day before. 'Still here?'

Nina lifted her chin defiantly. 'About bloody time. I thought you'd forgotten about me. I want to go to the bathroom.'

Coco ignored her and knelt to check the ties were still doing their job.

'And I'm hungry.'

Yesterday's mascara had gathered in the corners of Coco's eyes. 'Trust me, that's the least of your problems. And don't waste breath persuading me to let you go. In case you haven't noticed, I'm not Henry.'

She went to the landing and called downstairs. 'Julian, I need help up here!'

Nina watched Coco, hands on hips, waiting for him to join her.

With her slim figure and Kings Road accent, everything about her said money. Poland Street had been a run-of-the-mill robbery – one to add to the hundred a day in the capital – and until she'd shot the bodyguard the situation had been under control. But it wasn't just the act, it was the senselessness of it: the guard had been on the ground, barely conscious, the threat was zero. A merciless, unnecessary execution that raised the stakes to first degree murder. The jeweller had been a heat-of-the-moment reaction; if he hadn't grabbed the mask and seen Rafe's face, they'd have taken the gems and be in the car laughing all the way to north London.

7

Julian, another privileged wanker. Rafe, Coco, Julian– where did they get the names? None of them had done a day's work in their lives. Nina understood what she'd been dragged into – robbery wasn't the motive. These people were thrill-seekers. They did it because it felt good.

Coco pointed the gun at her head while Julian untied her. 'Let's be clear on one thing. I don't like you. All I need is an excuse to use this.'

'I'm lovely when you get to know me.'

Julian took hold of Nina's arm and led her to the bathroom on the landing. 'Leave the door open.'

'Oh, for Christ's sake—'

Coco laughed. 'You're such a perv, Julian, you really are.'

'Taking a chance to preserve her modesty doesn't make sense.'

Coco overruled him. 'Close the door. Don't lock it. You've got two minutes.'

The bathroom was small and, like the rest of the house, needed work. Nina ran a practised eye over it. Selling property was her business; Glass Houses had an impressive track record in London. If a client came to her with this place she'd advise them to upgrade it: the bath was old enough to be part of the original build – a feature; it could stay – but the black and white tiles were worn and cracked; in a corner of the ceiling a brown stain revealed an ingress that hadn't been properly attended to. No money had been spent on the place in decades.

Nina carefully pushed the window open, praying Julian and Coco wouldn't hear. Cold air rushed in, nipping at her cheeks, flushing her face. The sky was clearing, the snow had stopped, but the ground was a long way down; if she fell and broke her leg it would be a disaster. Taking her to a hospital was out of the question. They'd shoot her like a dog. No, the key to regaining her freedom lay in the fractured relationships of the people who'd taken her. Dangerous fools: Rafe and his girlfriend, overconfident, capable of anything; Julian, agitated and angry, at odds with both of them; and Henry, blindly following his brother, too young and naïve to be mixed up in this. Sooner or later, something would give. When it did, Nina would be ready.

* * *

Out on the landing, Julian glared at Coco. 'You shouldn't even be here.'

She stroked his cheek with her finger, daring him to react. 'Except, I am, darling. Be a love and get over it before I tell Rafe you raped me.'

'That's a lie!'

'I said no but you dragged me into a bedroom and tore my clothes off.'

'Rafe won't believe you.'

She scoffed. 'No? I can be very convincing. He'll kill you where you stand.'

'You really are a bitch!'

Coco mocked him. 'Rafe is ten times the man you are.'

'He's screwed this one up. We should've left her in Soho. This is too complicated. We could finish it and say she tried to get away.'

Coco disagreed. 'I suppose we could. But that would put us on the same side and I wouldn't want that, so have a little faith. Rafe knows what he's doing. Now, be a sport. Concentrate on the plan and try to forget I turned you down.'

Julian hammered on the bathroom door. 'Time's up! Out here! Now!' He whispered to Coco, the intensity behind the words spraying tiny particles of spit in an arc. 'Before this is over, I'll show you what a good sport I am.'

* * *

In the kitchen, Rafe shook another cigarette out of the blue packet, sensing his brother's unease. The trip out hadn't improved his young brother's mood; Henry was going to be a problem.

'What's wrong now?'

'I hate the smell of those things.'

'Okay, I won't light it if you tell me what's bothering you.'

Henry pointed at the ceiling. 'They shouldn't be left alone with Nina.'

'On first-name terms, eh? Cosy. And you mean Coco and Julian?'

'Yes.'

'Why shouldn't they?'

'Because they want to kill her.'

Rafe spoke quietly. 'But they won't, Henry. Unless I tell them to.'

'She hasn't done anything. Let her go.'

Rafe changed his mind about the cigarette. If Henry was going to be a pain, he might as well smoke. He leaned his elbows on the table. 'All right, let's say I do what you want – let her go – what do you think would happen next?'

Henry faltered. 'Nothing... nothing would happen.'

Rafe drew nicotine down into his lungs and blew it out slowly through his nose. 'You know, sometimes I wonder if you and I are from the same gene pool.'

'What do you mean?'

'I'm asking myself how any brother of mine can be so monumentally dim. You're fucking stupid, Henry. Or pretending to be.' He spread his fingers on the pine surface and studied them. 'Where are we?'

'What?'

'Tell me where we are. At this moment.'

'Julian's aunt's house.'

'Good lad. Now ask yourself, why?' Rafe answered his own question. 'Because, through no fault of our own, a silly woman who just happens to be the sister of the biggest gangster in London got in the way. Coco said it. She's seen our faces. She knows who we are. If we let her go, we'll be dead in a week.'

'But, say Nina promises to—'

Rafe roared. 'For Christ's sake, Henry, use your head! And stop calling her Nina! She can promise till the cows come home – it doesn't matter. Don't you understand? Luke Glass can't have it known somebody kidnapped his sister and got away with it. Not possible.'

Rafe forced himself to calm down. 'Let's examine our situation. The robbery went wrong. Two people are dead.'

'You said—'

'Forget what I said. Bollocks to what I said. Before it goes any further you have to get straight with this, brother. I've babied you long enough.'

If the conversation was meant to dispel Henry's fears, it had failed. His voice trembled; he didn't want to hear any more. Rafe – his hero – was as twisted and bad as the people upstairs.

'Okay, you said we'd be dead in a week – how will extorting him change his mind? She'll still know who we are.' Henry blanched as the awful truth arrived. 'Coco was right. You've never had any intention of letting her go, have you, Rafe?'

Rafe didn't deny it. 'Actually, no, and once she's dead there's no chance of Luke Glass finding us.'

* * *

Getting to Glass Houses had been easier than Mark Douglas had expected. Snow ploughs had cleared the main roads in the capital; beyond the centre it would be a different story and it was unlikely any of the staff would get through. He parked in the underground car park, took the lift to the fifth floor and let himself in. A blue spotlight shone on the GH logo mounted on the wall behind the reception desk. Burgundy sofas and outsized coffee tables casually strewn with copies of *Tatler* and *Elite Traveler* looked like the set of a play waiting for the audience to take their seats so the actors could wander on and the drama begin. During office hours, a bank of screens continuously showcased properties the company had sold. The first time he'd been here a scale model of Glass Gate, a new luxury development built by Luke's construction company, had dominated the space. Nina had sold every unit off-plan. Now her brother was on another project that, no doubt, would be equally successful. Building and property; natural synergy: legitimate businesses registered at Companies House, trading profitably and paying their taxes.

Impressive, but far from the whole story.

Nina's desk was neat, no scribbled message conveniently left on her computer explaining her sudden disappearance. Douglas hadn't expected there would be – Nina Glass was the strongest woman he'd ever known, one of many reasons he'd fallen in love with her. On his way downstairs, he remembered the doorman's name was Norman. Too many beers and the sedentary nature of his job had thickened the old soldier's middle and stippled his cheeks, but he hadn't lost the parade-ground posture and never would. He'd seen Douglas many times and recognised him.

Mark fought to keep his voice even. 'How long do you keep your CCTV tapes?'

The doorman took the question in his stride. 'Thirty days. Then we start again. Why?'

Douglas didn't have the energy for deception. 'I need a bit of help. Can I check if there's anything suspicious on them?'

Norman's guard went up. 'Suspicious like what?'

'I don't know. A stalker, maybe.'

'A stalker.'

'Nina – Miss Glass – is missing.'

'Have you told the police?'

Douglas went with the waiting-twenty-four-hours-before-filing-a-missing-person-report myth.

'It's too soon for them to get involved. When they do, they'll check the hospitals and contact people who know her. It'll take days. I can't hang around for that.'

'Maybe she needs time alone. No law against it. Feel that way sometimes myself.'

'We all do, except she was supposed to meet me last night.'

The doorman stepped back to get a better look at him. 'Don't take this personally... you haven't had a row, have you? Young people—'

Mark heard the harshness in his voice and regretted it. 'Things are great between us. What about those tapes?'

Norman stroked his chin. 'Nobody's allowed in the back room. Against the rules.'

'Fuck the rules. What if something's happened to her?'

'I might lose my job.'

'It'll be our secret. I'll owe you.'

'All right. Make it quick.'

Douglas followed him into a space no bigger than a cloakroom and listened impatiently while he explained how the system worked. 'It's cloud-based. That mean anything to you? Me neither. The previous technology was old – less coverage, poor image quality.' He laughed. 'To hear me talk you'd think I understood it. Believe me, I don't. All I know is it doesn't record all the time and is triggered by motion detection. We keep the tapes for thirty days. Thirty to ninety is standard.' He gestured for Mark to sit in front of the screen. 'I'll leave you to it.'

Douglas rolled the tape back ten days to check Nina wasn't being followed and started to watch. At twenty-minutes to five the previous day, her blue Alpine nosed out of the car park and pulled into the traffic. As far as he could tell, like every other day, nobody had followed.

Forty minutes later the doorman was back. 'Any luck?'

This time Douglas told the truth. 'She left here yesterday before five, earlier than normal, heading for Southwark Street. After that, I've no idea where she went.'

Norman sympathised. 'London's a big place, easy to lose yourself.'

Exactly what Mark was thinking, and, suddenly, he felt exhausted. Lines that hadn't been there cut into his face, his head was too heavy; he held onto the chair to stop himself from falling. The doorman noticed the change in him and put a hand on his shoulder, concern flickering in his eyes. 'She'll turn up, son, don't worry. Woman are strange creatures; they're not like us. How long did you say she's been missing?'

He could hardly get the words out. 'Fifteen hours. She's been gone for fifteen hours.'

8

The jeweller's name had come from one of Charley's girls, a stunning Colombian hooker called Angel who'd worked at LBC, the former companion of an American multimillionaire not slow to spend his money, until he'd traded her in for a younger model. Nina's association with Jan Stuka had been brief – just a few visits. The old Jew didn't engage in small talk, rarely smiled, and never asked anything that wasn't about the commission. He wore no jewellery himself, not even a wedding ring, and his hooded eyes were permanently sad. The revelation about his past explained why: Nina didn't know that the boy carried from Auschwitz in the arms of a Russian soldier on a bitter January day in 1945 had left part of himself behind.

But, where a million had perished, he'd survived.

Nina was determined to learn from his example. Luke would catch up with these people. She had to be there when he did no matter what it took. Rafe and his tribe wouldn't break her.

Nina gasped when she saw Julian alone in the doorway; she hadn't heard him on the stairs. The bowl he was carrying reassured her – they didn't intend to kill her just yet. Rafe had won another round. He knelt beside her, silently spooning tomato soup into her mouth, his hand trembling with suppressed lust and fury. She held his gaze, refusing to give ground when he put the bowl aside and undid the buttons on her blouse, staring expressionless, not even the contempt she felt for the spineless bastard on her face. His fingers traced the top of her left breast, watching for the reaction he was never going to get, savouring his power, moving inside her bra, roughly caressing her nipple: Julian had her where he wanted her and wouldn't be rushed.

'One of us is going to enjoy this.'

Nina's gaze was unflinching, her tone flat. 'Maybe, but it won't be you.'

Doubt stirred in his eyes; colour rose in his cheeks. The victory was slipping away – the bitch was acting as if he was the victim. His hand closed tightly around her breast, crushing the soft flesh, bruising the pale skin between his clammy fingers, his breathing hurried and shallow.

Rafe's voice cut the air like the crack of a whip. 'You really are a fucking sleaze, aren't you?'

Julian kept his eyes on Nina. 'I'm having fun. Wasn't that the idea?'

Rafe pulled him away. 'The kind that takes balls. Not this. If I catch you near her again, I swear to God, I'll kill you.'

Julian leered. 'Don't take the high ground with me. Admit it, you'd do her in a minute if Coco wasn't here.'

Rafe leaned forward and carefully closed Nina's blouse. 'Julian's a creep. He can't help himself.'

'I'm not scared of him.'

'I can see that.' Rafe stroked her cheek, allowing his touch to linger. 'In another world, Nina Glass.'

She tried to reach him. 'You must know this is hopeless. Give it up before it goes any further. Stop now and it's over. I promise you.'

'I'm afraid your brother wouldn't see it like that.'

'He would. I'd speak to him.'

Rafe smiled. 'But that would mean I'd lost and I can't have that.'

* * *

The white Georgian house in Denmark Hill was unchanged from when Mark Douglas had let himself in at two o'clock in the morning, opening the door with the key Nina had given him four weeks after the relationship began – a significant gesture from a fiercely independent woman. For Operation Clean Sweep, being Nina's lover was a giant step closer to discovering the identity of her family's police informant, bigger even than working as Head of Security for the club. Where Luke was guarded, keeping certain things from him, Nina was trusting and open. In time, she'd tell him everything. But finding out she'd been used would break her heart: Douglas couldn't let that happen.

In the lounge, a half-finished cup of coffee sat on the table. He leaned on the original mantelpiece under charcoal line-drawings and black and white photographs of Victorian London, imagining her checking her watch, scrabbling for her car keys, hurrying to get into the day. The first time she'd invited him in had been a surprise, the elegance on display not what he'd expected from a gangster's sister. It was all still here: the five-panel Rio Silver banana leaf mural, the polished hardwood floor and the white leather couch they'd made love on so often, solemnly watched by the set of African tribal figures carved in ebony. Everything where it should be, except Nina.

Douglas wandered through the house seeing nothing out of place, heading for the door when some sixth sense made him go back. In the walk-in dressing room, the shoes, the underwear, and the jewellery chosen to complement the black Kate Spade dress with the plunging V-neck to show off her décolletage – so new it still had the price tag – were gathered, ready to put on.

When Nina left Glass Houses, she hadn't come home.

Back in the lounge, he phoned the secretary at Glass Houses and paced the floor waiting for her to respond. The call was transferred. The girl hadn't made it into Glass Houses; she was at home. Mark introduced himself and asked the question he needed answered, knowing what she'd tell him before she spoke.

'This may sound strange. Bear with me. Did Nina have an appointment with a client last night?'

Her reply confirmed Douglas's fears. 'December is a graveyard month in the property business. We're lucky to have two viewings a week. January's the same. It won't pick up until April.'

The second call was one Mark Douglas hadn't imagined himself making; circumstances left him no choice and any doubt about his feelings for Nina disappeared.

In his office in New Scotland Yard, DCI Carlisle recognised the voice and immediately assumed correctly that something was wrong. In seven months, they'd met just once outside the Flask in Hampstead because security surrounding the operation was as tight as it was possible to make it.

This wasn't good.

The urgency in Douglas's tone told the senior officer he was right. 'I need to talk to you. Today.'

'What's wrong?'

Douglas ignored the question. 'Meet me in Victoria Tower Gardens.'

'Okay. I'll be there at twelve.'

'Fuck twelve, be there in thirty minutes.'

'Thirty... what the hell's happened?'

'Just be there.'

* * *

He parked on Great College Street and crossed Millbank to the small pocket of tranquillity in the heart of Westminster. During the summer months, tourists and people on their lunch breaks spread blankets on the grass and ate picnics. Today, deserted, with the temperature close to zero, it was hard to imagine. Rodin's bronze cast of The Burghers of Calais stood black against the snow but there was no sign of the DCI. Douglas made his way to the plane trees, dusted in white, lining the path along the north bank of the Thames and leaned his elbows against the frosted embankment wall to wait. The city was shaking off the storm, slowly returning to normal. Off to his right, a steady flow of traffic drove over Lambeth Bridge under a cold blue sky. Mark stared down at the brown river running faster than its usual sluggish pace and forced himself to not think about what might be happening to Nina.

Victoria Tower Gardens, in the shadow of the Palace of Westminster, was a three-minute walk from New Scotland Yard, the reason Douglas had suggested it, public and therefore unwise. But in a case of abduction – Mark shuddered at the word, not wanting to accept that was what they were most likely up against – every hour Nina was missing decreased the chances of finding her alive. Carlisle had access to almost unlimited resources. Today, Mark needed them. For sure, Luke would have his bent copper on it. Douglas wasn't willing to stand by and do nothing. The DCI would be expecting a breakthrough on the operation and wouldn't be happy to divert manpower for this. Fuck him! Mark Douglas had been undercover for more than six months, putting his life on the line for Operation Clean Sweep every day – the bastards owed him and he was calling it in.

He recalled the first time he'd met Detective Chief Inspector John Carlisle in Blackfriars bar in Glasgow's Merchant City. Dressed casually in jacket and jeans, the detective had still managed to look like a policeman. They'd sat in a corner, both ordering Siren – Mavka, though didn't get around to comparing the beer's chocolate, coffee, coconut and caramel notes. Carlisle had come straight to the point: was he prepared to abandon his career and take on one of the most difficult assignments imaginable?

With no family to consider he'd answered yes and waited to hear the details.

Carlisle had sipped his beer and wiped foam off his lips. 'Operation Clean Sweep's mission is to root out dirty cops at all levels. Only a handful of very senior officers are aware of it. You'd be one of several going deep undercover, inside and outside the force. You wouldn't know the names of the others or where they are. It's the most closely guarded secret in the Met.'

He'd stressed the risks involved. 'One slip – one unguarded word – and in all probability your body would never be recovered. It's a huge ask.' Carlisle spread his hands by way of an apology. 'Of course, you'd like time to think about it, except I need a decision now.'

Douglas's reply had been cavalier. 'Nothing to think about. When do we start?'

For all the DCI's assurances, Luke Glass had discovered his organisation had been infiltrated. Somebody tipped him off and almost got Douglas killed: somebody from Carlisle's inner circle. In a tense meeting in Hampstead, Mark had threatened to pull out unless they found who was responsible. It hadn't happened. Carlisle claimed they'd been unable to pinpoint the source of the leak.

Douglas believed a very different truth: the DCI had looked after his own and elected to cover for a senior officer. And in that moment, for him, it started to change.

At first, he wasn't aware of the shift in his commitment. Nina's disappearance – the reason he was leaning on a wall watching the river on its way to the sea – brought it home. These people, his fellow policemen, weren't worth the sacrifice he made every day, their behaviour no better than the corruption he was meant to be unmasking. If you belonged to the same clubs and exchanged funny handshakes in dimly lit rooms, you were exempt. Exposing others was fine – not their own.

Not one of the chosen.

On the banks of the river with a chill wind cutting into his face, the scales fell from Douglas's eyes and he saw the truth. The key he'd used to let himself into Nina's house was profoundly significant. She was a beautiful, successful, independent lady who'd had plenty of men and would have plenty more if she wanted them. Instead, she'd committed to him. Apart from the obvious advantages, to have their undercover detective sleeping with Nina Glass was a major breakthrough for Operation Clean Sweep. Being hired as her brother's Head of Security for LBC had been pure luck.

Until he'd fallen in love with Luke's sister.

Nina was more important than anything, even Operation Clean Sweep; his loyalty lay with her.

His phone rang in his pocket. He took it out and read caller ID: Luke was trying to reach him; they might have found her. He weighed the possibility against what he was about to do, then put the mobile away without answering.

John Carlisle hurried towards him, clearly uncomfortable with where they were. His first words confirmed the conclusion Mark Douglas had arrived at minutes earlier.

'Tell me you've discovered the identity of the copper working for Glass, otherwise you and I are going to fall out.'

Douglas wanted to throw him over the wall into the water below.

'I can't.'

Carlisle pursed his lips, on the edge of losing his temper. 'Then you better have a very good reason for dragging me here. You understand better than anybody how this works.'

'Nina Glass has been abducted.'

Carlisle snorted disbelief. 'Nina... are you serious?'

'Last night there was a party to celebrate the club's first birthday. Nina didn't show up. Nobody's seen her since she left Glass Houses late yesterday afternoon. Hasn't been home, either – the dress she was going to wear is still on the hanger.'

Carlisle tilted his head to look at him. 'You are serious. Christ Almighty, Douglas.'

'Somebody's lifted her.'

The DCI's eyes narrowed; he stared over Douglas's shoulder at traffic on Lambeth Bridge. After a while, he said, 'And in your estimation is this event likely to impact Operation Clean Sweep?'

'No.'

Carlisle nodded, frustration curling a corner of his mouth. 'In that case, why break the cover we've built?'

'Because I want you to find her.'

'Because you want us to find her.' Said slowly, deliberately, dripping disbelief. Carlisle walked away and came back, not bothering to rein himself in, stabbing an angry finger at Douglas.

'Understand something. I don't give a damn about Nina Glass. It's her brother I'm interested in. Him and the bent copper who's sold out to him. That's what this whole bloody charade's about.'

'It may be a charade to you sitting in your nice office on the Embankment – for me it's life or death. The only officers I've seen near Luke Glass are the greedy bastards running up a bill they've no intention of paying at his club. Want their names? No? Didn't think so.'

'You're out of order, mate.'

'Am I?'

'Bang out of order. I'd advise you to stop right now.'

Douglas hadn't slept in twenty-four hours; anxiety lay like a dead weight on his chest. He tossed caution aside. 'Your information reported Glass had a tame policeman, and maybe he had once upon a time when Danny was in charge south of the river. Perhaps you haven't noticed, John, Danny's not been around much, has he? My guess is the connection – if it ever existed – ended with him. Which means I'm risking a bullet and a lime pit in the New Forest on the strength of dodgy intel.' The veins in his neck stretched and thickened. 'Supplied by you!'

'Sounds like you've lost the faith, old son.'

'Does it?'

'Want to come in? That it?'

'That's not what I'm saying. But it's my life on the line, not yours, Detective Chief Inspector.'

Carlisle pushed back. 'The intel's solid. You're missing something. Luke Glass is keeping you at arm's length because he doesn't trust you.'

'Or because there's nothing to see.'

The exchange had left both men dissatisfied. Carlisle tried to repair the damage and failed.

'I'll double-check what we know.'

'You mean, what you think you know?'

The DCI let the slight go. 'If you're right about it ending with Danny, we'll get you out of there.'

'And what about Nina?'

Annoyance furrowed the detective's brow. Out on the river, two barges loaded with yellow containers were being towed by a tugboat. Carlisle let them pass before he spoke. 'What about her? She's the sister of the biggest gangster in London, not Mother fucking Teresa. I can picture the Home Secretary fielding questions from the opposition about how long the Metropolitan Police have been in the business of helping criminals. Hardly the optics the government or the Commissioner are after.'

'What're you saying, Carlisle?'

'I'm saying let her brother sort it.'

9

DAY 3: SATURDAY

The three men swaggered across the deserted bookmakers' floor like gunslingers in a cowboy movie, eying the silent TV screens with mild interest. Compacted snow stuck to their boots, leaving a wet trail behind them. The wall-mounted televisions wouldn't be switched on today: the length and breadth of the country, racing had been cancelled after cursory inspections by stewards from Wincanton to Catterick. They couldn't have cared less about the sport of kings – that wasn't why they were here.

Their leader was Thomas Timpson, a thug who hadn't done an honest day's work in his life and supplemented his social security money by coercing those weaker than himself. His mother called him Thomas, the name she'd given him thirty-one years earlier when she'd still had hopes he'd amount to something. Those hopes were gone. To the rest of the world he was TT, a confident, broad-shouldered, improvident petty criminal always on the lookout for the main chance. He wore a hooded leather jacket with Emporio Armani on the collar, stolen from Dover Street Market near Piccadilly Circus, and jeans from Primark, paid for with a credit card lifted off a tourist in Covent Garden. No one needed to remind TT how important he was – his arrogant half-smile said he knew. Under the jacket his body was an illustrated pastiche: a tattoo of an eagle in flight carrying a writhing serpent in its hooked beak, eyes mercilessly sharp, covered his chest; a complex 'full-sleeve' design ran down both arms as far as the wrists, at odds with the simple heart on his shoulder with the word MOTHER written across it; a roll of skilfully drawn folded dollar bills tied with a rubber band dominated his back. Every other spare inch of flesh, including his hands, had some emblem or lettering. To complete the hideous picture, a heavy gold medallion embossed with the satanic symbol of an inverted pentacle hung on a chain round his neck.

But it was his head that gave Timpson the intimidating presence of a guy it was wise not to cross – under the shaved skull, etched in blue ink, his face was a mask of The Goat of Mendes, the devil himself.

TT spoke to his cronies, mockingly respectful. 'Jet, Boz, this is where it all happens, where the big decisions get taken.'

Jet – short for Jethro – was a short-haired bearded Romany who smoked a pipe rather than cigarettes and wore long flat boots. He was smarter than Timpson and smart enough to keep it to himself. Boz was the most forgettable of the three: average height, a plain face and hair that looked as if he'd cut it himself; a nondescript character apart from the claret and sky-blue West Ham top.

Nobody knew why he was called Boz.

Boz and Jet didn't speak – that was TT's job.

Felix Corrigan waited for Timpson to drop the act and say what he'd come to say. The thug was enjoying himself too much to be hurried and Finnegan felt a stab of irritation. 'You asked for another meeting. You've got one. Don't waste our time.'

TT's eyes, still bloodshot from the previous night's drinking session, roamed the room from behind his goat face. 'I'm taking it in. Been a while coming.' He turned to Felix. 'Six fucking months and thirteen days to be exact. But who's counting, eh?'

Felix looked at his watch. 'I am. Spit it out.'

Timpson lit a cigarette and provocatively dropped the match on the carpet. 'You know why we're here, Felix?'

'Mr Corrigan to you.'

TT grinned as though he'd been told something funny. 'You know why we're here... Mr Corrigan.'

'Tell me anyway.'

'Same reason as the last time. The arrangement we had with Jonas Small. We want it reinstated.'

'What arrangement?'

TT lowered his shaved head. 'Now who's wasting time? Small was running the East End before I was born. He let us have from Aldgate High Street to East Smithfield.'

'Very generous of him.'

'Generous? Not really. I won't lie. Jonas was keeping it one hundred, recognising the advantages. If he had a problem and needed extra help, he gave us a shout. We're offering the same deal to your man Luke Glass.'

Felix summed it up. 'Let me check I've got this right. You've lost your earner and you want it back.'

'Spot on. Clever boy.'

'The answer's still no.'

Timpson realised the meeting was going to be short and changed tack. 'We've asked nicely twice. So far, nobody's listening.'

'Not true. Luke's been told.'

'And?'

'He questions if you appreciate that when the restaurant Jonas owned in Brick Lane blew up with him in it, your "arrangement" went with him.'

TT examined his nails and fingered the medallion on his bare chest. 'Ask him again. Point out the advantages of having us in the tent pissing out, rather than outside pissing in.'

Felix pushed a pen across the table. 'Is that a threat?'

TT rolled his tattooed shoulders. 'A suggestion.'

'I expect you know Mr Glass isn't famous for changing his mind.'

Timpson pulled himself to his full height and stepped away. 'I want to talk to him. Face to face.'

Felix sighed. 'I'm doing my best not to take offence here. You're dealing with me. Get used to it.'

TT held his temper in check. 'I expected a wrangle – you put your side, I put mine – a bit of harangue, no problem, then we meet in the middle and everybody goes home happy. This isn't it.'

Felix held out his arms in a gesture of powerlessness. 'What can I tell you? There's nothing to discuss. Everything that was Small's belongs to us, including the territory between Aldgate High Street and East Smithfield. You used to be in the picture. Now, you aren't and you're noised-up. I get it. Who wouldn't be? But it doesn't alter the facts. If you're short of cash, get your mate to go round the doors selling clothes pegs.'

A thin smile parted Timpson's lips; his eyes stayed on Felix. Over his shoulder, he spoke to his men. 'Hear that, boys? That's what's called a racial slur. Can't say stuff like that and get away with it. Not these days.'

Felix corrected him. 'You're wrong, it's a stereotype. There's a difference. A slur would be telling him to stick to fucking his cousin.'

TT shook his shaved head. 'You think you're cute.'

'Cute enough.'

'Well. You've made a bad choice. A very bad choice.'

'We'll live with it. Without wanting to damage your self-esteem, it's fair to say you bring fuck all to the operation.'

'You've no idea.'

'Oh yeah, what?'

TT cracked his knuckles like a pantomime villain and Felix wanted to laugh out loud. These clowns didn't have a clue: putting the grip on Luke Glass was the stop after crazy. Better men had tried and suffered the consequences. They didn't have to take his word for it. Jonas Small could've told them.

Timpson and his friends made a surly retreat, leaving the impotent threat hanging in the air. Finnegan saw them out, his flinty eyes watching them turn their collars up against the cold and head off to console each other and plot their next move. The Irishman understood them better than they did themselves: as Felix had said, they'd lost their earner and wanted it back. Fair enough. Unfortunately, blind to their shortcomings, they'd gone the wrong way about it. Trying to strongarm Luke was a loser's play. Finnegan's advice would've been to forget the past, accept things had changed and ask for a job rather than waste energy trying to force a result that couldn't be won. Not a message TT and his pals would've been keen to hear.

Luke wouldn't bend, that was for certain; he'd learned from his brother. Danny's reputation for ruthlessly holding onto what belonged to the family had been well earned. Nobody knew it better than Vincent Finnegan.

The signing of the Good Friday agreement in April 1998 made him and his kind redundant. The Cause was lost; fighting for it may have been noble but it didn't pay the bills and he'd arrived off the boat at Liverpool six months later with his friend, Sean Poland, an explosives expert with the same cocky swagger as Timpson; streetwise and full of it. Danny Glass understood what former members of the IRA could bring to his operation in south London and was a generous employer. Poland lived quietly but with more money than he'd ever had in his life, Finnegan bought clothes and cars and women as though there was no tomorrow, like Thomas Timpson, convinced he was invincible. Until the relationship with Danny went south and a brutal beating left him crippled, unemployed and unemployable. A chance meeting with Luke in the Admiral Collingwood pub changed his luck and for whatever time he had left on this earth, Vincent was Luke's man.

He locked the door, shaking his head. They hadn't seen the last of Timpson. But TT would learn. The hard way, probably.

Felix didn't identify with Timpson on any level. If he'd come looking for a job, he would've turned him down. His attitude told everything about him. Taking orders wouldn't sit easy – he'd already decided he was the smartest guy in the East End and wouldn't be convinced otherwise until he was in the dirt with a bullet, blood bubbling and popping on his lips.

Finnegan made a face and sat down. 'Another satisfied customer. Not!'

'Yeah, they'll be back. Sooner rather than later.'

'Timpson thinks he's better than he is. Classic mistake.'

Felix played with the pen. 'Did they really expect me to go with some half-arsed deal they'd had with old Jonas? Remembering how it ended for Small might've been instructive before brassing their case to the people who did for him.'

Vincent grinned. 'Amateur tough guys. Probably don't have two coins to rub together.'

'Nice jacket, though.'

'Nice nicked jacket. I feel sorry for them.'

'Don't bother, Vinnie. Aldgate High Street to East Smithfield wouldn't be the end of it – they'd want more and think they could get it.'

'What'll you tell Luke?'

Felix shrugged. 'Nothing to tell. When there is, he'll be the first to know.'

* * *

Vincent Finnegan was wrong. TT, Jet and Boz had the entrance money to the pub that had been their local since they were teenagers. TT bought three pints of Courage Directors and a couple of packets of crisps and pushed the cash over the counter to the barman, already planning to put the grip on his mother to finance the rest of the week. She'd come through for him, no problem; she always had. The small fortune he owed, accrued over years, never crossed his mind. Nor did repaying it – he was her son, for Christ's sake. A guy at the end of the bar stared into his beer, his mouth moving in silent conversation with somebody who wasn't there. By the window a grey-haired geezer studied the racing pages of *The Sun*, unaware every card had been cancelled.

In the empty snug, sarcasm rolled off Jet's words as he raised his drink to an imaginary victory. 'That went well. Now what?'

TT saw the mean look in his eyes, growing dark like storm clouds gathering on the horizon, and replied with his customary over-confidence. 'They've made a mistake, Jethro, and mistakes cost. It's up to us to show them the error of their ways.'

Jet's anger flashed across the table. 'Is that supposed to be a joke? Because it isn't funny. And don't call me Jethro.'

He was off on one. TT had to stop himself from battering the idiot's face off the wall. Jet was a moody bastard at the best of times, damaged by a father who'd lifted a name from Exodus and landed his firstborn with it. A boy growing up in the East End with that handle was in for a difficult time. After losing one playground fight too many, he'd dropped it for Jet. It sounded better – cool even – though his problems hadn't ended there; the consequences of living with a madman who spent all day and most of the night on his knees begging forgiveness for sins he hadn't committed weren't so easily eradicated. Occasionally, the anger inside him broke loose and some defenceless wrong-time-wrong-place drunk got an undeserved hammering.

TT and Boz were his family; beyond them he had no friends, no girlfriend; nobody.

Boz didn't like what he was hearing any better than Jet. 'You can't be serious, TT? Jonas Small tolerated us because he couldn't be bothered with the hassle. This is different. They gave their answer, loud and clear. The arrangement's off and it's staying off. They don't need us and aren't interested. Surely, that's the finish of it? Going up against Luke Glass would be crazy.'

Timpson hid his contempt for his companions and sipped his beer. Jet and Boz were losers – worse, cowards ready to fold rather than fight. He rolled the bitter around his mouth like a wine connoisseur, making them wait for a response. When he was ready, he answered. 'Said it yourself, Boz. Small could've seen us off any time he'd wanted. So, why didn't he? Simple, he preferred to live without the hassle. If we make a big enough noise, become a thorn in his paw, Glass will have second thoughts and do what old Jonas did.'

Boz disagreed. 'Jonas wasn't all there in the head. We laughed at him, remember? Always on about his wife – Lily did this, Lily said that – when all the while he'd caught her in bed with another man and done for both of them. Thirty-odd years back, yet it sounded like he'd just been talking to her. Mental. The Glass family aren't like that. Nobody in their right mind would've messed with Danny. Don't forget what he did to Rollie Anderson and his club. Burned it to the ground with Rollie in it. Fucking ruthless. The brother's cut from the same block. Wasn't keen to go into the business when he came out of Wandsworth, so I heard.'

Jet said, 'Well, he changed his tune, didn't he? Owns that poncey club up west. Raking it in, by all accounts.'

TT smiled. 'Exactly. Life is sweet for Luke Glass. He doesn't need the aggro. Giving up a few streets in the East End means nothing to him. And if he needs some extra muscle, we'll be on for it.'

'You make it sound easy.'

'It is, Jeth... Jet. Glass could snuff us out in a heartbeat, but he won't.'

'What makes you so sure?'

'My old granddad was born poor and died poor. He was convinced he was going to win the football pools. Never missed filling in his coupon. He'd mark an X in the box at the bottom, telling them he didn't want no publicity. Publicity brought people turning up at the door and begging letters, thousands of them.' TT wrote in the air. 'Our little Emma needs an operation to save her. Please give us money.' He laughed and ran a hand over his hairless head. 'Granddad put a stop to that before it got started, he did. That's how Luke Glass will see it. He'll say, "Aldgate High Street to East Smithfield. Fucking give it to them."'

TT was a fabulist who always had a story handy that proved whatever bollocks he was spouting at the time. Boz said, 'Somebody set the bomb that blew Jonas Small away. Who do you suppose that was?'

TT took the question in his stride. 'It was Glass, 'course it was, who else? Though it wasn't about a couple of roads in Tower Hamlets. Before we're finished, he'll be happy to see the back of us. Guys like him have better things to do. All we're after is what's ours. How more fucking reasonable can we be? Drink up. And smile, for Christ's sake. I've just remembered where I can get a sub.'

10

I hadn't seen Mark Douglas since the meeting in the King Pot when he'd let slip his insecurity about Nina, so I assumed he'd needed time to himself and gone off to find it. It hadn't done him much good: the difference in him was stark, shocking in its unexpectedness from a man with more guts than most; his eyes were puffy and wild with anxiety. He paced my office underneath the club, casting around for words he didn't want to hear himself say.

Fear was contagious: I felt his touch me as he replayed the story he'd told on the phone the night before. I let him do it his way. He said, 'A CCTV camera picked her up leaving Glass Houses.'

'Still no idea where she was going?'

He bowed his head, overwhelmed by his inability to answer with certainty. 'Nobody knows but she never made it to Denmark Hill. Her dress for the party was laid out. She hadn't been home. At twenty to five, Nina was fine. After that...'

Dark energy drifted like mustard gas across the room. In the battle with Jonas Small's mercenaries, Douglas had stopped something that would've been a bloodbath without his intervention. I'd hired him on the strength of how he'd handled himself. The man in the room with me wasn't that guy, visibly crumbling, desperately needing a sliver of hope to cling to.

I couldn't give it to him; I didn't have it.

'What about a client? Any chance of something there?'

'Not according to her diary. Her secretary says that as far as business went there was very little on.'

'What does that prove? This is Nina, an impossible woman to predict. It's what makes her who she is. You said she'd seemed secretive in the last few weeks. Had it happened before?'

Douglas played with his hands. After a while he lifted his head, steadying his darting eyes just long enough to fix me and get out what was inside him. 'You must have contacts you can call in.'

'I have and I have.'

'I mean police contacts. Somebody with more resources than us.'

three people can keep a secret if two of them are dead

It was tempting to tell him. Mark Douglas was in pain – knowing Superintendent Oliver Stanford was on the payroll and had been for years would reassure him. Instead, I kept it vague.

'Trust me, I want to find her as much as you do. I'm calling in every debt I can. No stone will go unturned. We'll find her, you have to believe that. She's only been gone a day and a half. I'm half expecting her to waltz in as if she'd been out to the shops.'

A sad smile cracked his face; he knew exactly what I was on about. At the door, he paused and I caught the panic Douglas was barely holding at bay. He spoke, his voice a whisper. 'Where the hell is she? I mean, where is she, Luke?'

* * *

I waited until Douglas left to pour a stiff whisky. Offering him one would've delayed his departure and I hadn't wanted that. He'd asked a question I couldn't answer. Pretending she'd gone off on some adventure of her own was meant to reassure me, not him. My fingers drumming the desk broke the quiet in the room and betrayed where I was in my head. Every atom of my being cried out for action. Douglas had urged me to call my contacts in the Met, assuming a man in my position would have some. He wasn't wrong, though he wouldn't hear it from me – the family's association with Oliver Stanford had survived because I'd taken on board Danny's jaundiced maxim about keeping a secret. In a perfect universe two people wouldn't need to die because I'd be the only one who knew about the relationship. That particular ship had sailed but the circle was closed: nobody else would be admitted – not even my head of security, a strange response given he'd proved his loyalty more than once.

Being in love with Nina put him at a disadvantage – thinking clearly and unemotionally would likely be beyond him. George Ritchie, Felix Corrigan, even Oliver Stanford were better placed to deal with the situation.

And what was that, exactly?

Light caught the liquor in the glass; warm and welcome. I pushed the whisky away and started to count.

One: Nina had been in an accident – ruled out in the early hours.

Two: my sister had gone walkabout, alone or with someone else – considered and dismissed.

Three: improbable as it seemed, someone had taken her – with the other options ruled out it was the only possibility. But who? Who'd be crazy enough? And why hadn't we heard from them?

I reached for the alcohol I'd rejected. The city was awash in small-time outfits fighting for ownership of the streets, squabbling over scraps. So long as they remembered their place and didn't get over-ambitious the easier option was to let them get on with it. The players – the real players – were well known; the Glass family was one of them. The Irishwoman – Bridie O'Shea – controlled the West End. Like Jonas Small, Kenny and Colin Bishop had made some poor choices and were out of the business, leaving Kenny's nephew, Calum, in charge of what was left of their former north London empire.

I hadn't spoken to him and didn't intend to unless it was necessary.

Unless he made it necessary.

But it was George Ritchie's throwaway comment in the King Pot that crawled in my brain.

'Nuisance value. Don't worry about it.'

He'd been careful to leave whatever Felix was up against in the East End unspecified, his dismissal of it intentionally casual. Felix had taken over from Jonas Small and was new in the job. Could be George was protecting him. There was only one way to find out. I swapped the whisky tumbler for my mobile and called him.

The first words out of his mouth told me I was wrong. 'Luke, any news?'

'Nothing so far. I'll be honest with you, George, and I wouldn't say it to Mark Douglas, but I'm worried. This doesn't feel right.'

'I agree. I've spent more man-hours than I can count chasing around this town looking for your sister. This feels different.'

'Ideas?'

'Unfortunately, none.'

'You mentioned some business in the East End with Felix – what's that about?'

An exasperated breath blew down the line. 'It's fuck all.'

'Tell me.'

'A couple of losers trying to cut themselves in.'

'And.'

'Got told, didn't they?'

'That's it? That's all? No connection to Nina?'

Whenever he could, Ritchie avoided speaking in absolutes. Experience had taught him anything could happen and often did. 'Even a *doylem* would realise going that road doesn't end well.'

Hearing him revert to Geordie slang reminded me of his northeast roots and the reputation that had travelled ahead of him when he'd come south. Ritchie was a straight shooter, a good man to have in your corner. I needed that from him now.

'So, you're telling me... what?'

He didn't answer right away, choosing his words like he always did. 'Best guess is it's Nina being the Nina we know and love. We'll keep looking and won't be surprised if she just shows up. You're her brother, the last man I should say this to.'

'Except, you're going to.'

'Except, I'm going to. Douglas has his work cut out there. I don't envy him.'

A spark of annoyance flashed in me – there and gone – because it was the truth and we both knew it. 'Call me the minute you find anything.'

'Depend on it.'

His final comment might've been an attempt to reassure me and take his unflattering, though unfortunately accurate, assessment back. He'd said, 'I've had my differences with Nina, wouldn't deny it. She's not the easiest girl to rub along with, least not where I'm concerned. Got no time for me and I'm okay with that. But when they made her, they broke the mould. I'd put my money on your sister any day of the week. Against anybody.'

A nice try, George.

It didn't help.

* * *

I pictured him glaring out over a bitterly cold London from his office window high above the Victoria Embankment, his snarling mouth so close to the phone I could almost smell the Thai curry he'd had in the New Scotland Yard canteen on his breath. He'd be alone behind the door with:

SUPERINTENDENT
O STANFORD

stencilled in black letters, halfway through another day dedicated to keeping the capital safe from the likes of me; studying his pension statement, playing with the projection for the umpteenth time as he figured how much it would take for him and his fragrant wife to retire to the Cotswolds. Oliver better not have factored in any of my money because the gravy train he'd been riding was coming to the end of the line. It should've done before now. When and how depended on his response to our latest crisis.

Stanford let me have it. 'What the hell do you think you're doing? We agreed you wouldn't contact me here. You're endangering both of us.'

I had to admit, he had a point. If the roles were reversed, I'd have gone through him. His anger triggered some of my own: I wasn't on to discuss how his prize marrows had survived the coldest night of the year; he'd do well to remember it. My sister was missing; his job was to locate her car and be quick about it. Clearly, he didn't share my urgency – the reason I was calling the lazy foot-dragging bastard. Perhaps in the dim and distant, a younger, more idealistic Stanford had been a decent copper. That guy hadn't been around in a while. What remained was an individual weighed down with fear of discovery and the shame it would bring on one shoulder, and greed for the life dirty money could buy on the other.

'I can't believe this. Have you lost your fucking mind?'

I ignored him. 'Any sign of Nina's car?'

He remembered where he was and lowered his voice. 'What? Oh, come on, Glass, it's bloody London we're talking about. It could be anywhere. I told you. It'll take time.'

'What're you doing to find it?'

'What am I doing...? Everything I can. How many parking spaces do you think there are?'

'I pay for results. Excuses don't interest me.'

'I'm not giving you excuses. Twenty years ago, there were 6.8 million. Want to guess how many there are now?'

Stanford was a dick. Then, I already knew that. I said, 'For Christ's sake. You're going about it all wrong. Would you leave a fifty-thousand-pound car out on the street? Neither would Nina. It's under cover somewhere. Try car parking in the centre. There aren't millions of them.'

'If it's so bloody easy why don't you do it?'

Oliver Stanford needed a slap.

'You mean, have a dog and bark myself? Find that car. I won't ask twice.'

That cottage in the Cotswolds was getting sweeter by the minute.

He hit back. 'Your expectations aren't reasonable.'

'Listen, Superintendent, because I'm only going to say this once. I don't give a flying fuck. You've had a tasty drink off the Glass family. Find that car or you're finished, understand? No more bloody waffle, just do it.'

I'd been too busy tearing a strip off Oliver Stanford to notice her come in. And as anxious as I was about Nina, Charley took my breath away: she was wearing a quilted grey satin coat trimmed in what looked like fox fur, with black metallic accents at the belt buckle and zip. When she opened it, a silver crucifix gleamed against the light-grey polo neck underneath. Everything matched, including the leather boots laced up to just below the knee. Charley was stunning and, in spite of something with claws and sharp teeth eating me from the inside, I thought of Shani, the Egyptian lady who'd seduced me with a flicker of her eyelashes, keeping me interested and at arm's length at the same time.

Fear makes you horny. Nobody talks about that, but it does.

Charley's question was the same as George Ritchie's. 'Any news?'

'Still waiting.'

She nodded; it was what she'd expected. 'I'm going to drop into Glass Houses and chat. Girl talk. Wouldn't be surprised if we ended up in the pub. If Nina's involved with somebody else it'll come out after we've had a few drinks and told each other a few lies.'

'Wait until Monday, there's nobody there today.'

'Okay.'

'But you're wasting your time. Douglas says everything's great between them.'

Charley shot a look at me I'd seen before. 'Yeah,' she said, 'except, he's a man. What would he know?'

11

The heath's barren moonscape was no longer visible now night had fallen. Apart from the odd car throwing up slush, the road was deserted. Above Rafe Purefoy, smoke from his cigarette hung like a spectre. He rolled the brandy round his tongue – fifteen-year-old Asbach Uralt: sweet and thick; dark fruits, pepper and a hot rough finish – replaying the events that had led to them cautiously navigating their way out of the city through the storm. Coco's face had been bright with disbelief and elation.

They'd done it. They'd actually done it.

The robbery had been his idea, born out of a conversation Julian had had with a bodybuilder in a gym, teasingly suggested to Coco in the afterglow of sex and yet more drugs that she join them in their little criminal adventure, pitched to appeal to the thrill-seeker in her. Recently, he'd caught her barely listening when he was speaking, and sensed he was losing her. Suddenly, he'd had her undivided attention. She'd lain naked, staring at the ceiling, smooth thighs parted, hands behind her head as Rafe stroked her breasts, lightly brushing the nipples with the tip of his finger.

Coco hadn't noticed, too busy thinking. 'We'd need guns. Can you get guns?'

'We already have them. More for fun than anything. They make people want to do what you tell them. A bloody hoot, actually.'

Rafe had made a pretend weapon with his fingers.

Coco wouldn't be distracted. 'And a car?'

'That, too. My friend's aunt is in South Africa; we're using hers and her house in Hampstead as a base. We've got clothes and stuff there in case we need to lie low.'

'Is he driving?'

'No, my brother Henry will do that.'

'Does he know?'

Rafe had laughed. 'Not yet.'

'Will he do it?'

'If I ask him to, of course.'

'When?'

'When the stones are where we need them to be. In a couple of days.'

'What'll we do with them?'

'Sell them in Amsterdam.'

'You and me?'

'And Henry. Don't forget Henry.'

'The three of us? What about your friend?'

'We aren't really friends. He was my partner from the Jolly Boys at Sangster-Devlin and, yes, he's involved, too.'

'Who? What's his name?'

'Julian. You don't know him.'

'Can you trust him?'

'Do you trust me?'

'No.'

'Well, then.'

* * *

Killing the guard and the jeweller had taken it to a new level. Folding the gangster's sister into the mix opened up an even greater adventure. Rafe was ready for it, but in the aftermath of the adrenaline rush, he felt edgy and depressed. Afraid, even.

He heard Coco come into the room and stayed as he was, not wanting her to pick up on his mood. Her arms snaked round his waist, she kissed behind his ear and he smelled the faintest trace of scent. She whispered, 'They're on their way. Henry was asleep – at least, he said he was asleep. I'm not sure he was telling the truth. The Glass bitch is really getting to him. Keep him away from her. He's weak. He isn't coping. You'll have to speak to him.'

'I already have. Henry will be fine.'

'Julian was on the edge of his bed, staring into space. Don't trust him, I think he's up to something.'

Rafe untangled himself from her embrace. 'I don't trust anybody. Told you that already. And if you're wise, neither will you.'

She moved closer to kiss him again. 'Anybody? Not even me?'

He pushed her away. 'Especially you.'

She faked hurt. 'What makes you say that?'

How could she ask? She'd shot the bodyguard for fun. From now on, he'd be sleeping with one eye open.

'Because—'

She put a finger to his lips, stopping him from saying something she didn't want to hear.

'We've done magnificently, thanks to you.'

'Yes, but—'

Footsteps on the stairs interrupted him, then Julian and Henry arrived together. Henry sat in an armchair by the fire and didn't look at his brother. Julian slumped onto the cranberry-check Laura Ashley sofa that matched the curtains and the rectangle of carpet on the oak floor, clearly unhappy with being summoned, already bored by whatever Rafe had to say. He'd removed his shirt, his pale skin stretching across taut biceps a reminder that the idea about Poland Street had sprung from a conversation he'd had with the guard in a gym in Finchley.

Julian spoke like a surly teenager. 'How does the heating system go on? I need a shower.'

Rafe said, 'It's on. The temperature outside is zero. In here, the radiators are jumping off the walls. How d'you imagine that happens?'

The reply was cheeky. 'Yeah, well, make this fucking quick, will you?'

Rafe raised an eyebrow. Coco had called it wrong: Henry wasn't the weakest link. Once again, that was Julian. He'd pushed the investment scam too far, otherwise they'd both still be with Sangster-Devlin and raking it in. Senior management weren't blind and they weren't fools, either. The Jolly Boys had reached an earnings threshold too good to be true. What they were doing had to be dodgy. The final straw had come with almost the last trade of a long week, when he'd aggressively sold shares in a Dutch paper company to drive the share price down. Within minutes of it plunging he'd placed a buy order, effectively trading with himself. The following Monday morning they'd been called into Toby Lennox's office and suspended, pending an investigation. The outcome was never in doubt: both were dismissed.

Their fall had been as spectacular as their rise. And it needn't have happened if Julian hadn't been so fucking greedy. Now, he was acting out because he wasn't getting it all his own way. He didn't seem to understand that when Rafe pulled the trigger in Poland Street, he'd crossed a line. Taking the awkwardness too far wouldn't end well for him, though he was too much of an arrogant moron to realise it.

Rafe stood in the middle of the floor, a self-assured half-smile on his lips, eyes assessing them in turn. Henry: honest and naïve. Coco, the opposite: devious, always thinking about what was best for her. And Julian. Rafe struggled to define his former colleague in his head and settled for angry and resentful.

A poor selection for the contest ahead.

But it was what it was.

He said, 'I'll keep it short. As you know, our guest upstairs isn't any ordinary female. She's Nina Glass. Her brother is probably the most dangerous man in London. We didn't know that when we brought her with us.' He fixed on Julian and moved on to Henry. 'Some of you believe we made a mistake, that we should let her go. Forget it. That isn't an option and, thanks to the old jeweller, it never really was. She can identify us.'

Julian saw an opportunity to be disruptive and took it. 'Then kill her.'

'We will, eventually.'

Henry shifted uncomfortably in his seat. Rafe saw him and apologised. 'Sorry, Henry, we don't have a choice. Meantime, we do what we agreed we'd do.'

Coco said, 'To have fun?'

Something in her tone set Julian off. 'Listen to yourself. Fucking Coco? You were plain old Charlotte the night I met you in Chelsea.'

'You mean, the night I told you to get your paws off me and take your halitosis somewhere else?'

The insults bounced off; Julian carried on. 'Charlotte Boothby-Bell. Your family's claim to fame is that, by an accident of birth a hundred and fifty years ago, your father wound up distantly related to the Queen. So distant they've never actually been in the same room at the same time. Doesn't stop the gossip columns mentioning the connection whenever Uncle Freddy gets caught coming out of a massage parlour. Which he seems to do rather a lot. "Coco" is a pathetic attempt to make you interesting. Fine, if it worked. Except, it doesn't, you aren't interesting. You're a bored, reckless little rich girl. Why Rafe's besotted with you, Christ knows.'

'Leave her alone, Julian. I mean it. If you want to pick on someone, pick on me.'

Rafe nodded to Coco and returned to what he was saying. 'Last night I had a look at what the Net has to say about the Glass family. It made for an interesting read. Two brothers and two sisters. Wikipedia devotes a whole section to Danny, by all accounts a psycho who brought up his young siblings when their alcoholic father drank himself to death. Luke spent seven years in Wandsworth for his part in their rival Albert Anderson's death. Danny did the rest. Before he left the stage, everything worth having south of the river belonged to him. Fortunately, he's not around these days.'

For the first time Henry looked across at Rafe, the shadows in the corners of his blue eyes showing the strain of coming to terms with the knowledge the brother he'd trusted had lied to him.

'Where is he? Where is Danny?'

'Nobody knows.'

'You mean—'

'I mean nobody knows, Henry. Luke's the boss and he's taken the family in a new direction. They're legitimate business people now. They'll want this settled without a fuss.'

Luke Glass had gone to prison for throwing rival gang boss Albert Anderson off the forty-third floor of a building. Rafe left those details out. It was better they didn't fully understand what the man they were fucking with was capable of; it wouldn't settle nerves already on edge.

Rafe took a coin from his trousers and pointed at the ceiling. 'The sister upstairs may seem like a well-dressed tart. Don't be deceived. She owns one of the top estate agencies in the city. Luke's the force behind Glass Construction and a private members club in

Margaret Street called LBC, short for Lucky Bastards Club, apparently.'

Coco said, 'LBC? The card I found in her handbag.'

'Correct. The other sister – Charley – is involved, too. She's a bit of a mystery.'

Julian interrupted. 'Pardon me, Rafe. This may all be fascinating but what relevance does it have to us? Forget the history lesson and get to the point. And don't start fucking about with that bloody coin trick. We've seen it. We're impressed. Let it go.'

Rafe tossed the coin in the air and caught it in his open pocket. 'That is the point. On the surface, their criminal past is behind them. Except, it isn't. Their kind don't change. They were born rubbish and they're still rubbish. Fucking them about is almost our duty.'

'Yeah, unless they catch us. I still say put a bullet in the bitch and dump her body.'

Rafe slipped the gun from the waistband of his trousers and held it out. 'Okay, Julian, if that's what you want go ahead. I won't stop you.'

Julian hesitated. 'Keeping her alive is asking for trouble.'

'Maybe you're right. Maybe you've been right all along. You know where she is, so do it. Coco shot the guard. I shot the jeweller. That makes it your turn, doesn't it?'

'Not here.'

'Mmmm. If you don't mind me saying so, that sounds like a bit of an excuse to me. You're not up for it after all, are you? Then, do me a favour, shut the fuck up until you've grown some balls.' He spoke to the others. 'Anybody else have something they want to say? Coco? Henry? That's what I thought. We'll go with the plan.'

Julian didn't learn; it wasn't in his nature. 'There's a plan?'

Rafe pulled out the gun and stuck it under his chin. 'I've told you once already, Julian. One more word and four becomes three.

Understand when you're winning and don't push me any further. Choosing between Nina Glass and you wouldn't be hard. She'd get the vote every time – and not just because she's better to look at, although she most certainly is.'

'You wouldn't dare.'

'Wouldn't I? Sure about that, are you?' Rafe put the gun away. 'As I was about to say, Glass will have men scouring the city, calling in every favour he's owed, at the same time expecting somebody to contact him demanding money in exchange for his sister. By staying patient we'll have softened up big bad Luke so that when we break our silence, he'll be so relieved he'll fall over himself to give us what we want.'

'And what *do* we want?'

'Coco said it. "To have fun". Have fun messing with a gangster.'

Julian laughed. 'Until he finds out who we are and the "fun" really begins.'

'How exactly would he do that? Who's going to tell him? You? Me?' Rafe shook his head. Julian didn't grasp the basic laws of life. 'We can't lose because we're Luke's worst nightmare – people who actually don't give a fuck. Beautiful, isn't it?'

Julian sat forward. 'So, tell us – what is this great plan?'

'Okay, we'll wait another two days before we make contact.'

Julian couldn't help himself; he jumped in. 'Glass will trace the call. It'll only be a matter of time till he's cutting your head off. No, thanks, Rafe. I'm out.'

Rafe let him bluster. 'And if that was the plan, I'd agree with you 100 per cent, Julian. It isn't. For as long we need to, we'll make contact from public places. Maybe supermarkets not near here with plenty of people around.'

'Aren't you forgetting something?'

'Am I? What?'

Julian pointed to the velvet pouches on top of the fireplace. 'The stones.'

'The stones aren't a problem. When our business here is finished, Coco and I will fly to Amsterdam and sell them. If the jeweller was to be believed about the quality, it shouldn't be a problem. We'll meet up and split the money.'

Julian stood up. 'Got it all figured out, haven't you, Rafe?'

'Most of it.'

'Yeah, well, good for you. I'm going to have a shower.'

* * *

Voices travelled up the brick chimney from the room below like the drone of a fly against a windowpane. Nina couldn't make out the words. She didn't have to; they were discussing their next move, arguing about what to do with her. During the first long sleepless night, the temperature had fallen, the heat had gone out of the air, and the timbers in the old house groaned and contracted. The pins and needles nipping her wrists and ankles were replaced by an ache that throbbed and faded as her hands and feet went numb. Alone in the darkness, Nina had taken strength from being a Glass. Her family had known more adversity than most and come through it. More than come through it. Come out on top. She'd played the drama she'd been dragged into in her head, still not able to believe it – Coco's execution of the guard, the foolish courage that had cost Mr Stuka his life, and her own failed attempt to escape in the snow. In the shadows, her lips had parted in a humourless grin: Rafe and Coco had probably imagined having sex was their idea. It hadn't been. In the aftermath of the robbery, adrenaline had released dopamine in the lovers' nervous systems, bringing a sense of well-being. But that had been yesterday. Today, the mood had been very different.

The house was in Hampstead, across from the heath, no more than four or five miles from the club, yet it might as well have been a thousand. Luke would move heaven and earth to find her. On streets all over London, word of her abduction would be whispered. George Ritchie's men would give every likely character from Barnet to Bromley a hard time in an attempt to slap information they didn't have out of them. Mark would be going insane, thinking she'd left him for somebody else. The absolute absurdity of it made her smile. Nina would never know another lover. Poland Street had been a secret; her secret. And it had worked against her.

She was on her own.

* * *

Thomas Timpson's mother was a good woman who had done her best bringing up her only son by herself. But in attempting to make sure the boy lacked for nothing she'd overcompensated, indulged him and ignored the reality that he was his father's son, an untrustworthy waster. When he'd said he needed money, as usual, she'd given him most of what was in her purse. TT tossed an empty promise to pay her back over his shoulder and closed the door on his way out.

In the pub, Boz nervously eyed the clock behind the bar. He said, 'Are we sure this is the way to go? I mean, are we really sure?'

TT mocked him. 'What? You scared, Bozy?'

Boz didn't apologise. 'As a matter of fact, TT, yeah, I am. Not sure this is one we can win. They'll know it's us.'

'No, they won't. They'll put it down to vandals and make a few bob on the insurance. We step in like we did for Jonas Small and offer our services.'

'Don't see them going for it, TT.'

'Even if they don't, they'll be glad to do without the aggravation.'

'I wish I had your confidence.'

'You and me both, old son.'

* * *

It was bitterly cold on the high street. At half-past one in the morning they had it almost to themselves. A taxi with its FOR HIRE sign unlit passed on the other side of the road. TT, Jet and Boz ducked into an alley until it was out of sight. The firebombs, like the arsonists themselves, were crude – empty beer bottles three-quarters filled with petrol and a torn piece of cloth held in place at the neck by an elastic band.

TT said, 'Time to teach the fuckers a lesson.'

Boz weighed the brick in his hand. 'Doubt torching his shop will make a difference to Luke Glass.'

TT punched his shoulder, playfully. ''Course, it won't. But it will to his flunkies.'

He put his bottle on the snowy ground, flicked a disposable plastic cigarette lighter and triggered the spark; a soft-yellow flame, blue at the base, sprang into life. TT sheltered it with his palm and spoke to his companions. 'Ready?' Jet and Boz nodded. 'Then, let's do it.'

Boz ran into the street and hurled the brick at the bookies' window. The glass smashed, fell to the ground and shattered into a thousand pieces. TT and Jet let the burning bottles fly, aiming for the opening Boz had created. The effect was instant – the blaze raced up the walls, devouring the television sets, licking the ceiling tiles.

Jet tugged TT's arm. 'C'mon, before somebody sees us.'

TT shrugged his hand away, fire shadows dancing on his grinning face, and spat on the ground.

'Fuck you, *Mr Corrigan*.'

12

Felix Corrigan kicked a charred piece of wood with his shoe into the pile of blackened timbers and tiles that had crashed to the floor when the roof caved in. Through the hole, a sky heavy with rain waited to release its load. The early-morning air was acrid and smoky; Felix tried not to breathe it. The bookies wouldn't be opening any time soon. Maybe never. Felix hoped Luke had checked Jonas Small's insurance payments were up-to-date when he'd taken over. Outside on the pavement, Vincent Finnegan stood with a uniformed police officer. Guessing what was being said wasn't difficult. When the conversation ended, Finnegan picked his way to his boss through tiny lakes left from the river the firemen had hosed on the burning building.

'They've found pieces of bottle glass. Reckon it's deliberate, probably kids. Very little chance of catching them.'

Felix nodded. 'Deliberate, yes, kids, no. What did you say?'

'Nothing. I let him do the talking. You think it's Timpson and his troops retaliating for getting knocked back?'

'One hundred per cent. And the coppers can leave the catching to us.'

* * *

In Douglas's office, the tech guy he'd installed was monitoring incoming calls. His feet were up on the desk; he was relaxed, reading a titty mag and smoking a cigarette. When he saw me, he dropped the magazine and sat straight, pretending to watch something on his screen. Until the kidnappers made contact, all he could do, like the rest of us, was wait.

No news was definitely not good news. We'd assumed someone had abducted Nina but what if we were wrong? What if she'd had enough and left? I'd considered it myself more than once. She'd seemed happy; maybe that had been a front and Charley's throwaway comment was on the money – Nina had gone off with somebody else and wasn't coming back.

Mark Douglas had asked a question I couldn't answer. A sleepless night trying to come up with something, anything, that made sense didn't change it. This morning, Douglas looked the way I felt, eyes tired and gritty, though better than he'd been the day before. Talking would've meant going over the same ground yet again, so we didn't. Every other minute he glanced across, expecting the great Luke Glass to step in and fix what needed fixing.

He wasn't alone. So was I.

Finally, he said, 'She can't just have disappeared, it isn't possible.'

Douglas was wrong – it was all too possible, though I wouldn't be the one to educate him. Dropping out of your life wasn't a crime. Close to sixty thousand people went missing in the capital every year and the longer we heard nothing, the more I wondered if Nina was one of them.

Douglas got up and paced the room, firing out accusations and questions without waiting for a reply. 'What about her car?' He shook his head. 'That car sticks out like a bloody sore thumb. Somebody must've seen it.'

My mobile ringing brought his relentless stalking to a halt. I lifted it and turned away when I saw who was calling. Oliver Stanford said, 'We still haven't found the car. Not much to be done until it raises a flag somewhere. Anything your end?'

I didn't answer. We weren't friends. I said, 'Stay in touch,' and hung up.

Mark Douglas leaned on the desk, crowding me in his eagerness for news. 'Who was that?'

My standard reply would be, 'None of your fucking business.' He was hurting so I let it go.

'One of my contacts checking in.'

'And?'

'And, sod all. He'll keep searching.'

The hope that had briefly flared in his eyes died and he went back to chasing shadows.

'George Ritchie has had his ear to the ground for twenty-five years. Surely...?'

'As soon as he finds anything he'll be on the blower. Depend on it.'

He wasn't reassured. 'Call him anyway.'

'It's a waste, Mark. George knows the score.'

'Yes, but—'

My mobile rang for the second time in a minute. Ritchie's ears must've been burning. Before he spoke, I sensed he had something to tell me. 'What've you got?'

'On Nina, so far it's a blank. Got guys all over the city working on it. We had a bit of bother in the East End last night.'

'What kind of bother?'

'One of our bookies was torched. The police are blaming it on kids.'

'I'm hearing a but, George.'

Ritchie sighed down the line as though he'd rather not get into it. 'You'll remember Jonas Small let a couple of locals have a few streets in exchange for a bit of extra manpower when he needed it.'

'Vaguely.'

'Yeah, well, they weren't best pleased when we took over and they lost their patch.'

'They suggested doing the same deal with us. Felix sent them on their way.'

'You're right, he did. Yesterday, they turned up again and got kicked into touch a second time.'

'And Felix thinks it was them?'

'No proof, but yeah. The leader's an arrogant arsehole, name of Timpson.'

'Break his legs and see how arrogant he is then. Meanwhile, stay on Nina.'

'Will do. Nobody in London has the balls to mess with Luke Glass.'

'I hope you're right, George, I really do. Except, if a few tossers in the East End can try it on, there's bound to be others.'

* * *

Charley had only been to Glass Houses twice before. After she showed up claiming to be Nina's long-lost sister, the rivalry between the women had been undisguised, occasionally downright hostile. Time had mellowed them, though they were careful to stick to their own side of the street: Glass Houses – one of the fastest growing estate agents in the capital – was very definitely Nina territory.

A fresh-faced girl behind the reception desk wearing an oatmeal polo neck and a jade necklace smiled when Charley pushed the door open. 'Good morning. Welcome to Glass Houses. How can I help you?'

The spiel was rehearsed but the delivery was warm and if Charley hadn't known better, she might've believed it. The office was as she remembered it, functional and stylish at the same time, not unlike its owner. Beyond the entrance, a double line of computers sat silent. In the run-up to Christmas, property obviously wasn't the business to be in.

Charley softened her American accent and said, 'Is Nina around? I'm her sister.'

'Sorry, she hasn't come in today. Is she expecting you?'

'Yes, we're supposed to be having lunch. Been trying to reach her. Her phone doesn't seem to be switched on. I'll wait to see if she turns up. Will that be all right?'

The girl heard the American accent and took in the expensive clothes; her boss hadn't mentioned she had a sister. 'Of course. Can I get you anything? Tea? Coffee?'

'That's sweet of you, coffee would be lovely.'

Charley grabbed the opportunity. The receptionist wouldn't be Nina's confidante but there wasn't much she wouldn't see or hear. If Nina had brought another man here, this girl would know.

'How do you take it?'

'Black no sugar.'

'Black no sugar, it is.'

'Perhaps you'll join me?'

'Oh, I'm not sure Nina would like that.'

'Nonsense. I'll tell her you were keeping me company.'

'Okay, I will.'

'What do I call you?'

'Vivian.'

'Vivian. What a lovely name.'

13

I had to get out – anywhere that made me feel like I wasn't sitting around waiting for the news my sister's body had been found. When I picked George Ritchie up, he seemed glad of the distraction and asked where we were going. I told him and watched his face fall. For as long as I'd known him, his MO had been to assume everybody knew something, even a little something, he hadn't heard. His first instinct was to listen rather than talk: a man who made the Sphinx seem like a blabbermouth. This morning he looked at the world beyond the window and stepped out of his normally taciturn character, damning our destination in a few not particularly well chosen words, spoken to himself.

'Darkest Walthamstow. The arse-end of nowhere.' He turned to me. 'How does a south London boy know somebody in this neck of the woods?'

He made it sound as though we were in a canoe on the Orinoco on our way to meet a lost tribe, instead of Seven Sisters Road, heading for a scrapyard and an old 'associate' of my brother's.

But it was a fair question.

To answer it properly would mean divulging information only a couple of people had. Instead, I gave him the short version, the one that didn't incriminate me. 'Hughie was Danny's connection. The first time he brought me here I was a teenager. Said he'd business to discuss and told me to stay in the car. Believe me, George, when I saw what was out there, I was fine about that.'

Ritchie mused out loud. '"Business to discuss". Anybody I might've known?'

He didn't expect a reply and didn't get one.

'I've heard rumours about this guy. What's he like?'

My mouth spread in a private joke. 'Like nobody you've met or would want to meet. As for his story...' I hesitated. 'All I can say is he's been around as long as I can remember.'

'Why go near him?'

A woman ran in front of us, talking into her mobile, hurrying towards Blackhorse Road Tube. I braked to avoid hitting her and almost stalled. George said, 'Good reflexes. She has no idea her day almost changed.'

For a second, I thought he'd forgotten what he'd asked. No chance: this was George Ritchie. He waited quietly until I answered. 'Because he hears things, and right now anybody who might get a whisper about who has Nina and where they've taken her is worth a visit. Even to "the arse-end of nowhere".'

He let that sink in. 'How did Danny know him?'

'I'm guessing you had something to do with it.'

'Me?'

'Yeah, you. He was at the start of the war with your old boss, Albert Anderson, building alliances with all kinds of people. Hughie was one of them. For a while they were pretty tight.'

'Hughie what?'

'No idea. Only ever known him as Scrap Hughie. But a word to the wise, George – whatever you do, don't let him catch you staring at him. He doesn't appreciate it.'

'Why would I stare?'
He'd know soon.

* * *

We drove through the shuttered remains of what had once been an industrial estate, down the side of a red-brick railway bridge covered in purple graffiti. Apparently, Spider loved Lady: good to know. Patches of moss sprouted from where the lime mortar, put there by the Victorians who'd built it, had slackened and fallen loose. Danny had brought me here – still a teenager and very much the junior partner I'd remain. Back then, he'd been my hero: in his best moments I'd wanted to be him.

Further on, the road narrowed to a single track overgrown with long grass at the sides that had, so far, managed to survive the English winter. Then the high fence came into sight, topped with barbed wire, and the cars piled on each other like broken toys, mountains of them. When we reached the entrance, I rolled down the window and pressed the intercom. No words were exchanged; the gate parted and soundlessly closed behind us. The earth was glazed with frost, rutted and hard under the tyres, forcing me to crawl towards a grey Portakabin with a bottle-green door near a crusher. At the back of the site there would be hills of plastic, glass, wood, rubber and upholstery separated out before the giant claw that hung in the air lifted the mangled vehicles and fed them into a hydraulically powered maw to be flattened like pasta dough. Above it, a bird with large wings circled in the overcast sky joined by its mate, and it was easy to imagine we'd crossed into a dystopian world of rusting steel and twisted metal.

I wasn't alone. Ritchie sensed it, too. He said, 'Who else is here?'

'Just Hughie.'

It wasn't true: I caught a black blur out of the corner of my eye.

The last time it had been Dobermanns. Big mothers. These were Tibetan mastiffs and there were three of them. The dogs raced from their hiding places under the wrecked chassis, not barking until they were almost on us. One stopped in its tracks, balancing like a dancing bear on its hind legs, breath like white clouds on the cold air, snarling while the heavy chain attached to the collar round its bull-neck tightened and did its work.

I turned the wheel and pulled away, not quickly enough to prevent a paw from denting the panel on the driver's side.

The two others prowled, growling low and baring their teeth. In the passenger seat, Ritchie hadn't moved. I'd been here before, yet it had caught me off-guard. The next words out of his mouth surprised me. 'Where's the other one?'

'The other one?'

'These are pack dogs. Has to be another one. The leader.'

That there could be a beast smart enough to hang back until we'd made a move was a sobering thought. I hammered the horn, adding to the canine cacophony, till the cabin door opened and Scrap Hughie appeared. He shouted something I couldn't make out and the barking stopped. Ritchie put his hand on the door, about to open it when I said, 'Not yet.'

The animals weren't for security. Their real purpose was the stuff of nightmares and there were always people ready to hire their services, my brother among them.

Hughie waved us to him. When we stayed in the car he came over and launched into a spiel he'd had plenty of opportunities to spout – the 'surely you aren't afraid of a couple of harmless little dogs' speech. He leaned in the window, filling the car with the sweet and sour fumes of cider.

'They can smell you're scared. Don't be, they won't touch you.' His round face cracked in what passed for a smile. 'Unless I tell them to.'

We didn't reply – he was playing with us.

Hughie said, 'If you're here to jaw, we jaw inside. Otherwise, fuck off out of it,' and went back to the Portakabin. Scrap Hughie had to be seventy years old. Financially, life had been good to him: his business was a goldmine. Recycling had made him a fortune. He'd have more money in the bank than he could spend in a handful of lifetimes. As far as I knew, he'd never married, so there was no Mrs Scrap to help him get through it. Physically, he hadn't been so lucky: his beat-up leather jacket was too big for his thin frame. The stoop made it impossible to guess his height, though he couldn't have been more than five one or two, and there was a tinge to his skin that spoke of some kind of liver disease. His fingernails were cracked and dirty and the nicotine stains weren't limited to his fingers; his teeth were brown and yellowed. A hump bent him at an angle of sixty degrees when he walked. Taken together they explained his single status. Partnered with a glass eye, the overall effect was too much for most people.

Maybe the dogs were his way of evening up the score.

To say I'd met Scrap Hughie that first time would be wrong. I hadn't, not in any real sense. I was there – that was as much as there was to it. The nearest I got was watching him and Danny talking in the middle of the metal mounds.

Seeing them together was the beginning of my understanding just how much I didn't know about my brother. And wouldn't, until it was too late for both of us.

On our next visit, Danny insisted I get out. Back then, Hughie operated out of a wooden hut – a glorified garden shed that leaned to one side. When my brother introduced me, the scrap man settled for an almost imperceptible nod. The meeting itself was unmemorable, chit-chat that didn't include me about faces they both knew, punctuated with lewd comments about women that had both of them laughing.

It didn't last long. My presence wasn't required and I was beginning to wonder why we'd made the journey from south of the river when they drew away, moved closer and lowered their voices. As they spoke, Hughie single-eye-studied me. Whatever or whoever they were discussing was on their way out, even if they didn't realise it.

Then, it was over and we were back in the car.

Since then, an ocean of water had gone under the bridge.

* * *

The stench in the Portakabin hit me like a blow; sweat and cigarette smoke hung in the confined space and the walls were bare – not even an out-of-date calendar with the obligatory pictures of naked women – apart from dark marks I didn't allow my mind to speculate about; flimsy net curtains covered the filthy windows; the only furniture was two plastic chairs and a heavy wooden desk. Scrap Hughie sat behind it. At the other end, a camp bed with a mottled duvet and a grubby pillow told the story of a lonely, unwell man's withdrawal from the world. An almost empty cider bottle stood beside it on the floor; another one had rolled into a corner.

Hughie poked a black finger at Ritchie. 'I know you, you're George Ritchie. Albert Anderson's brain, they called you. That whole crew's dead. Except you. What happened, George, fall into the river and come out with a salmon?'

The implication was nasty and over the line. I stepped in before Ritchie hauled the manky bastard over the desk and straightened out his hump for him. 'George runs everything south, Hughie. He's on my team now.'

Whatever point he'd been making was made. Or was it? He scratched a jaundiced cheek and turned on me. 'Danny still AWOL, is he? Not like him. Hope you're taking care of his interests.'

I let him speak.

'That club of yours – what's it called again?'

'LBC.'

He drew on his cigarette and coughed. 'That doesn't sound much like old Danny. Can't see a man with his opinions going for that. Heard they let all sorts in.'

'All sorts'. I could add racist to Hughie's long list of defects.

Reacting was exactly what the bastard wanted. I didn't disappoint him. 'LBC belongs to me, Hughie. So does Glass Construction. Me and Nina are in Glass Houses together. My brother has fuck all to do with them. If and when he decides to put in an appearance, I'll be telling him the same. Now, any other observations or can we get on with why we're here?'

He chuckled and stubbed what was left of a butt in a battered-tin ashtray. His work was done.

'I made some calls.'

'And?'

'Nothing. Nobody know where she is, which tells me the people you're dealing with are outsiders.'

'Keep trying.'

'Don't hold your breath.'

I already was.

Hughie said, 'Anything else?'

'When there is, we'll be in touch.'

He nodded as though he didn't believe me. 'You're the boss, boss.'

Outside, the cold air nipped our faces but it was the sweetest I'd ever tasted. We were at the car when he called from the door. 'Hey, George, what's it like to work for somebody as smart as yourself?'

Ritchie faced him. 'Where's the other one?'

Hughie grinned a yellow grin. 'I heard you were a bright guy.

Sure you want to meet him? I mean, you almost wet yourselves with the puppies.'

Ritchie's expression didn't alter. 'Where is he?'

Hughie laughed and slapped his hand on his thigh. 'Wait there.'

He disappeared doubled over at a crazy angle between the metal canyons. I said, 'What the hell're you doing, George? Thought you were anxious to get out of here.'

'Seeing what he's got.'

'And then?'

'Then we know.'

I wasn't prepared for what happened next. Neither was Ritchie. Scrap Hughie came from behind the crane. Trotting beside him was the biggest animal I'd ever seen outside Regent's Park zoo. Its head was massive above muscular shoulders melding into a long black coat. The dog leaned affectionately into its master's leg, at a guess, all two hundred pounds plus of him. As they got closer, without breaking stride, Hughie slipped a chain over its thick neck and wrapped the end round his hand. He wasn't strong enough to control this animal. It was a gesture, no more, and I felt dread stir in me.

They stopped eight feet from where we were. 'Here he is, George. The guy you were so keen to get acquainted with. What do you think?' He flashed his terrible grin and squinted at us; he'd got the reaction he was expecting – the only reaction possible – and was pleased with himself.

Ritchie tensed but held his voice steady. 'What's his name?'

'Freddie. His name's Freddie.'

'Usually, it's Sabre or Khan.'

'I prefer Freddie.' He clapped the giant, his hand lost in the folds of fur. 'Just a big softy, aren't you, boy? Look at those eyes.'

I did look; they were kind and sad and for a moment I almost forgot what this aberrant monster was. A pink slab of tongue darted between its jaws, sliding over rows of teeth and incisors bigger than my thumb.

Hughie's good eye stayed on us not wanting to miss a second of our discomfort. He was showing off. Suddenly, the smile froze on his ugly face. He whispered in the animal's flap of an ear and braced. In an instant, Freddie morphed from a loveable pet into something from a genetic nightmare. His great head half turned, the top of the jaw drew back, eyes on fire, a growl rumbling like an underground explosion beneath our feet.

And where there had been sadness, I saw death. Agonising, bloody, horrible death.

It didn't last more than a couple of seconds. While it did, it was the most terrifying thing I'd ever witnessed. My brain measured the distance to the car. Reason told me I wouldn't get there, those enormous paws would crash into me, the sheer weight of the impact breaking my back. Images of sticky drool and hot fetid breath on my neck made it hard not to panic and run. But if I did, those pictures would become reality: Scrap Hughie couldn't stay with him – not a chance; he wasn't strong enough – he'd be pulled off his feet and the animal would be free.

Hughie whispered again and, like a magic trick, the beast – I couldn't bring myself to think of it as 'Freddie' – reverted to a docile cuddly toy any kid would love to wake up to on Christmas morning.

Hughie gave us a history lesson. 'Tibetan mastiffs can kill a lion. It's what they were bred for. A word from me and he'll rip your throat out. Be over before you can scream.'

'I believe you, Hughie. It's safe to say we're impressed.'

He wasn't finished. 'Once he's loose, there's no stopping him. I can't. Nobody can. Commands won't work. Triggers – forget them. His primitive nature kicks in. He'll drag what's left behind the crusher and play with it before he eats you. Seen it with my own eyes.'

Of course, he meant eye; it wasn't the time to correct him.

* * *

On the drive back Ritchie was quiet even by his standards.

'Something wrong, George?'

'Wrong, no, not exactly. I'm trying to figure why we came all this way for a one-minute conversation you could've had on the phone. He hadn't a thing, not a fucking thing, to tell us. I don't get it.'

It was tempting to roll out my own history with Scrap Hughie. Tempting, but unwise. And Ritchie was lying; that wasn't what was on his mind. I knew because the same thing was on mine.

We were skirting a bleak Finsbury Park when the truth tumbled out. In the passenger seat, he couldn't hold onto it any longer, shuddered and said, 'Freddie. Fucking hell.'

14

Nina's defiance with Rafe and Julian had been an act, a stubborn refusal to let them see how scared she really was. But with the prospect of another terrifying night ahead, fear began to overwhelm her. As the shadows lengthened, rising like ghosts around her, she assessed her situation honestly, seeing the truth. A harsh laugh broke from between her lips in the darkening room. It was hopeless. No matter how much money Luke paid, they wouldn't let her go. Because they couldn't.

The worst of the storm had passed. A wind rattling the wooden window frames reminded her of the world beyond her prison. Believing her brother would save her was all she had to hold onto.

But, as the hours passed, doubt eroded Nina's faith, and she believed a little less.

By now, they should have contacted him with demands for her safe return. Nothing about them suggested they had. What the hell were they waiting for?

Had they realised they'd bitten off more than they could chew?

Would they simply walk out of the door and abandon her? Leave her to die?

Nina tried to shut out the questions torturing her mind. Her stomach churned; acid rose in her throat and she forced herself to calm down. 'Focus on them. Focus on them.'

The mood in the house had been different again today. That didn't prove anything. These people were volatile – factions with no love lost between them.

Her heart rate slowed but the fear was still there. She flexed her hands and feet against the bonds lashing her tightly to the chair. If by some miracle she managed to break free, she'd need to be able to use them.

Nina heard them go to their rooms. No one bothered to check on her. Bastards, what if she needed to go to the toilet? She closed her eyes as the night-time sounds of the old timbers contracting triggered another wave of terror, making her dread what tomorrow would bring. Hours later – or maybe it was minutes – a noise startled her. Someone stood at the door, their face hidden in the gloom. When they didn't speak, Nina dared hope Henry had disobeyed his brother and sneaked back to help her.

In the darkness, she whispered his name. 'Henry?'

The figure didn't reply and she bowed her head, realising how foolish she'd been to even consider the boy would be brave enough to cross his brother. And if it wasn't him, only one option remained: Julian had returned to finish what he'd started.

Nina pressed herself against the chair and called out as he silently moved across the floor – his palm closed over her mouth, he bent and brushed her lips with a kiss, then left. The unexpected tenderness took her by surprise. Julian wouldn't be capable of gentleness – not when there was the opportunity to slake his lust at some helpless female's expense. Before she could consider what it meant, she felt hot breath on her neck and Rafe was fumbling to free her breasts, breaking the clasp of her bra. His wet mouth found her nipples. Breathlessly, she whispered, 'Not here. On the bed.'

'No.'

'Untie me.'

'No.'

'You need to so we can both enjoy it.'

'I said, no.'

She pleaded with him. 'Please, Rafe.'

His voice came from a place deep inside him, raw and mistrusting. 'Okay. Try anything stupid and I won't wait for Coco to kill you. I'll do it myself. Understand?'

'Yes, yes, I understand.'

He hastily undid the rope, both of them pulling at her clothes. When she was naked, he gasped and threw her onto the bed. Rafe kicked off his shoes. Then, he was between her thighs, his face buried in the soft skin of her throat, Nina's long legs circled him, binding them together, panting, 'Yes. Yes. Yes.'

She unzipped his trousers and arched her back to take him.

Blinded by the need that had brought him to the room, Rafe didn't see her fingers claw in the dark until they found what they were after. The brass Victorian antique lamp was cold and heavy in her palm. At the last second, he sensed something and cried out as it crashed against his temple.

A terrified Nina lay still, expecting one of the others to burst in. When they didn't, she pushed the unconscious Rafe off and grabbed the pink dressing gown from behind the door. Every atom of her body wanted to finish him – beat his face to a bloody pulp. Instead, she got on her hands and knees and searched the floor in the dark for his shoes – big, but better than bare feet – all the time listening for the voices that would mean they were coming. She heard nothing and began to believe she'd get away with it.

On the stairs, too unsteady on her feet after so many hours in the chair, she sat on the top and edged down, knowing one groan from the old boards could betray her. Like the amateurs they were, convinced she wasn't a threat, they'd left the key in the lock. Nina turned it thankfully and ran as best she could out into the night. At the end of the drive she stopped and looked up. A light came on in the bedroom: through the glass Coco's angry face glared hate. The shoes protecting Nina's feet from the freezing ground were impossibly large but she dared not kick them off. The freezing air seared her lungs, pain burned in her chest and it was difficult to breathe. Two options presented themselves – neither of them great. On her right, the bleak expanse of the heath stretched to Highgate. Nina wouldn't make it; they'd catch her long before she got there. The second was fifty yards further on, a rambling red sandstone set back from the road. If she could reach it, the people who lived there would call Luke and she'd be safe.

She staggered towards the house, leaving a trail of footprints. Behind her, boots crunched on the virgin snow. Nina struggled up the steps and banged on the door, praying someone would be there. 'Help me! Help me! Please, help me!'

When no one answered she turned to face her captors. The dressing gown spilled open revealing her nakedness; she didn't care. Julian leered, savouring the show, enjoying her humiliation. 'You really are the unluckiest bitch in the world, aren't you? There's nobody here. The owners live in New Zealand.' He laughed. 'Though, I do have to compliment you: nice tits.'

Coco was coming up the drive, taking her time, certain they had her. Nina stared her down, the old defiance alive in her eyes. 'Think I'm going to make it easy? Well, fuck you!'

She fired a shoe at Julian. It caught him on the shoulder; he stumbled on the icy ground in front of Coco and Nina ran down the side of the building to the garden. At the bottom, under an apple tree, a summer seat beside a wooden fence dividing it from the next property offered the only escape route. She reached for the lowest branch, cursing the weakness in her arms, hauling herself up until her foot was on top of the connecting fence.

Before she could jump, firm hands caught her ankles and pulled her down. She landed heavily and this time Julian took no chances; his fist smashed the side of her face and drew back to deliver a second blow.

Coco stopped him. 'Enough! She's mine.'

A knife flashed in her hand. Julian put himself between the women. 'Not here. We'll take her to the house and you can do what you like.'

* * *

Rafe stood at the door watching Coco drag the beaten Nina by the hair, his face ashen, a bruise at his hairline. Coco glared at him, pushed past into the lounge and spoke to Henry. 'You do know your brother's a fucking idiot, don't you? Thanks to him, this bitch almost got away. Get out all of you. I'll handle it.'

Rafe found his voice. 'Like hell. I made a mistake. It won't happen again. But understand this, Coco. I'm still running the show.'

She turned on him. 'You're kidding yourself. Henry thinks the sun shines out of your arse. He's wrong. You're pathetic.' She stabbed a finger at Nina. 'You creep out of my bed to fuck this trollop, this... piece of street trash.'

Rafe sneered. 'Oh, spare me the righteous indignation. If you got half a chance, you'd do her brother. Don't deny it.'

Julian's ironic laughter cut the tension. 'Saint Rafe. Our leader. What a joke. Coco's spot on, you've lost it. Well, understand this, old chap, spending the next twenty years of my life in prison because you couldn't keep it in your trousers doesn't appeal to me.'

'That isn't going to happen and you know it.'

Coco drew the knife. 'We should've finished her in Poland Street, that's what I know!'

Before anyone could stop her, she lunged at Nina's face, missing her eyes by inches. Nina cried out as the blade continued its downward arc and slashed her breast. Rafe grabbed Coco's wrist and forced it back until she dropped the weapon. He picked it up, breathing heavily, and spoke to the group. 'Listen to me. We're either in this together or we aren't in it at all. You decide. "This trollop" is Luke Glass' sister. And she's ours. We said we wanted excitement, remember? Well, no one can say we haven't got it.'

He pointed at Nina, moaning, clutching her chest, blood trickling through her fingers. 'Henry, take her upstairs.'

'She's hurt, Rafe. She's bleeding.'

He pulled Nina's bloodied hand away: the knife had cut a line an inch from her left nipple. She'd been lucky; there would be a scar, but it wouldn't kill her. Rafe dismissed the wound. 'She'll live. I'll be up in a minute. You'll get your wish, Coco. When the time's right you can do what you like to her. Now, let's stop fucking about and get some sleep. Tomorrow we'll introduce ourselves to Mr Luke Glass. I'm sure he'll be happy to hear from us.'

PART II

15

Oliver Stanford sounded pleased with himself and I pictured the smug smile on his still-handsome face. Maybe our paths had crossed in another life but when Danny introduced us, I'd disliked the policeman on sight. This morning, the insufferable superiority oozing down the line was welcome – it meant he had something.

His tone was light, conversational. Devoid of urgency. He might've been on to tell me he was thinking about booking a holiday in Majorca instead of drip-feeding crucial information.

'I said these things take time and I was right.'

He pushed my buttons without trying. He couldn't help himself; it was who he was. As soon as he spoke, my heart jumped in my chest; I knew this could be the break we'd hoped for. My gut told me my sister was in trouble. The great Luke Glass was powerless and impotent. Stanford wasn't a fool. He understood exactly and teased it out with an unwanted lesson in geography. 'It's easy to forget how large the city is.'

He was winding me up, making me wait. I didn't appreciate it. All the old enmity resurfaced and I growled at him. 'Get fucking on with it, copper.'

'All right. We've found your sister's car.'

'Where?'

'Soho.'

'Where in Soho?'

'A parking place in Poland Street.'

'What the hell was she doing there?'

Barking wouldn't make him go faster; he was enjoying himself too much. 'You mean, you don't know?'

'If I did, I wouldn't be asking you.'

A rustle of paper told me he was reading off the details. 'According to Q-Park, a blue Renault Alpine A110 matching the registration you gave was left on Thursday at twenty-minutes to six in the evening. The owner hasn't come back for it.'

The news took us a step closer to understanding where Nina had gone though not why. It was what I'd wanted but it wasn't enough. 'That it? There's no more?'

He paused. 'Actually, there might be.'

'Then spit it out.'

'Does the name Jan Stuka mean anything?'

'Should it?'

'I've no idea. Two bodies were discovered at an address in the same street as the car. One of them was Stuka. He was a jeweller. The other, we assume, was his bodyguard. They'd been shot. The safe was open and empty. We found several diamonds on the floor, which suggests there was a robbery and it didn't go as planned.'

'You've lost me. What has that got to do with Nina?'

Stanford thrived on being in control. He said, 'Her name was in Stuka's book next to sketches of a necklace and a bracelet. There was an inscription. "From N to M – all my love."'

He'd saved his bombshell till last, relishing my silence.

'You're saying Nina got caught up in a robbery?'

'It's a possibility.'

'Except, it doesn't make sense. They'd already killed two men, why not shoot her and be done with it?'

'We don't know enough to answer that.'

'Okay. What do you know?'

The rustling started again. He'd risen above being personally involved in cases; a detective inspector and his team, names I'd never hear, faces I'd never see, had done the legwork. Thanks to me, Stanford had a part of a puzzle his colleagues weren't aware of: Nina's abandoned car and its significance.

'The bodies were found on Saturday morning. Forensics put the time of death at thirty-six to forty hours earlier.'

'Not long after Nina parked. Too much of a coincidence. What about cameras? Soho's bound to be crawling in them.'

Stanford chuckled as though I'd said something amusing. 'You'd think so, wouldn't you? Q-Park has them, of course. Private firm and all that. The investigating officers reviewed them – one of the first things they did. Problem is, they weren't looking for your sister. She'll be on there. I don't doubt it. You may remember Westminster Council axed fixed cameras in 2016 to save money. Claimed the old ones didn't meet police needs. Bollocks, of course. They promised to reinstate them but they've dragged their feet. I'm told that at four o'clock in the morning Soho looks like a scene from *Dawn of the Dead*.'

He was at it, showing me Nina was my problem, not his. It was clear my sister's car had no part to play in her disappearance. I said, 'What did they get on the robbers?'

'So far, nothing. Either slick operators who knew what they were doing or, more likely, thanks to the lack of CCTV, just some bastards who got lucky.'

The policeman had been reining himself in. Faking concern.

Not so secretly, he'd be delighted, fulfilling my order and sticking bad news to me at the same time.

Happy birthday to him.

He wasn't wrong. Stanford detested me – anything that caused my family pain was fine by him; he loved it. His next question turned the screw. 'Has anybody contacted you?'

'If they had I'd be handling it myself.'

He let a moment pass, then dropped his poisoned pebble into the pond and waited for the ripples. 'Mmmm. Taking their time, aren't they?'

I wanted to snap his worthless neck. 'What're you saying, Stanford?'

'Only that the robbery was on Thursday night and now it's Monday. What's keeping them? Unless they don't have her.'

He meant don't have her alive.

'Nina's out there and I'll find her.'

'Well, if there's anything the Metropolitan Police Service can do, don't hesitate.'

He had the advantage and was determined to use it.

'You really are a low-life bastard, Oliver. I'll tell you what you can do.'

He rang off before I could get it out. But his card was marked – he'd had the information since Saturday. I wouldn't forget it.

My next call would be to George Ritchie. In an hour his men would be swarming all over Soho. And unlike the police, they didn't have to be polite.

* * *

Before she'd met Mark Douglas, Nina had used men for sex and moved on to the next pretty face without a backward glance. She was a Glass – tougher than the majority of males who'd wandered across her path. The exceptions were her brothers, Danny and Luke; hard acts to follow in more ways than one. For a relationship to have any chance of working, her partner had to be someone she could lean on. Somebody strong. Strong enough, if need be, to end it. Mark was all of that and more. The most difficult part of the nightmare she'd unwittingly been caught up in was knowing how badly her abduction would affect him.

Her second attempt to escape had been as hopeless as the first – they'd caught her easily and brought her back. This time the consequences had been more serious than a broken heel.

At first, Rafe had stood between her and the other two. That protection was gone; humiliating him had lost her her advantage. She looked down at the ugly gash on her breast, knowing she'd been lucky – it had been aimed at her cheek and Coco was still angrily banging doors because she'd been stopped from finishing her handiwork.

Aggressive voices drifted through the house, followed by periods of silence before the arguing began again. After a while, Nina heard the front door close and an ignition spark to life. The car pulled out of the drive and she realised they'd put their differences aside and reached a decision.

It was finally starting.

* * *

Rafe turned off Camden Road into the busy Sainsbury's car park. Grit cracked underneath the wheels but apart from discoloured mounds of impacted snow here and there, the storm might never have happened. He pulled into a space between a Fiat and a Mondeo.

From the back seat Coco said, 'Remind me why we're going to all this trouble.'

She was still in a mood over Nina. He said, 'You know why. I've told you why.'

'Well, tell me again.'

'Don't play silly buggers, Coco. It was sex – it meant nothing – you'd take her brother on in a heartbeat. This is no different.'

'I should have killed the little whore. I wish I had.'

Rafe took a deep breath. There was nothing to be gained by losing his temper: Coco wasn't jealous. She was restless and uptight. He didn't blame her. 'Look, forget her, she isn't important. What we're doing is. Can't you feel it? As soon as we make contact our advantage disappears. Glass has been expecting a call for days. He'll be set up to trace it, have people ready to go the minute he has a location.'

In the rear view he saw Coco smile. She said, 'When they come for us can we stay and watch?'

'What?'

'Stay and watch. I've never seen a gangster in the flesh.'

Rafe couldn't tell if she was serious or just stupid and felt his patience slip. 'Fucking hell, don't you get it? We'll be more at risk than at any time since Poland Street. We keep our heads down and stay on the move. Camden Town today. Next time, we'll use somewhere where there are lots of people, well away from Hampstead.'

Julian said, 'Do you think he's involved the police? If he has, the place might be crawling with them.'

Rafe scratched his chin. 'Difficult to say. A man in his position is bound to have a few tame ones. He'll handle it himself. You know, send out the right message and all that.'

'How much money are we asking for?'

'Does it matter?'

'No, but how much?'

Rafe took a coin from his pocket, changed his mind and put it back. 'I rather think we'll leave that up to him. It'll be interesting to hear what value he puts on his sister's life, won't it?' He opened the car door. 'Let's do this thing.'

* * *

In the old days, Nina would swan off with some loser she'd met five minutes ago and not be seen for a week. Danny would go crazy and I'd laugh, knowing she did it because it wound him up. When she finally showed they'd have a row – or, more accurately, he'd have a row, threatening all kinds of stuff that was never going to happen. She'd ignore him until he ran out of steam and carry on being Nina, doing what she liked. Danny Glass was the most feared name in London but with her he'd met his match. Wherever my sister was, I hoped that same spirit was burning.

Mark Douglas was a tough cookie – he'd proved it more than once. Nina's disappearance had sucked the will out of the Glasgow ex-copper. I didn't judge him. People coped in their own way. Mine was to tear the city apart, brick by brick, until I found her.

Stanford – just thinking about him made me angry – had delivered his news in instalments, teasing out the details like an interesting puzzle that had fuck all to do with him. Not clever. Nina's car and a double murder in the same street at the same time was significant and the policeman knew it.

As for George Ritchie's team – who the hell was I kidding? It was a bloody waste of time.

So was Charley's visit to Glass Houses. Her 'girl talk' had produced sod all, otherwise she would've been back with it. Her non-appearance told the story.

A wave of despair washed over me. We were feeding on scraps, pretending the search was moving forward when in reality we were busy bloody fools.

I hadn't had a decent night's sleep since last Wednesday,

surviving on a diet of coffee, alcohol and not much else. Suddenly, the dam broke and my resistance crumbled. I rested my head on my arms and closed my eyes. How long I stayed like that, I couldn't say. The hum of my mobile pulled me back.

I read the caller ID and ran down the corridor to Douglas's office. The guy with the headphones was already on it; he gave me a thumbs up and I answered the phone. 'Nina? Nina, is that you?'

Silence.

'Can you talk? Where are you?'

Nothing.

'Nina? Nina, speak to me.'

The voice was plummy and educated, dripping the assurance only money could buy. I hadn't heard it before – I would've remembered – although I'd suffered many like it in LBC, talking loud, laughing louder, convinced the world and everything in it belonged to them and always had.

'Good morning, Mr Glass. It's time we had a chat considering how much we have in common, don't you agree?'

My fingers closed round the phone's hard plastic case. 'What've you done with Nina?'

The question amused him. 'Nina's fine, don't worry about her. She sends her regards.'

'If you so much as harm a hair on her head—'

The amusement faded; it had never been real. 'You'll do what?'

'Trust me, you don't want to know.'

'I'm disappointed in you, Mr Glass. Can I call you Luke? I'm disappointed in you, Luke. Threatening me isn't wise. I might take it personally and do something rash.'

'Who are you?'

'Who I am isn't important.'

'How much do you want?'

The laugh returned, forced and fake. 'Surely, what matters is how much you want to pay?'

'Stop playing games. How much?'

He sighed. 'You're not listening. I'm asking what your sister's worth to you. For the moment, whether it's enough is neither here nor there.'

'You say she's fine. I want proof.'

'Can I be pedantic and point out I'm using her phone?'

'Not good enough.'

'Mmmm. Perhaps an ear sent to a newspaper would convince you?'

'I don't have time for this. How much?'

The urbane tone taunted me. 'Again, that's for you to decide. I'll give you until tomorrow to think about it.'

* * *

Henry would've preferred to go with them rather than be left in the house with Nina. Not happening. Rafe couldn't depend on Julian or Coco. Given the chance, they'd harm her. At the right time he wouldn't stand in their way. That time wasn't now. The Glass sister had a part to play; they needed her. He'd taken his brother aside and explained. At the end, he'd said, 'So you see, Henry, it can't be anybody else, it has to be you. Tell me you understand why.'

'Because Julian will kill her.'

'He will, and there will be nobody to stop him. I'll be back as soon as I can. Stay away from her and everything will be fine.'

For an hour Henry watched TV and looked out of the window at the few remaining patches of snow on the heath. Eventually, inevitably, he switched off the television and went to the room. Nina's chin rested on her chest, her eyes were closed; at first, he thought she was sleeping. As he turned to go, she slowly raised her head – her face was tired and puffy; dried blood crusted on the wound at her exposed breast – and spoke quietly, softly, trying to touch something in him. Certain it was there if only she could reach it. 'Henry. Henry. Please, Henry. Look what they've done. If you don't let me go, you'll be a murderer, a murderer just like them. You'll spend the rest of your life in prison.'

He didn't want to listen, didn't want to hear. Nina sensed she was getting to him and kept talking. 'You've no idea what that's like for a handsome young man – the things they'd do to you. Awful things. You wouldn't survive.'

Henry put his hands over his ears. 'You're trying to scare me.'

'You're right, I am. Because you should be scared. You should be terrified. Being brutally raped, forced to take some stranger's—'

He screamed. 'Stop! Stop it! Rafe won't let that happen!'

Nina's mouth twisted in a sneer. 'Rafe. Rafe. Always fucking Rafe. If you believe that, then you're a fool, a poor weak boy blindly following his crazy brother. Prison will be the easy option, believe me. When my brother catches up with him, Rafe won't be able to save himself, let alone you.'

Henry looked away. Nina thought he was going to cry. 'Even if I wanted to, don't you realise, I can't?'

'Yes, you can. Of course, you can. Rafe made a mistake – you heard him admit it – why can't you?'

Henry's voice cracked with emotion. 'In case you haven't noticed, I'm not Rafe.'

* * *

In the lounge, he slumped on the couch and turned the TV on again. What she'd said, the pictures she'd painted – he couldn't get them out of his mind. His head hurt; he felt sick. But one thing he was sure of: prison wasn't for people like him.

'You wouldn't survive,' she'd said, and she was right: he'd be found hanged in his cell.

Henry paced up and down, as confused and depressed as he'd been in the boarding-school dorm when his father had shaken his hand, told him to be 'a good little chap', and left him alone with the suitcase his nanny had packed at his feet.

He'd cried himself to sleep that first night. Rafe had phoned the next morning and every week after that, making him laugh with funny stories. Without him, Henry wouldn't have been able to stand it. But that had been a different Rafe – the Rafe he loved.

His brother had let Nina escape; he could hardly point the finger at him. Henry would claim he'd been taking her to the bathroom when she'd pushed him down the stairs. Nobody would believe it. He didn't care. This was wrong.

* * *

Nina saw him standing in the frame and knew her prayers had been answered. As he untied her, she mouthed a silent thank you. Henry was pale, reluctant and obviously unhappy.

Rafe had trusted him. He was betraying that trust.

Nina said, 'You're doing the right thing.'

'I'm not a murderer, I can't let them hurt you. I just can't.'

She hugged him. 'You're a good guy, Henry. When this is over – and it'll be over soon – we'll get to know each other properly.'

'The police—'

Nina pursed her lips. 'There won't be any police. My family will deal with this themselves. When Luke—'

Tyres crunching on the gravel drive cut short her vision of future retribution. They were back.

She took his boyish face in her hands and kissed him. 'I'll never forget this, Henry, never.'

He pulled away. 'Go. Get out. Quickly.'

Nina struggled downstairs and along the hall to the kitchen, more mobile than she'd been though still stiff and sore. A heavy key, discoloured with age and probably original, hung on a hook. She slipped it into the lock and opened the rear door – they'd see it and assume that was where she'd gone. The snow had melted. At the far end of next door's garden she saw the apple tree and the summer seat, reminding her of how close she'd come to regaining her freedom. Nina was tempted. Except, they'd caught her before and would again. She slipped into the pantry, pressed herself against the shelves and held her breath.

Yards away, Coco cursed. 'We've lost her. The fucking bitch, we've lost her.'

Julian said, 'She'll make for the road. We need to be out front. Come on.'

Rafe didn't chase after them: Coco and Julian would handle it. He stood at the bottom of the staircase, hands on hips, staring down at his brother sprawled on the floor, rubbing his leg, glancing nervously towards the kitchen. There was disappointment in Rafe's voice, a genuine regret that hadn't been there before. 'Henry, Henry, Henry. What have you done?'

He walked up the hall to the kitchen. In a cupboard he found two mugs, put them on the granite work surface and filled the kettle from the tap. Over his shoulder, he shouted, 'I'm having coffee. Want one, Nina?'

The door opened; Nina came out of the shadows, holding herself, biting back fear and frustration. Rafe heard her behind him and said, 'I assume you take it black, no sugar.' He smiled. 'Because you're sweet enough, right?' He handed her a mug. 'The only reason you aren't dead already is because you might be valuable to me. Coco and Julian disagree. They want us to get rid of you and wouldn't think twice about putting a pillow over your face. Until now, I've stopped them. But when you turn my own brother against me, I have to wonder if maybe I'm wrong and they're right.' Rafe came closer. 'So, here's the deal. If you value your life, you'll take it. This time it's black coffee. Next time it'll be a bullet in your brain. And one more thing. Henry's young, leave him alone. Or I'll smash your pretty face so bad even your fucking brother won't recognise you. Cheers!'

16

The King Pot had been the scene of so much over the years. All this time later and even without the photograph of the Queen on the wall and the juke box blasting 1960s pop classics, the spectre of Danny was still here. It was hard to shake the feeling that the door would open and he'd come waltzing in, grinning the manic grin that meant he wasn't happy and somebody was going to be sorry.

Felix Corrigan leaned his elbows on the desk, talking quietly with George, probably bringing him up to speed on the 'nuisance value' in the East End Ritchie had casually mentioned. The conversation ended abruptly. On another day, I would've been suspicious and asked what they were discussing. Right now, I couldn't have cared less.

Felix was lucky to be alive. He'd screwed up big time when Albert Anderson hit the pub, getting himself a drink at the bar, instead of guarding the front door like he was paid to do. Danny had gone ape-shit and ordered somebody to put a bullet in his head. I'd stepped in – not to save Felix; I hadn't known him from a hole in the wall – but because the pub was full of witnesses, some of them coppers. Shooting him in front of them was a one-way ticket to Broadmoor and Danny would've had one of the nutters who'd hacked corporal Lee Rigby to death near the Royal Artillery Barracks in Woolwich for company.

My brother had been a racist and a xenophobe.

He'd have loved that. Not!

As ever, Charley was dressed to impress, but her stylish clothes couldn't hide the strain of the past few days, though it was nothing compared with Mark Douglas; he was really suffering. He took a seat without acknowledging anybody and stared at the floor, as lost as any man I'd ever seen. What I had to say wouldn't make him feel better. Oliver Stanford's news and the phone call painted a clear picture: Nina had been caught up in a robbery and the thieves had decided to go for gold.

Before I could start, Douglas spoke, his voice thick, on the edge of hysteria. 'What's happened?'

He was drunk.

I spoke quietly. 'There's been a development.'

'What kind of development? Is Nina all right?'

It was easy to sympathise with him and I did, except what we were up against needed clear heads, not boozed-up lovers who'd lost the plot. 'Mark. Mark. Everybody understands what you must be going through. We feel the same. But unless we keep cool, we haven't a hope of getting Nina back.'

He seized on my words. '"Getting her back." You mean you know where she is?'

'Let me tell it my way.' I spoke to Felix. 'Get some coffee in here. Black. Sweet. Lots of it.'

Douglas snapped, irritable and aggressive. 'If that's for me, I don't want it.'

'It is for you and you're fucking drinking it, even if I have to pour it down your throat myself. Now, as I was saying, there's been a development. We've found Nina's car.'

'Found it where?'

'In a parking place in Poland Street.'

'Poland Street? What the fuck was—?'

'A jeweller's was robbed around the same time. It looks like Nina got caught up in it.'

Douglas ran a hand through his hair. 'What the hell was she doing in Soho?'

'I think we can answer that. The jeweller's name was Stuka – he's dead by the way. So's his bodyguard. Nina's name was in his notebook.'

Alcohol had dulled Douglas; he wasn't getting it. 'In his notebook? Why would Nina's name be in his notebook?'

I hesitated. He wasn't going to like it. 'She was having stuff made.'

He screwed up his face. 'Stuff? What kind of stuff? She didn't mention it to me.'

'Because some of it was *for* you. There was a wax model of a necklace and another of a bracelet with the inscription "From N to M – all my love". I'm guessing it was a surprise Christmas present.'

Douglas bowed his head, crushed. From where he was, he probably felt it couldn't get much worse. I wasn't so sure. He said, 'How... how do you know this?'

three people can keep a secret if two of them are dead

'Doesn't matter. The thieves took her with them.'

'I'm not following. They'd killed two people, why not Nina?'

'For the same reason anybody gets kidnapped, Mark: money.'

'Then, why haven't they made contact?'

'They have.'

* * *

Days ago, we'd celebrated LBC's first birthday in a packed club bursting with the great and the good. Apart from Shani, I hardly remembered it. From Douglas's call in the middle of the night to the stranger laughing down the phone today was like being trapped in a bad dream.

Felix Corrigan was a smart guy, a shrewd operator who'd risen from the ranks to run the East End streets for me. After his poor start, he'd earned his seat at the table. He set a pot of coffee down in front of Douglas and poured. Douglas ignored it. So far, George Ritchie had settled for listening. When his question came it was typically on point. 'Have you actually spoken to Nina?'

'No, George, I haven't.'

'What about tracing the call?'

'There wasn't enough to get an exact fix. It was made from a supermarket in north London. Nothing stands out. Unfortunately, there was no CCTV from the car park. It seems nobody in London can get a fucking camera to work.'

The blunt Geordie in him slipped out. 'Not much bloody good to us, is it?'

'No good at all, George. Might as well be the fucking moon.'

Charley went where Ritchie had chosen not to. 'We can't be sure she's still alive.' She glanced an apology at Douglas. 'How much do they want?'

'They didn't say a figure.'

'What did they say?'

'They asked how much Nina was worth to me.'

Charley's brow furrowed. 'They asked how... I don't understand.'

'They're letting me decide.'

'Wha...? Who are these people?'

The toffee accent laughed in my head, chiding me, mocking my helplessness. 'I don't know.'

She said, 'Are they insane? Do they know who they're dealing with? Before we pay a penny, we need proof Nina's okay.'

I hesitated again out of respect for Mark Douglas. He didn't need to hear this. 'They've suggested sending an ear to a newspaper.'

Douglas buried his head in his hands. George Ritchie got up and knelt beside him, whispering empty reassurance. Charley said, 'Christ! I don't believe it. Are they serious?'

'Absolutely serious. They're calling tomorrow and they expect an answer.'

* * *

George Ritchie watched Luke go; George didn't trust people and had rarely been wrong. There were exceptions – admittedly few and far between, but they existed – Luke Glass was one, Felix Corrigan another. Originally from Newcastle, Ritchie was a wise old owl who didn't act without reason or speak unless he had something pertinent to say. His preference for caution was legendary – rumour had him taking a different route home at the end of a day, never the same way twice. Excessive, maybe, though in a world where life was cheap, he'd survived longer than his peers. Most of the people he'd started out with were no longer around. Seven years after his old boss, Albert Anderson, had taken a dive off the forty-third storey of a building under construction in Bishopsgate, a fire in a disco called the Picasso Club had effectively wiped out the whole organisation, including Anderson's son, Rollie – everyone apart from George Ritchie.

The findings of the public enquiry in the aftermath of the tragedy that claimed so many young lives still hadn't been released. Nobody knew what had started the blaze or who was responsible. Although Danny Glass was the odds-on favourite.

With his boss and crew gone, Ritchie had considered retiring until Luke changed his mind. If the offer had come from Danny, he'd have turned it down. Since then, he'd spent more hours than he could count with the younger brother, drinking whisky, discussing books, films, politics, religion, philosophy and the best place to get a doner kebab at two in the morning. Every topic under the sun... except the Picasso Club fire and what had really happened to Danny.

Luke's empire was growing and it would've been easy for Ritchie to add the East End to his territory south of the river. Instead, he'd passed. Felix Corrigan was a good guy; he deserved it.

While the others were arriving for the meeting, Felix had pulled him aside. 'Need a word about that bit of bother.'

Over his shoulder, George had seen Luke. 'Okay, catch up with me at the end.'

Now they were alone, Felix opened up. 'Thought I should check what level to take it to.'

'When're you sorting it?'

'Tonight.'

'How much damage?'

'For us, nothing the insurance won't cover. For them, I'm thinking broken legs and skull fractures.'

Ritchie nodded, slowly. 'Yeah,' he said. 'Sounds about right.'

Constance Greyland had had a shitty day. Not good: Constance didn't do shitty. Florian had huffed and puffed on the sun lounger by the hotel pool, sighing, making his dissatisfaction obvious. The voice that had charmed her in Chelsea had taken on the unattractive whine of a lawnmower going in somebody's garden at eight o'clock on a Sunday morning when she had a crashing hangover from the party the night before. The famous old hotel in the shadow of Table Mountain was a friend; at sixteen on her first visit with her parents, she'd lost her virginity to a middle-aged Turkish wine buyer in his room overlooking this very swimming pool. Connie hadn't known his name then and didn't know it now: Enis. Ender. Emre – something like that. What she remembered was his wide smile, his deep-brown eyes, and the totally unnecessary lies he'd told to get her into bed.

That was the beginning. Later, she'd married Simon and for six years stayed faithful until he killed himself. Connie had given him a good send-off for the sake of appearances, then picked up the pieces of her own life with a series of men: every year a different one, always young, always good-looking, always – though they didn't know it – passing through. The deluded would've called them love affairs. Constance had a different name. They started with long passionate afternoon sessions – all legs and lips and athletics – and died three or four months later from neglect. Some of her partners kidded themselves into believing they couldn't live without her; the notion made Connie smile. Bloody fools. They were using her as she was using them. Fair exchange and all that. She waited until they landed back in England, then she put them out of their misery. Occasionally, one would cry and she'd feel for him. Most recognised they'd had a good innings and took it well enough.

Surprise, surprise – it hadn't been true love after all.

* * *

Dinner in the Mount Nelson's wood-panelled old writing room was worth looking forward to – beautiful food, great service, and the sun setting behind the flat top of Table Mountain. Time seemed to stand still. This evening it had been a disaster. The confrontation that had been building for days came to a head in the afternoon when she'd finally tired of Florian's childish behaviour and reminded him he was lucky to be here. He'd thrown a bottle of suntan lotion at her and stormed off. Later, Constance had found him in the suite's other room in bed with one of the maids.

He'd spent every minute in the restaurant desperately trying to undo the damage, totally spoiling a perfectly delightful lobster bisque, telling her he was sorry, begging her to give him a second chance. It wouldn't happen again. He promised.

Too fucking right, it wouldn't.

Connie didn't do second chances.

* * *

The pub in Little Somerset Street was decent, a lot better than the boozer they usually used – the beer was okay, reasonably priced, and there were so many screens you were guaranteed to see the match. The game at Stamford Bridge had gone ahead in spite of the rock-hard pitch; most of the players wore gloves. Ten minutes from the full-time whistle, West Ham were awarded a penalty and scored. Boz punched the air. 'Yes! Yes! Get in. Get in!'

As a Hammers supporter, he'd listened to older fans' stories about the glory days of Bobby Moore and Geoff Hurst. A bloody long time ago – there hadn't been much to cheer about since. Tonight's victory took them to within a point of the top four and qualification for the Champions League. If it had been April, cause for hope. Unfortunately, it was December and there was a lot of football still to be played. God knew where the team would be in May. Mid-table probably. Tonight would be just a memory and he'd be back to hearing about the outrageous volley Paulo Di Canio had scored against Wimbledon when Boz was six years old.

He swallowed the last of his pint, zipped up his jacket, and headed for the door. He hadn't seen TT or Jet. They'd agreed to stay out of sight for a while. Very wise. In hindsight, torching the bookies was bound to bring a swift backlash. Boz and Jet had been against it. TT saw it differently. For him it was a matter of honour – a concept he only vaguely grasped. His logic was simple: Luke Glass had royally screwed them. The only way to get their old patch back was to be a thorn in his paw. He'd used his mother's money to buy them a drink and lay out his half-arsed plan like a general before a battle.

Jet had said, 'Before you start, TT, this is crazy. It isn't going to work.'

'Going against them head on, I agree, we'd have no chance. We don't. We've asked nicely and been knocked back.'

Jet said, 'What madness are you suggesting?'

'I'm keeping it one hundred, people. Burn the place down. See what they think of that.'

'I can guess exactly what they'll think about it. They'll do us in. We'll get slapped up all over the place.'

'No, we won't. It'll get their attention; they'll realise we're ballsy and are making a point.'

'And change their minds? Not in a million.'

TT had agreed. 'You're not often right, Jethro, but you're wrong again. It's on. Get used to it.'

The night air was bitter. Boz remembered the football players and their gloves. The difference was they were getting paid a fortune to be out in it, he wasn't.

He took a shortcut to the Tube station, off the main road, along an unlit lane. About halfway down, Boz heard a noise and turned to see a cat scurry across the cobbles from a bank of bins against the exposed brick wall. His nerves were on edge. Dealing with TT, no wonder. Further down, he kicked a stone and raised his arms in the air pretending he'd scored the winner in the cup final just as two men stepped out of the shadows, two more appeared behind him, and cut short his celebration.

17

Henry lay on his bed, hands behind his head, staring at the ceiling. Since the attempt to let Nina escape failed, he'd stayed in his room so he didn't have to look at his brother or the others. He hated them. Saw them as they really were and was ashamed of being so easily led. Julian and Coco were cruel and twisted but he'd trusted his brother – his whole life he'd trusted him – and Rafe had repaid that trust by lying to him.

The original plan to rob the jeweller's and scare a few people, including themselves, had sounded stupid – he should never have allowed himself to be talked into it – but it hadn't included murder. When they'd had their fill, they'd kill Nina and there was nothing Henry could do about it, not if he wanted to stay out of prison himself.

The door opened, Rafe came in and sat on the edge of the bed. He looked unhappy and Henry caught a glimmer of the brother he'd loved and trusted.

'You shouldn't have done it, Henry. You really shouldn't.'

'Yes, I should, this has gone too far.'

Rafe toyed with a loose thread on the covers. 'I came to tell you we're leaving in twenty minutes. You're coming with us.'

Henry fired back. 'Oh, I'm leaving all right, make no mistake about that. But not with you. I'm out.'

'Forget it, you're driving.'

'No, I'm not.'

Rafe shook his blond head. 'I'm very much afraid you're not getting it. Coco and Julian think you're a problem – a problem that needs to be resolved.'

'Resolved? You mean—'

'The only thing standing between you and a bullet is me.'

'That's ridiculous.'

'Is it? They believe you'll go straight to the police.' Rafe teased a loose thread from the bedcover. 'Honestly, Henry, I'm not sure they're wrong.'

'I'd never do that. You know I wouldn't.'

'So, you'd just go on with your life and forget Nina Glass tied up waiting for the bullet that will end her pointless existence?'

Henry didn't reply and Rafe stood; he had his answer. 'Twenty minutes. You're driving.'

'Driving where?'

'Liverpool Street Station.'

'Can't you see this is madness? You have to end it, Rafe. Let Nina go. I swear she won't give us up.'

Rafe dropped the thread on the carpet, pulled out the coin and gazed across the room at a collection of photographs in heavy gilt frames taken at a garden party on a sunny day, the men in morning dress, the ladies print frocks and hats. In one, a handsome woman he guessed was Julian's aunt Connie smiled on cue for the camera.

His lips pursed and he brought his attention back to his brother. 'Henry, Henry. You're so naïve. Perhaps she won't give you up. The rest of us would be a different story.' He laughed and cut it short, suddenly serious. 'Always remember Julian's a loose cannon. He wouldn't hesitate and I can't always be there.'

'You can tell them they don't have to worry. No matter what happened I wouldn't give their names. On my word.'

If only it was so easy.

Rafe said, 'On your word as a gentleman? A bit late for that, old chap. Julian and Coco don't trust you. Neither do I. You royally fucked up when you let her go, and you did it all by yourself. There are consequences to what we do or don't do.'

'Somebody has to stay.'

'It won't be you and, no, they don't. Coco's taking her to the toilet. Julian's going to double-tie her hands and feet and gag her. The door will be locked from the outside. She won't get away again.'

'But, Rafe—'

Rafe had done all the talking he was going to do. 'Downstairs in twenty minutes. And a word to the wise. In the car, keep your mouth shut and maybe they'll forget you almost got us caught.' At the door he turned, slowly, reluctantly. 'You keep telling me you're not a child. Well, you'll get a chance to prove it. When this is over, you're on your own, Henry. As far as I'm concerned, I don't have a brother.'

The announcement was expected to rattle Henry; he met it full on. 'If that's your decision, then fine. But I won't be part of this.'

Rafe gripped the brass handle. 'I hoped you'd learned your lesson and were ready to see sense. Julian promises me you won't suffer.'

'What...?'

'He'll make it quick for you.'

Henry screamed at him. 'Julian's a sociopath and your girl-friend's barking! What does that make you?'

'A man who doesn't want something bad to happen to you. Last chance. Get yourself down there or he's coming up. Your choice.'

On the landing, Rafe closed the door and leaned against it. Coco and Julian were right. Henry was going to be a problem.

* * *

Blood from the cut on her breast had dried all over the pink dressing gown; she'd been fortunate. Another inch and Coco's blade would've sliced off her nipple; the 'nice tits' Julian lusted after wouldn't be so nice any more.

Yesterday's failed attempt to escape was the worst of the three. Hiding in the pantry, daring to think she'd fooled them, until Rafe's mocking question asking if she wanted coffee landed like a hammer blow, crushing her belief there was an end to this horror show.

Since then, there had been no sign of Henry. He'd betrayed them: there would be a price to pay. Maybe she wouldn't see him again.

The room door swung open. Coco stood, hands on hips, savouring the fear in her prisoner's eyes. Behind her, Julian held something in his hands and Nina understood a new phase in her abduction was about to begin.

Coco dragged her hair back and said, 'I'm taking you to the toilet.'

'I don't need to go.'

She punched her in the kidneys. 'That isn't my concern. You're going.'

When they came back, Julian kicked the chair aside and tied her wrists and ankles to the bed. Coco grinned as his hands wandered over her helpless body. Nina turned her face away so they wouldn't see the revulsion in her eyes and realise he was getting to her.

He checked the ties, satisfied with his work. 'I bet you're wondering where Henry is, aren't you? Sorry to be the bearer of bad news but your young friend won't be coming. Not today. Not any day. He's... shall we say... otherwise engaged.'

Julian stuffed a piece of cloth in her mouth. 'How's that? Comfortable enough for you? We'll only be a few hours.' He ran his tongue over his lips. 'Then the fun will really get going.' He leered. 'To be honest, we can't decide who gets you first. Coco says it should be her. I disagree – she can have what's left, although there won't be much.'

A lone tear trickled down her cheek; Nina couldn't stop it. From the start she'd pinned her hopes on the fact that these people were amateurs. Counting on them making a mistake that would lead Luke and Mark to her. It hadn't happened. It wasn't going to happen.

Julian leaned closer. 'As a matter of interest, who would you prefer?'

* * *

Henry had taken his brother's advice and said nothing on the journey from Hampstead. It wasn't hard. None of the others spoke to him. The atmosphere in the car was charged. Rafe hadn't lied: he couldn't protect him from these people – that time was past. What that meant for him wasn't hard to guess. They'd gone from bored young rich kids playing a game for the hell of it, to cold-blooded murderers. Two people were dead. Nina would be next: her brother didn't have enough money to stop them. Because it wasn't about money.

It was about this – the high, the adrenaline rush: the newly discovered thrill of the kill.

In the rear view, Coco and Rafe held hands, her head resting against his shoulder, their eyes glazed, shining with an inner light – they were loving it.

Henry was terrified. Rafe's words echoed in his head.

I can't always be there

He was already not there.

They turned left into the traffic on Euston Road. In the passenger seat, Julian's fingers tapped the waistband of his trousers, as though just knowing the gun was there made him powerful. He said, 'Why couldn't we have contacted this guy from somewhere nearer instead of driving halfway across bloody London?'

Rafe couldn't be bothered telling him again. To keep the peace, he did. 'A couple of reasons. The second I connect they'll know where we are. Glass probably has men spread all over the city in the hope he'll get lucky and be close enough to catch us.'

Julian conceded the point. 'Okay, I'll give you that, what else?'

'Glass doesn't have a clue about us. It's important it stays that way, which means being nowhere near Hampstead when I phone him.' Rafe leaned between the front seats to hammer home his point. 'When I say they'll know where we are, Julian, I mean *exactly* where, in a nano-fucking-second. And "this guy", as you blithely call him, is Luke Glass. Worth a look. Plenty of stuff about the whole family.'

'Like what?'

'Like do your own homework, you lazy bastard, before you diss somebody. I guarantee you'll get why this is such a blast. The Glass family are the real McCoy. Genuine, 100 per cent gang lords. And his club in Margaret Street is the place to be seen. Coco found a platinum membership card in her bag, remember? I'm guessing it'll get anything you want.'

'And we've got one.'

Rafe clapped him on the shoulder as if they were friends. 'And we've got one, Julian.'

18

They'd been gathering in my office from early morning. George Ritchie first, followed by Mark Douglas, Felix Corrigan and Charley. The same group as yesterday with one important difference: yesterday the trouble Nina was in had no name. Now, it did, and it had changed all of us. They didn't talk, silently speculating about what was going to happen when the phone rang, none of them sure what I'd say to the bastard at the other end of the line. They could join the club. Because neither was I.

Dawn had broken over the city at seven twenty-seven. By then, I'd already been up for three hours, making one cup of coffee after another and forgetting to drink it till it was almost as cold as the hard light in the December sky. Growing up motherless with an alcoholic father, it had been our brother who'd taught us family was everything. A younger me had heard his 'Team Glass' mantra and laughed behind his back. I wasn't laughing now.

Family wasn't just everything: it was the only thing.

The previous day, Douglas had been in his very own world of pain, no good to himself or anybody else. I'd half expected him not to show up. He was better than that. Now we knew what we were up against, he'd found the strength to pull himself together, still pale, eyes dark and hollow, but my head of security was in the building.

The guy with the headphones sat in the corner – no feet on the table, no mags or cigarettes. He'd miss them because it might turn out to be a very long day. I said, 'How much time do you need to trace the call?'

He wasn't more than twenty years old – some wizard Douglas had sourced – smugly proud of his infinitely superior knowledge. 'That's old hat. They can hang up before you answer. Won't matter if a connection's been made. We'll have the GPS coordinates in seconds.'

'Shouldn't I keep them talking?'

He grinned, remembered who I was and why we were here, and smothered it. 'The radio signal travels to the satellite and back. Establishing the origin of the call won't be a problem.'

The wonders of technology.

Unfortunately, that was no more than a beginning point – getting to them through the London traffic was something else again. In reality, most likely we'd know where they'd been, rather than where they were.

Charley took my arm and drew me aside so the others wouldn't hear and whispered. 'Luke, listen. You're the boss, the head of the family. I'll go with whatever you decide.'

Nice of her.

'Only, I've been over and over this, over what they said.'

'And?'

Her painted nails bit into me. 'A million pounds. Offer them a million. In cash. If they want more, give them more. It's only money. And we're drowning in it.'

She read my mind and gasped. 'Oh, God. Oh, God, no.' Shock paralysed her features, her lips parted and her hand dropped from my arm. In her eyes, sadness and disappointment stared at me, the same emotions that had been there the day I'd asked her to meet me here, when I'd believed she was the insider – the mole in the organisation – and come within seconds of shooting my own sister.

The only thing missing was the gun pointing at her beautiful face and my finger on the trigger.

She faltered. 'You... you aren't going to pay, are you?'

'Charley...'

'They've asked what Nina's worth to you and...'

'Whatever we give them, it won't be enough. Can't you see that? They'll kill her anyway – they may already have. They showed they're capable of it when they shot the jeweller.'

The words didn't register. Her mouth screwed up in contempt. 'Don't play games with these people. Don't do that.'

'I'm not, Charley, trust me, I'm not.'

But she didn't trust me. Maybe she'd never trust me again.

'Just for once, forget you're Luke Glass. Forget it. Be Nina's brother and save her.'

The others realised something was going on. George Ritchie stood up, ready to move if he had to. Charley took hold of my lapels, pulling me to her in one last desperate attempt to reach me.

In my face. Trembling. Close to tears.

She'd lost her family before and was afraid she was about to lose them again. Charley pleaded with me. 'Please, Luke, please. This is our sister's life we're talking about.'

I grabbed her wrists and pushed her away, unable to control my anger. 'You think I don't know that? You honestly imagine I'm missing the danger she's in? One million. Two million. Ten fucking million! They can have it. Have it all. Except they still won't let her go.'

Over her shoulder my mobile rang on the desk. The guy with the headphones gave a thumbs up and I was aware of sweat on my palms. I said, 'That isn't how it ends, Charley.'

'Then, how? How does it end? Tell me. I need to hear you say it.'
I lifted the phone and held my hand over it. 'Like this.'

* * *

His voice boomed in the room, echoing through the speaker phone.
'Good morning, Luke.'

My chest tightened and my mouth was dry. I'd spent the wee
hours and beyond stressing about the call and what was riding on
it. Now, it was here: whether Nina lived or died might depend on
the next ninety seconds. The people in the room had overheard the
heated exchange with Charley; their anxious eyes were on me. Luck
– good and bad – had a bigger part to play than I wanted to admit. If
it was with us a CCTV camera somewhere would show what this
bastard looked like. And I'd have him.

If it was the last thing I ever did, I'd have him.

'Did you sleep well?'

I ached to break his face.

'Let me speak to Nina.'

'Ah, I guessed you'd say that. Not possible, I'm afraid. You have
my word she's safe.'

Mark's guy waved a sheet of paper in the air. I read the message
scrawled in blue felt-tipped pen and for the first time since the
nightmare started, began to think it might be all right.

Liverpool Street Station
  Main concourse

Charley's dark eyes fixed on me; Mark Douglas was on his feet;
George Ritchie whispered into his mobile – his men would already
be on their way. It had taken less than three seconds to kick off.

I managed a laugh that sounded weak and hollow. 'You expect

me to hand you a shedload of cash on the strength of your word? What're you smoking and where can I get some? Get my sister on the line!'

He was a confident fucker and he was ready for me. 'You're used to people jumping when you bark. I'm afraid I'm giving the orders and you're taking them. It'll be helpful if you remember that.'

'Here's something for you to remember. I'm going to tear your smug fucking head off your body with my bare hands.'

He wasn't fazed. 'Threats don't impress me, Luke, empty threats especially. I'm disappointed in you. Let's get back to the point, shall we? Yesterday, I asked how much she was worth to you.'

'Bring Nina.'

'What's your answer?'

'You're getting fuck all until I'm satisfied she's okay.'

'Then you leave me no choice.'

'Listen, you bastard, you think I won't find you? You're wrong. I know more than you realise.'

'Really?'

'Really. I'll give you two words: Poland Street.'

He lost his composure, only for a moment, before certainty returned to his voice. 'Well, well. Who's a clever boy? Impressive, though, really, what does it change? We still have your sister and I'm still waiting for an answer. How much to get her back? I'll help you out. Take the number in your head and double it.'

'Nothing's happening until I speak to my sister.'

'Mmmm. An ear or a finger? Which tabloid rag would you prefer? Is the *Daily Mail* all right, or shall I go with *The Sun*?'

I was losing control – he was holding all the cards and he knew it.

'Last chance, Luke. Make a decision.'

This was what I'd tossed and turned and struggled with during the longest night of my life, while every atom of my being screamed for me to do the easy thing and give in to them. But the reality was clear: these people wouldn't hand Nina over – not in a million years. It wasn't in their plan. They'd grab the money and run. Words, angry, defiant words I'd thought I'd never say, tumbled into the world. 'Okay, you bastard, you want my decision? Here it is. Kill her! Kill her and be done with it! Is that decision enough for you? Put a bullet in her fucking brain and stop this thing.'

'You aren't serious.'

'No? Try me. And don't contact me again.'

I ended the call and closed my eyes. There was a rushing sound in my head and for a second, I felt alone and overwhelmed. Charley had pushed me where I hadn't wanted to go: to the hardest truth. And, as she'd pleaded with me to pay them, pay them anything they demanded because we could, I'd known with shattering clarity that if I did, we'd never see Nina alive again.

On the other side of the office Mark's guy took off the headphones, tossed them on the desk and searched in his jacket pocket for the fags I'd forbidden him to smoke – a symbol of how fast and how far I'd dropped, even in his estimation. Felix spoke quietly to George Ritchie and left. Douglas, unable to process what he'd just witnessed, was riveted to the spot, his fists balled and bone-white at his sides, while Charley cried into her hands, sobbing uncontrollably. 'Luke, Luke, what've you done? What the hell have you done?'

* * *

They hated me. Despised me. I didn't blame them. I felt the same.

Charley wiped her eyes. 'I thought you were a man. I was wrong. As long as I live, I'll never speak to you again.'

'Charley—'

Mark Douglas made a noise somewhere between a snarl and a moan and threw himself at me, his hands circling my throat, digging into the flesh. We fell to the floor locked together. The depth of his rage gave him an unnatural strength and I couldn't break his hold. If Ritchie hadn't dragged him off, I wouldn't have survived.

He caught him in a bear hug, spitting and kicking, flailing his arms, screaming, 'Let me go! Let me go!'

'Not until you understand what's happened here.'

I got to my feet and staggered to a chair, every breath agony. Douglas stopped struggling and Ritchie said, 'You're too close to see it. Luke did the right thing, the only thing in the circumstances.' He didn't hold back. 'Face facts. She was dead the minute she crossed their path in Poland Street. And there's another thing.'

Douglas said, 'Yeah?'

'What if we've got it the wrong way round? What if they'd known she'd be there?'

I said, 'They were after Nina, the two men got in the way and ended up dead?'

Ritchie nodded at me. 'I think it's a real possibility.'

The anger drained from Douglas's face; along with the rest of us he'd been happy to accept that nobody in their right mind would be stupid enough to abduct Nina Glass.

Ritchie scratched his ear. 'I'm not telling you that's definitely how it was, but the family are high profile so we have to consider it. The truth is, there's something off with this. Professionals don't leave valuable stones behind, and they don't take hostages when they don't have to. Serious people, people who intended to make an exchange, would expect to be asked for proof of life and give it. Unless they couldn't.' He paused to let his words sink in. 'Luke tossed the ball back into their court. Let's see how they respond.'

His tone softened. 'Waiting is hard but falling out among ourselves is the worst thing we can do. We're in this. All of us.' He stared at Douglas. 'Right now, we need the copper to step up, not the lover. That means dealing with what is, and considering the reason they can't show us Nina is because she's dead.'

The statement, spoken in George Ritchie's strong, quiet voice, was like a punch to the gut. But it brought us together and he pressed his message home. 'We've no idea who these bastards are, let alone what they look like. The call came in at 11.43. Felix is on his way to get a cut of the CCTV footage from the station.'

Charley said, 'They won't give it to him just like that, will they?'

Ritchie smiled. 'Not just like that but they'll give it to him. When he gets back, we'll take a look. Until then, I suggest we settle down and wait. Anybody got a better idea?'

19

Coco angrily dragged off the hoody and pitched it onto the ledge at the back window. Rafe had insisted they all wear them. It reminded her of what she'd never known, never would know, and was strangely afraid of: the world of ordinary people. She didn't need to speak – her body language gave her away. Going into the station, Rafe had insisted they split up so they weren't seen together. It made sense, except she was tired of Rafe automatically assuming he was in charge – he'd fucked up Big Time with Nina Glass, something he seemed to have forgotten.

'What did he say?'

'He told me to kill her.'

'Kill her! His own sister?'

'And then he hung up.'

Julian swore under his breath; they should've done it at the start and saved themselves a ton of hassle. 'Let's take him at his word.'

Rafe turned to face him. Julian's parents had wasted their money on his expensive education – he was thick. 'You're missing it, Julian. Whether Glass knows it or not, he's joined the game. Exactly what I was hoping for. Result.'

Henry followed the route taken on their way in, nosing through the lunchtime traffic towards Euston Road. Rafe had advised him not to speak but the others were missing the point. He raised his voice so there would be no mistake; everybody had to understand the danger they were in.

'This could be our last chance to let her go. We may not get another one.'

Julian slapped the back of his head. 'Shut up, Henry. Nobody's asking you.'

The car swerved into the middle of the road. Henry pulled it back. 'We're all going to die. Unless we—'

Rafe cut him off before he could get started. 'It pains me to admit it, Henry, Julian's right. Just drive. And keep your mouth shut. Surely, that isn't too difficult.'

He grinned and flashed the platinum membership card Coco had found in Nina's bag. 'Luke Glass just upped the stakes. Let's call his bluff. It's time we met the lion in his den.'

Coco blew him a kiss. 'Game on, lover.'

* * *

At the Mount Nelson, breakfast was served in the Oasis Bistro, a lovely spot overlooking the swimming pool. Today, its elegance escaped her. Constance sat back in her cane chair, sipped her organic Earl Grey St Clements and frowned. Her annual trip to South Africa was meant to be fun: a respite from the cold and the wind and the rain in London. So far, it had been a bloody disaster and she blamed herself. Men – especially young men – needed to be carefully managed, otherwise they ruined everything with their immature tantrums. Connie Greyland had a Golden Rule she hadn't broken in twenty-five years: as soon as a companion – she thought of them as companions – became difficult, it was over. Last night, Florian had caused an ugly scene in the dining room and stormed away. She hadn't seen him since and this morning discovered he hadn't come to bed.

Connie pushed the smoked salmon scrambled eggs around her plate, too angry to eat. Angry at herself for tolerating his behaviour and for not realising in Hampstead that bringing him here would end in tears. His, not hers.

Their affair was in its fourth month – most of hers hit the rocks long before this – but it was well and truly over. When he returned, as inevitably he had to since he didn't have two farthings of his own, she'd break the news. Hardly unexpected considering the state of the relationship. Perhaps whatever trollop he was with would foot the bill for the endless stream of G & Ts that so reminded her of Simon, her late husband.

The waiter appeared at her elbow like a ghost with a copy of *The Times*. The familiarity of the news was comforting: the stock market was up and down on the slightest whim, the weather was awful, and the government was making a pig's ear of things – so no change there.

On page eleven, near the bottom, a headline got her attention: Two Dead in Soho Robbery.

Connie shuddered and moved on; she didn't need to read the details.

England had gone to the bloody dogs.

* * *

Outside the intensive care unit of The London Hospital on Whitechapel Road, TT and Jet watched their friend from a corridor. Boz was unrecognisable, like a mummy under the bandages. At the side of the bed, a machine monitored his heart rate, blood pressure and the level of oxygen in his cells; an IV line and tubes carried fluids, nutrition and medication, while a catheter drained bloodied urine into a bag. The last time his mates had seen him he'd been laughing. He wasn't laughing now.

TT hated hospitals. Everything about them put him on edge. He'd been nineteen years old when he'd visited his mother after she'd had the cancer cut out the first time. For Timpson, seeing her pale and exhausted had been a frightening experience; and he hadn't gone again. The smell and its association with sickness and death had terrified him then and still did.

He hid the anxiety building in him and cautiously asked his question, knowing he wasn't ready for the answer. 'How serious do they think it is?'

'Too early to be sure. He was unconscious when they brought him in. They're waiting to see if he comes out of it to find out how much he's affected. Boz's old lady quizzed the doctor about his chances.'

'What did he say?'

'Wouldn't commit himself, just repeated what he'd already told her. They did a CT scan. The sister says he's going for an MRI this afternoon.'

'And that'll tell them what they want to know, will it?'

Jet shook his head. 'I think they already know; they just aren't saying it. Apart from the skull fracture, his left arm, his nose, and three of his ribs are broken. He's bleeding inte—'

'All right, he's bad. I get it.'

'I'm only telling what—'

TT ground his teeth and turned away. 'Let's get out of here. I need a drink.'

* * *

They hung a right onto Stepney Way and walked to the Good Samaritan. It had rained and the pavement was wet. TT gratefully breathed in the fresh air. Now they were out he felt better. They ordered Guinness and took them to a table. Jet sipped the creamy top off his. 'Brick Lane's half a mile away. Probably still finding bits of Jonas stuck to the wall.'

TT wasn't listening. From the moment he'd got a whiff of that fucking awful disinfectant and seen the tubes coming out of the unconscious Boz, he'd made up his mind. He said, 'I'm not going back in there.'

'What do you mean?'

'I won't be back until we've put the bastard who did this in the ground.'

Jet wasn't sure. 'Is that wise? I mean, if this is a reprisal for torching the bookies—'

TT snapped. 'Fucking grow a pair, Jethro.' He drained his pint without tasting it. 'Dying would be the best thing that could happen. For his family and for him. Would you fancy somebody changing your nappy for the rest of your life?' Jet stared at the table and TT said, 'Yeah, me neither. He's gone, man. Boz is gone. Luke fucking Glass finished our mate because we demanded what was due.'

'So, what're we going to do about it?'

TT wiped his mouth on his sleeve. 'They took one of ours, we'll take one of theirs.'

* * *

Upstairs, the steady hum of a vacuum cleaner filled the deserted club; twelve hours from now it would be very different. A man in overalls at the top of a ladder was cleaning the crystal chandelier hanging in the centre of the room, spraying each teardrop and wiping it with a cloth, then going on to the next. Careful work. Patient work. All it would take was one slip, one false move, and the whole thing might come crashing down. The irony wasn't lost on Mark Douglas.

He sat at the bar, absently shredding a beer mat, glad to be out of the office. Douglas wasn't a fool. Nobody needed to tell him what he'd just done was madness. Attacking the head of the Glass family! Insane! People had died for less. But when he'd heard Luke say, 'Kill her! Kill her and be done with it!' he'd snapped.

Charley's reaction had been the same as his, except she was his sister; she was allowed. Douglas expected Luke to fire him. No big loss. So far, he'd been a fucking liability.

And for the first time he asked himself the question he'd been avoiding: why? Why had he moped like a lovesick schoolboy instead of focusing on catching the bastards who'd taken Nina? The answer he'd buried under a mountain of excuses forced its way to the surface, demanding he confront it.

Guilt: he'd been prepared to use Nina to bring down her brother and the corrupt police officer DCI Carlisle was certain existed without a second thought, even though it would destroy her.

Liking him and loving her had never been in the plan.

In the last eighteen months, Douglas had blown up a promising career with Police Scotland in Glasgow and worked as a celebrity security guard, stepping stones in building the backstory that would get him close to the Glass family. All gone. Because now it was crunch time and he was picking his side.

At some point, he'd tell Nina and Luke the truth about who he was and what he'd been doing and take his chances. Thankfully, that was for another day. Before then, he'd contact John Carlisle and tell him he was out. His handler would be furious. Mark couldn't have cared less. DCI Carlisle's reaction – or rather, his non-reaction – to Nina's kidnapping in the park on the banks of the Thames had soured a relationship already on the turn.

The detective was using him as surely as he'd been using the family.

This was the end. It was over.

The only thing that was important was finding the woman he'd fallen in love with and hurting the bastards who'd taken her.

* * *

Mark Douglas was at the bar by himself, shoulders sagging, shredding a cork beer mat with his fingers and dropping the pieces on the counter. I slid onto the stool next to him. He didn't acknowledge me until he said, 'I owe you an apology. Two apologies. Since the first meeting in the King Pot I haven't been worth a damn. You were right. No matter how much cash you give them they aren't going to let Nina go.'

'They didn't come ready to do business. Today was a hustle.'

'You were calling their bluff to buy time.'

'Let's hope it worked.'

'Assuming she's still alive.'

'We have to believe she is, Mark.' The conversation was in danger of going down the wrong road; I changed the focus. 'The CCTV might tell us what they look like.'

'I doubt it. You heard his voice – he was laughing. They're toying with us, playing a game.'

I let him get it out.

'What worries me most is proof of life, the first thing anybody asks for before they hand over money. They didn't offer any. That doesn't feel good.'

I agreed with everything he'd said. This wasn't the moment to reveal my own fear, the one I'd been carrying since the beginning.

Douglas guessed what was coming and was ready for it. 'Luke, about downstairs... don't know what to say.'

'Then, say nothing.'

'Yeah, but...'

'Here's the deal, Mark: you're upset about Nina. So am I. Getting her back is the top priority. When we do, you'll go after the people who thought lifting Luke Glass' sister was a great idea and change their minds. You and Nina love each other. You have a huge stake in this. Felix will be here soon with the CCTV from the station. The more eyes we have on it, the better.'

'You're nor firing me?'

'No, at least, not today.'

20

We huddled round the PC – me, Mark Douglas, George and Felix, watching the techie load the first disk in the computer. Charley hadn't spoken a word to me and I felt anger rise in my chest: did she really believe calling the kidnapper's bluff, maybe risking Nina's life, had been easy? Sister No. 2 was a smart cookie, but she wasn't thinking straight or she'd have realised the guy was enjoying himself too much: we were being scammed.

Ritchie had been right to be confident about getting the railway station CCTV footage. In his experience, money, if you offered enough of it, would buy you anything. Felix said, 'There are two cameras on the area we're interested in. Got them to burn a copy of both and the three exits.'

'Did you look at them?'

'Saw a bit. Assumed it was more important to get back here fast as I could.'

At first the screen was black, then it flickered into life. The techie offered an early critique.

'Colours are off. There's a problem with the white balance settings.'

He'd lost me already. I didn't care as long as it gave us what we needed: a fix on who we were dealing with and what they looked like. The position we'd got on the mobile was accurate up to fifty feet. Not a big space until you filled it with scores of people coming and going, every other one of them on their phone. Picking our guy out would be difficult. And on the first pass, I didn't. The second time the techie paused the picture at exactly 11.43 on the clock in the top right-hand corner. We silently scanned the frozen image. Beside me, Mark Douglas edged closer, his finger searching for the fucker who'd taken his woman. I counted thirteen people making or taking calls, seven of them female. Of the six men, three wore suits and carried briefcases. Somehow, in spite of his accent, I didn't picture Nina's abductor as a shirt-and-tie type. That left three, one of them in a wheelchair, a tartan shawl over his legs, pushed by a younger lady, probably his daughter or his nurse.

The last two had their backs to the camera. Douglas barked at the techie as though we'd miss something if he didn't hurry. 'Play the next disk! Get it going!'

Mark Douglas was back. Good news. We'd need him.

The angle from the other side of the concourse was wider. When the techie zoomed in it narrowed: the seven women were there, so was the guy in the wheelchair and the suits, moving through the crowd without breaking stride. Every few seconds the picture flickered and I cursed those white balance settings I hadn't heard of a minute ago. The remaining two men were in the shot. One carried a backpack and wore a hat. Suddenly, he waved and rushed cross the concourse to an older couple who were obviously his parents; they threw their arms around each other. The last guy was standing side on to the camera, his face hidden under a grey hoodie. He passed the phone from his right hand to his left, doing something with his fingers, maybe to emphasise the point to whoever was on the other end of the line. In this case, me.

I willed him to look up. Instead, he shook his head, slipped the mobile into his pocket and hurried away. Mark Douglas clicked his fingers. 'Enjoy the moment whoever you are because we're coming for you, you fucker. Switch the disk.'

Ritchie glanced at me, both of us thinking the same thing: Douglas was a different man, the most invested person in the room. Even more than Charley or me now we had an enemy we could see. The fear that had crippled him had given way to anger and a need to avenge the wrong done to his woman, leaving him pumped and ready.

Felix explained his thinking while he changed the disks. 'We knew there were two cameras on that part of the concourse – a no-brainer. For sure he'd be on one. But which exit would our boy take? He had three options – Bishopsgate, Liverpool Street, or the Broadgate Development.'

Felix was building his part. I didn't appreciate it; we'd had our share of drama and didn't need more. He grinned, pleased with himself. I felt like slapping it off his face.

'Which exit did he take?'

'Bishopsgate.'

I said, 'Did you—?'

'Get the street view? Damn right.'

'Good work, Felix. Let's see it.'

The man in the grey hoodie strode briskly and stopped, keeping his head down so we still couldn't see his face.

Douglas was like a coiled spring. 'He's waiting for somebody.'

George said, 'Whoever was in Poland Street with him.'

He was right – two figures, then a third joined him, dressed in the same featureless hoodies. They gradually disappeared into the crowd and didn't turn round.

Douglas stopped the disk and pointed at the screen. 'One of them's a female. Watch her hips.'

I couldn't see it. George Ritchie said, 'Well spotted, Mark.'

Douglas leaned forward, rewound the disk and let it play. 'Definitely. Look at her walk.' He was animated, eyes shining; clutching at straws. I didn't share his enthusiasm – even if he was right it didn't take us any closer to getting Nina back.

He pulled off his jacket and rolled up his sleeves. 'I'm going to go over the internal supermarket stuff. See if I can get a fix on these people. Now we're starting to piece it together—'

I interrupted. Mark Douglas had gone from despair to deluded. 'Mark... Mark... what're you talking about? We're being led around by the nose. They're aware they're on camera, calling all the shots, that's what the hoodies are about. This is a performance for our benefit.'

He stared at me, something in his eyes that hadn't been there. It didn't have a name. 'You're not wrong about that. But we've learned a helluva lot.'

'Like what?'

He held up his hand and counted off on his fingers. '*One* – pros would've set a timetable, turned the screw on the money. No doubt about it. These people didn't. *Two* – they didn't offer proof of life, which means Nina might be dead. On the other hand, it could be more evidence that they're amateurs. *Three* – not demanding a ransom makes them the first kidnappers in history to go that road. But they did because money has no part in this. Maybe because of what they got from the jeweller's, though I don't think so. *Four* – after today we can say with certainty we're dealing with a gang that's four strong. Posh Boy on the phone is the leader and one of them is a woman.' He paused to let me catch up and I saw George's eyes narrow; he was on it. Douglas was on a roll. 'Let me ask you a question: what kind of kidnappers aren't in it for the cash? Who does that, Luke?' He breathed deeply and went on. 'Don't bother answering, I'll tell you. Nobody. Absolutely nobody.'

'Agreed. Where does it leave us?'

'You spoke to the guy. You heard his reaction when you told him to kill Nina. The bastard was disappointed because you wouldn't play his game. Asking how much Nina was worth to you. Remember?'

Douglas drew the corners of his mouth back, his teeth bared in a rictus of hate as the fury in him boiled to the surface. He'd held the floor and was giving a good account of himself.

'I believe Nina's alive. For how much longer, I've no idea. Otherwise, what was the point in taking her? It's their move. We'll soon find out what they come up with, but, I'll tell you, we'll be hearing from them, and soon. They're having too much fun to quit. These fuckers are having a laugh. A laugh at our expense.'

21

The Glass family were unpredictable people. Oliver Stanford hadn't expected his involvement with them to last as long as it had. For years he'd reaped the rewards. Getting Luke the information about the car hadn't won the policeman points and with the relationship bumping along the bottom, grinding to a conclusion that might very well leave him face down in the river, it was time to consider his exit strategy.

Luke wasn't Danny and never would be; Stanford didn't rate him. Danny had been a beast but, though he'd loathed him, it was impossible not to admire his strength. In the old days, if he'd spoken to him the way he'd spoken to his brother, Danny would've dragged him across his desk under the framed photograph of the Queen and beaten him until he couldn't stand.

Back then, Stanford was a DI and Scotland Yard had still to make the move to the Curtis Green Building on the Embankment. Knowing where the bodies were buried, not just metaphorically, demanded he put in more hours than other officers to keep their secrets intact: he still did. His efforts had been wrongly identified by those on high as a well-developed work ethic. Added to timely whispers from the south London gangster that meant he contributed to a clutch of high-profile cases, he'd climbed the greasy pole. Pretty successfully, even if he said so himself.

Elise had the bit between her teeth, on at him again to retire: take the gold watch and head for the hills while he could. For her sake, he'd pretended the idea appealed. In truth, the prospect appalled him. But it was the right thing – the only way to bring the deteriorating situation to a natural conclusion. Breaking it to Glass wouldn't be easy and he'd wait until this business with his tart of a sister was resolved.

Out of the Met with his power gone, his usefulness to the gangster would be over.

Where would that leave him?

Perhaps Luke would have more Danny in him than he imagined, see him as a threat, a loose end, and invite him to one last meeting in the derelict factory in Fulton Street.

A terrifying thought.

Meanwhile, he'd play the game for just a little longer. Then Elise could have her husband back.

* * *

There was no news. No more contact. I was on edge, in a foul mood, ready to lash out. As usual, George Ritchie, the loyal soldier, arrived first. He guessed how the wind was blowing and parked himself in a corner. George was a man of few words. I liked that; it made him easy to be around. After five minutes of empty air, I said, 'How's Felix doing? Meant to ask him yesterday. Didn't get a chance.'

'He's all right. Felix is one of those guys who's always all right.'

'You said he had a problem.'

'Not any more. It's sorted.'

I nodded. 'Pleased to hear it.'

By the look of him, Mark Douglas had managed a decent night's sleep. He sat down and launched into what little there was to report. 'We spent four hours comparing the supermarket film with the station. The car park cameras aren't working and the gang definitely aren't on the internals.' He turned to me. 'We were both right. The first time they made sure we didn't see them. The next, they went out of their way to make sure we did. Like you said, Luke, Liverpool Street was a show. These bastards put discovering their identities at risk for fifteen minutes of fame. Ramping up the danger. Definitely amateurs. Absolutely, a professional would do the opposite.' His expression hardened; he slowly shook his head and delivered his verdict. 'Can't second-guess fools acting out some fantasy of their own. No tradecraft. The idiots are making it up as they go along. Unfortunately for us, it doesn't augur well for getting Nina back.'

Ritchie said, 'For idiots, they aren't doing too badly.'

* * *

Nina hadn't seen them all together since the car journey out of central London through the snow. The dynamic hadn't altered: Rafe was still in charge, Julian a leering spectator; Henry was quiet, very much the junior. Coco sat cross-legged on the floor, rocking backwards and forwards, languidly twirling strands of hair between painted nails. Grey smoke trailed to the ceiling from the joint in her hand and her eyes were glazed; she was high.

Rafe smiled at Nina and held out the phone. 'Are you ready for your close-up? Gonna make you a star, kid.'

She spat hate at him. 'You'll wish you'd never been born when my brother gets you. And he will.'

The threat sounded unconvincing and, for all the effect it had, she might never have spoken. He laughed and went on setting up the shot. 'You can thank him for this little bit of theatre. He wants proof you're alive. Doesn't trust us, I'm afraid. Can you believe it?'

Nina was so accustomed to the ties chafing her wrists, she no longer noticed the pain.

'I'm not doing any fucking hostage video. You can't make me.'

Rafe didn't argue. 'Of course, you're right, though the other option may be worth bearing in mind – cutting off a finger and sending it to him. A pinky, maybe? Or a thumb. Fancy that, do you? Personally, I'd go for the video but that's just me.' He smiled again. 'Your decision. Don't let me influence you.'

Julian let Rafe get on with it. His view hadn't changed. None of this was necessary. He tore the dressing gown open, exposing the dried blood on the wound. 'This time it was your tit, next time it'll be your throat.' He weighed Nina's breast in his palm and squeezed. 'Before that, we'll have some fun, you and me.'

Coco sneered. 'Christ Almighty, Julian, you really are a sleaze-bag. I'd rather be dead. And by the look on her face, so would she. Can't stand to be in the same room as you, never mind anything else. What's it like to have such a devastating effect on women?'

Rafe ignored the squabbling and spoke to Nina. 'Look on this less as an appeal for help and more as a last adieu to a cruel world. Be as dramatic as you like. Mention of us or where you are, we'll stop and start again. Simple as that. Imagine Luke watching, seeing the state his sister's in, knowing he could've saved her and chose not to.'

He did the thing with the coin, then stuck it in his pocket before delivering the final cruel blow. 'Because, make no mistake, he had the chance.'

Nina screamed, 'You're a liar! A fucking liar!'

Coco got to her feet. 'Actually, he's telling the truth. Rafe asked what you were worth to him. Your darling brother said, "Kill her."'

'"Kill her and be done with it" to be exact.'

Coco tilted her head in mock-sympathy. 'Oh, dear, Rafe. The poor deluded thing was convinced he was coming for her. Sad.'

Nina sneered. 'You stupid, stupid cow. My only regret is I won't see you taken apart. Stay high – it'll dull the pain as he drives a fucking nail into your skull.'

'Your brother sounds exciting.'

'You've no idea.'

* * *

Behind the Tom Ford 'Tallulah' sunglasses, Connie Greyland closed her eyes and let the warm air soothe her body. She'd expected Florian to show up begging to be forgiven, telling her he was sorry and deeply ashamed. Except, he hadn't. When men behaved differently from her expectations, it prodded her insecurities, stressed her: Connie didn't do stressed.

She was still a good-looking woman but accepted the days of flaunting her figure and revelling in the lascivious glances of male admirers were in the past. While it lasted, it had been fun. A great deal of fun. One afternoon on her second trip to South Africa after Simon passed, she'd attracted the attention of two Swedish brothers by the pool she was lounging beside now. Twenty years on, she didn't remember the boys' names; it was possible she'd never known them. She did have a vivid recollection of their lean, tanned bodies, the creaking of the bed that seemed to go on and on, and the monotonous whir of the overhead fan as first one, then the other, then both of them had her.

Constance didn't realise Florian had joined her until his shadow blocked the light. She peeled off the shades, shielded her eyes and stared at him with rehearsed anger that had, somehow, become real. 'Where the hell have you been?'

Florian was like Simon: weak, and not just where alcohol was concerned. Her late husband hadn't stood up to her. Hadn't been man enough. Florian gazed at the dipping fronds of palm trees moving in the breeze. 'The porters are moving my cases.' He left the statement there, as though it required no more explanation.

Connie turned onto her side and stretched impatiently for her cigarettes. 'The porters are... what the hell are you talking about, Florian? Are you drunk? When we get back to England you're going into the Priory. I'm sick and tired of—'

'I'm perfectly sober. It's very simple, Constance. This isn't working.'

She snapped at him. 'What do you mean? We're in one of the best hotels in Africa. Of course, it's bloody working.'

'You don't understand. It isn't working for me.'

Slowly, the words began to make sense. 'The porters are moving your cases? Where? To the fucking staff quarters? Wouldn't have thought that was your style. Oh, don't tell me you've fallen for the pretty little housekeeper.'

Florian found something on the floor to study. Connie was speechless. She was the one who ended affairs; it was almost a tradition. This was a new experience.

'Where were you last night?'

When he didn't answer, she asked another question. 'You're leaving the hotel? Our return tickets are in the safe. How will you get back to the UK? I'm bloody well not paying.'

'I'm not going home just yet. I've been invited to stay.'

'You've been...' Connie lost her temper. 'You arrived with me and you'll leave when I decide.' She lit a cigarette and blew smoke out of the side of her mouth in short annoyed bursts. 'I thought you understood the rules, Florian. What do you mean you've "been invited to stay"? Who invited you?'

He'd known this moment would come and was ready for it. 'Rosamund.'

She'd assumed he'd been rutting with the chambermaid *again* – an unpleasant enough thought, but this. Connie spat the name out. 'Rosamund?' She couldn't believe what she was hearing. 'Rosamund Symington? She's here?'

'Yes. Rosie has a studio flat in the grounds of her house in Richmond Hill and asked if I'd be interested in taking it.'

'Rosie? Fucking Rosie, is it? I'll say this for you, you don't let the grass grow.'

Connie scanned the terrace for a waiter; she needed a drink. Florian kept his tone neutral. 'I'm not sure why you're upset, you must have realised it was winding down. We've been here since the middle of November and only had sex twice. Not very good sex at that. I'm amazed you didn't see it.'

She faced him, her expression a snarl. '"Rosie", as you call her, was my best friend, once upon a time. We were inseparable. Until I came home early one day and discovered her in *my* bed with *my* husband. They were having an affair. Of all the women in the world... I hate her. And I hate you.' She threw the lighter at him; it struck his shoulder and fell to the floor. 'Don't you realise what you've done? When this gets out, I'll be a laughing stock.'

'I'm sorry.'

'If she's been here, why haven't I seen her?'

'She's stayed in her room most of the time, having her meals sent up so she wouldn't run into you.'

'How long have you known she was here?'

Florian went back to looking at his shoes; he shook his head. 'She said you'd be angry.'

'Angry doesn't begin to describe it. Where did you meet?'

'At the party we went to in the Café Royal.'

'You were seeing her when you were supposed to be with me?'

Florian didn't reply; it wasn't necessary. 'Nobody planned it, it just happened.'

Connie's lip curled. 'You're pathetic and you're stupid. She's using you – can't you see that?'

'You're wrong. Why would she?'

'Because it wasn't just an affair. Simon wanted to marry her. When I caught them, she scurried away and he asked me to give him a divorce. I refused.'

'And?'

'His investments had gone bad and he was drinking heavily.' The memory was painful; suddenly, her face was bone-white. 'We lived in Knightsbridge in those days. Simon went to his study, locked the door and shot himself.'

'God, how awful. I'd no idea. I would've told you eventually.'

'How very considerate.'

'I didn't want to hurt you. You have to believe me.'

She watched him through a cloud of smoke. 'No, I don't, Florian. I don't have to believe anything. You're a fool. And actually, the bitch has done me a favour. I intended to end it with you the moment we touched down at Heathrow. You aren't important. Rosamund Symington is my enemy. She blamed me for his death – can you credit the irony of it? – and swore she'd get me back. It's taken twenty-five years but now she has.'

'Nobody's getting back at anybody, it isn't like that.'

'Oh, fuck off, Florian! Do you forget I caught you shafting the maid? Does your precious Rosamund know?' Fear darted in Florian's eyes and Connie smiled a slow smile. 'Don't worry, I won't tell her. It'll be our little secret knowing that when you're between her legs you're thinking about somebody else.' She lowered her voice; people were listening. 'Enjoy it, because it won't last. Don't get too attached to the studio flat. You won't be there long enough to unpack properly.'

Florian stuck his chin out. 'Anyway, I've told you. Rosie can't spend much more time in her room, but we'll do our best not to cross paths.'

Connie stabbed the cigarette in the ashtray and waved to the waiter hurrying towards her.

'That won't be an issue. I won't be here.'

'Where will you be?'

Florian was a pawn in a game that had been running for a quarter of a century. Soon, he'd be like the Swedish boys: Rosamund would struggle to remember his name.

'On the first flight out tomorrow.'

22

Vincent Finnegan hadn't been in the Admiral Collingwood for years. Tonight, he'd abandoned the boozers in Whitechapel and Mile End to revisit his former watering hole and its once-familiar charm. He hadn't found what he was hoping for. Like everything, including himself, it had changed. The tables old men had huddled over wordlessly playing cards and dominoes had been replaced by plush red-leather booths. Against the far wall dotted with signs advertising karaoke, a guy tapped the sides of a whirring fruit machine, his concentration absolute; the lighting was subdued and rap music pounded monotonously from a speaker. Whoever had taken the place on had ripped the heart out of it, gone plastic and modern in an attempt to attract a younger demographic. Finnegan recognised nobody and leaned on the counter, swirling the last of his pint, studying his reflection in the mirror behind the gantry. Maybe because of the changes in his old local or maybe because he was a lonely maudlin old bastard and it was Christmas, but a sadness, a feeling of being left behind, washed through him like a rising tide. There was no wife at home, no kids. Vincent had never married and hadn't regretted it. Until now.

As the alcohol worked its magic, his mind wandered to when he'd arrived in Liverpool with Sean Poland early on a chilly October morning off the overnight boat. In London, their talents were in demand. Almost twenty-five years ago they'd sold them to an up-and-coming south-of-the-river hardcase called Danny Glass and with money in his pockets, dressed to impress, Vincent had attracted more than his share of women, all but a few of them forgotten.

But with a psycho like Danny, it wasn't destined to last. After his wife and daughter were killed in a car bomb, the IRA men were caught up in the purge that inevitably followed – Poland was found hanging from a tree in Norwood Park hours after Finnegan was attacked in his flat by a gang armed with baseball bats. He'd had no part in the bomb. To his knowledge, neither had his countryman. In fact, Vincent hadn't known about it till he saw it on the TV news – but his days as a Lothario were over; they left him unconscious to see out the rest of his life as a cripple surviving on disability benefit.

A chance meeting in this very pub with Danny's younger brother, Luke, fresh out of prison, had turned it all around. Danny was gone now. Luke was in charge – more thoughtful, more approachable, less reactive: a good guy who'd given him a break. Finnegan smiled. Telling lies to females had got him what he'd wanted. He drew the line at lying to himself: Luke wasn't so different from Danny; the same blood flowed in his veins. His brother had been unhinged. A madman. Luke wasn't that, but he was a Glass; whoever had lifted his sister might not appreciate what they'd done – the poor buggers were as good as dead. Danny had hanged Sean and almost killed Vincent. Luke would be more measured, though the message wouldn't alter: nobody messed with the family and lived to tell the tale.

He ordered again and felt the edge of his mouth twitch when the barman did his best not to see him. Finnegan raised his voice to get his attention – 'Guinness, and a large Bushmills for luck' – smiling at the toast he hadn't used since the old days.

The barman put the drinks up and took his money without a word. Vincent made himself a promise; he wouldn't be back. Like Danny, Sean Poland and the long list of girlfriends, the Admiral was the past.

A group of young guys loudly playing darts in the corner drew his attention, cheering or booing every shot. They didn't know their days were numbered; their sport didn't fit the new look. Six months down the line they'd be looking for another venue. From their accents they were local boys, full of it, mistakenly believing they understood the streets. Finnegan's dismissive grunt caught in his throat. They understood fuck all. Yards from where they laughingly downed their lagers and threw their arrows was a London they'd never known – if they were fortunate, never would know.

He turned away, pitying their naivety, and lifted the Bushmills; the whiskey was like honey, warming his throat on its way to his gut. He tipped the dregs into his pint, seeing them stipple the creamy surface, and downed the lot in one go.

The beating had left one of his legs shorter than the other, the swagger replaced by the limp – a small price to pay for avoiding a wheelchair. Out on the street, Finnegan considered hailing a cab and going home, deciding instead to walk for a bit to clear his mind. He didn't hear the figure falling in behind him, his wide nose flat on his unsmiling Gypsy face, or see the hand grip the thick shaft of an axe at his side high up near the head.

For Vincent Finnegan, one-time IRA hitman, womaniser and gangland enforcer, revisiting the pub had opened a portal to a yesterday that hung heavy on him. He imagined Sean's strangled cries in Norwood Park, his legs wildly kicking the cold early-morning air in the moments before his neck snapped and his life ended, while his assassins laughed like the darts players.

Christ Almighty! What was wrong with him tonight?

A man strode confidently from the alley, blocking his path, his shadow a dark cloud falling across the pavement. He tapped a slow deliberate rhythm with a length of iron against his thigh.

Finnegan saw the shaved, tattooed skull and stopped in his tracks.

TT slapped the iron bar into his palm; it thudded against the skin. He said, 'What is it about people, eh? They don't listen, do they? Don't want to know unless it affects them. Your boss underestimated us. Disrespected us. Treated us like shit on his shoe. We weren't greedy. We didn't demand what wasn't ours. Even when he told us to fuck off out of it, we gave him time to reconsider and tried again. But there's a limit. And you say to yourself enough is fucking enough, know what I mean? Firing the bookies...' TT searched for the words, gave up and moved closer '... is what it is.'

Over Finnegan's shoulder a shoe scraped concrete and Vincent realised he wouldn't be going home after all.

TT continued. 'The guy you slapped up's in hospital. He's brain-dead. A fucking vegetable. His old mum's in tears because her son's coming home in a box. Tomorrow they're switching off the life-support machine.' He looked up and down the street and back to the alley. 'Can't go unanswered. Wouldn't be right.'

Finnegan's southern Irish accent thickened as it always did when he was under pressure.

'Go to hell.'

TT ran a hand over his shaved scalp. 'Thought you'd say that.'

The iron crashed against Finnegan's good leg; something gave and he dropped to his knees. The second blow broke his collarbone – the pain was excruciating, almost as bad as the hammering Danny had sanctioned. The last thing he saw was an image of Sean Poland struggling like a rag doll and the streetlight glinting off the axe.

TT said, 'Think of yourself as a message, a message to Luke Glass.'

He nodded. Jet raised the axe and buried it in the Irishman's head.

His Bushmills luck had finally run out.

* * *

Rafe tipped the white powder onto the coffee table's glass top and shaped it with the platinum membership card, cutting and re-cutting until it formed three lines. He rolled a twenty-pound-note into a thin cylinder and admired his work. Coco and Julian watched the ritual they'd witnessed many times. Her eyes were wide and Rafe realised she'd had a bump off her fingernail when no one was looking. Accusing her would mean a scene – it always did – just when they needed to be on the same page. She squeezed next to him. Close up her pupils were dilated. Her hand wandering between his legs. He brusquely removed it. 'Later.'

Her cocaine-inspired arousal wasn't new; since he'd known her, she'd been a horny bitch, always looking for it, insisting they do it in the street over the bonnets of parked cars or up against a wall a stone's throw from the pavement. The more public, the better, the risk of getting caught an added thrill. Rafe knew her wanton exhibi-tionism wasn't because of his animal appeal.

In the beginning, the drug made their couplings last longer, the orgasms shatteringly intense. He'd been happy to keep it occa-sional. She'd insisted on using every time. Maybe she hadn't noticed the decline in their performance, but he had. Climaxing required more and more effort. Often, they didn't reach it and pulled apart exhausted, distant and dissatisfied with themselves and each other.

She had a solution. More. Always more. And always, it was never enough.

What nose candy gave, nose candy took away: Coco was a junkie.

Her fingers mischievously sneaked back to where they'd been. Rafe wasn't in the mood and roughly pulled them away. 'I said later.'

She pouted her lips, her voice hoarse. 'What's the matter? Don't you love me any more?'

His answer was harsh. 'Be told. Stop being a silly girl and behave yourself.'

Julian watched the exchange and smothered a smile: the love-birds were tiring of each other. Coco was a bitch – no two ways about it – though he'd have her in a heartbeat if Rafe didn't want her. He said, 'Where's Henry? Anybody seen him?'

'He's in his room. Where else?'

'I worry about him.'

'Don't, he'll be fine.'

'What's the plan for the video? Do we even have one? When are we sending it?'

Rafe leaned over the table, snorted, gasped, and fell back – the hit almost taking his head off. Then, the magic started to work. Any war on drugs was doomed to fail for one reason and one reason only – drugs were fucking great, a fact no amount of warnings would change.

Coco took the rolled-up note from him and Julian asked again. 'The plan. What is it?'

Rafe said, 'Relax, Julian, you'll love it.'

'Yeah, so you say. Give me the details and see if I agree with you.'

Rafe was floating. 'Bugger details. You'll love it. Now, shut up.'

23

DAY 8: THURSDAY

It was still early but I couldn't sleep and had had it with trying to control my crazy mind. I was leaving for LBC when George Ritchie called and asked me to meet him at the King Pot. I clutched at a straw. 'Is it Nina? Have you got something?'

He answered quietly, speaking slowly, understanding I'd be disappointed. 'It isn't about Nina.'

'Then, what?'

'It's Vincent. Vincent Finnegan. Somebody ambushed him outside a pub and left him on the ground with an axe in his skull.'

This was all I needed right now.

'What? Have you told Felix?'

'He's here with me. We need to talk, Luke.'

Driving through the south London streets I tried to make sense of what it meant. Finnegan had played a big part in my life. Now he was dead I was struggling to come to terms with it.

Felix was waiting at the door of the darkened pub. I followed him upstairs to Ritchie's office and a scene reminiscent of the morning after my sister had gone missing. I dragged a chair out, straddled it. 'Okay, I'm here. What the fuck happened?'

George pushed a whisky across the desk and let Felix tell it. 'Not everybody was happy when we took over from Jonas Small. One group in particular thought they'd been hard done by.'

I fired a look at Ritchie; he didn't look back. 'Is this the "nuisance value" you mentioned? I understood that was sorted.'

'It was. Least, we thought it was.'

Ritchie roused himself and spilled what they'd been keeping from me. 'A couple of nights back, one of our bookies got torched.'

'You said, George. You also said it was being dealt with.'

Felix shrugged. 'We knew who was behind it and taught them a lesson. Should've been the end of it, except it wasn't.' He fidgeted with his fingers. 'Seems we went over the top; the guy's brain-dead. Vincent is their retaliation.'

Lately, anger had become my default setting. And here I was again, having to rein in my emotions before they erupted like I'd seen my brother do more times than I could remember. Knee-jerk reactions rarely ended well. Temper was a luxury few people could afford; it hadn't stopped Danny.

'Let me be straight on this: some tuppenny gangbusters were upset and set a shop on fire. You put one of them on life support, so to get back at us they killed Vincent?'

The admission fell reluctantly from Felix's lips. 'Right.'

'Then the problem hasn't gone.'

Felix and George were hurting, it was on their faces. Taking my frustration out on them would've been easy and I wanted to. But it wouldn't help. They'd fucked up and didn't need me to remind them.

I ignored the whisky; I wasn't in the mood. 'Contact these people. Say we want to talk. Maybe we can work something out with them.'

Ritchie wasn't happy and didn't hold back. Unwise, considering he'd left me in the dark while him and Felix royally got it wrong.

'Not the way to go, Luke. These fuckers are flies on a bull. We should've rinsed all of them instead of just the one – that was the error. If we had, Vincent would be alive instead of in a refrigerated cabinet in Lewisham with a tag on his toe.'

'Can it, George. You had your chance and blew it. We're doing this my way.'

Of the three of us, Felix had been closest to Finnegan; they'd become friends. He said, 'After what's happened... it might be too late.'

'Convince them. Say I'll meet them myself, and take them to Fulton Street.'

'Fulton Street. They'll run a bloody mile.'

'Then don't tell them, just get them there. How many are there?'

Felix didn't answer my question. He processed the order, doubt drifting like rain clouds across his eyes, unable to credit what he was hearing. 'Luke, these bastards stuck an axe in Vincent's head. If we're even thinking about doing business with them, then sorry, I'm out. Effective as of right fucking now.'

Ritchie lifted his glass and reassured him. 'Take it easy, Felix. The only business we have with them is putting them down.' He glanced at me for confirmation. If he didn't get it, I'd be three men short instead of one – Vincent Finnegan, Felix Corrigan and George Ritchie.

'That's right, isn't it, Luke?'

'Absolutely right. Get the hole dug; they're going in the ground.'

* * *

George Ritchie waited until Luke had gone before turning to Felix. To pick up on the nuances behind the words, you had to know who you were dealing with and what he was capable of. These days the former street fighter from Newcastle preferred to use his brain rather than his fists.

He didn't shed blood easily. When he did, it would be a river.

Felix Corrigan knew he was witnessing a master at work, doing what he did best – managing a tricky situation, giving him his place while at the same time subtly controlling the action they were about to take. Ritchie noticed the lines around Corrigan's tired eyes that hadn't been there twenty-four hours earlier; the younger man was discovering there was more to being a boss than barking orders and scaring people. No doubt he'd prove himself an apt student. He was smart, ruthless when he had to be, and, more importantly, fiercely loyal to the family, especially Luke. In the past, according to urban myth, Luke had talked Danny out of shooting Felix downstairs in the bar of this very pub.

He'd used up one of his namesake's nine lives that day.

The brutal murder of Vincent Finnegan was his first big test since taking over. The Irishman had been his right hand and a friend. Felix was in pain, needing someone to point him in the right direction. He needed George Ritchie.

Felix said, 'The two of them are at his mother's place.'

Ritchie steepled his fingers and took his time responding; he'd learned the valuable difference between acting and reacting. However much you wanted to, the latter was almost always a mistake.

'How do you think we should handle it, Felix?'

Corrigan recognised the guile in the question and smiled. George was a pro, in his way, a gentleman, giving him his due and testing the water.

'If it was up to me, I'd bust the door down and slit the bastards' throats. The last thing they'd hear would be their agonising gasps for breath as they drowned in their own blood.'

Ritchie's gaze was unwavering; he spoke quietly, his tone neutral, giving nothing away. 'It is up to you. Is that the plan?'

'No, it isn't.'

'Why not? Would be no more than they deserve after what they did to Vincent.'

Felix stared at the window over Ritchie's shoulder and the darkness beyond. Underneath the desk he flexed his fingers: nothing would give him greater pleasure. But that wasn't the response George Ritchie was looking for. He said, 'Vincent was one of the good guys. Sure, I'd relish the chance to deliver justice to his killers. Except...' he hesitated '... that isn't happening. At least, not yet.'

'How so?'

'The timing isn't right. Got enough going on with Nina. There's a better way.'

'Better than wiping scum off the face of the earth? Tell me.'

'I'd prefer you told me, George. Because, in the end, that's how it's going to go.'

Felix wasn't allowing anger to cloud his judgement. Good to know. Ritchie said, 'Okay. You're spot on about Nina. Until that's sorted, anything else, everything else, is a distraction. Luke's worried about his sister. Looking for something to lash out against. Left to himself he'll get too close. That can't be. We handle the streets. You and me, Felix. The better way is this: we give Vincent a decent send-off – he deserves that much – and keep an eye on this guy and his sidekick in case they decide to move. When we don't come after them, they'll assume we're reconsidering. In a couple of days put it out that we're willing to talk. They'll come to us.'

'And we show them the inside of Fulton Street?'

'That we will, Felix, that we will.'

* * *

The British Airways stewardess was young and blonde and slim. Everything Constance Greyland had been but wasn't any more. She hated her. The girl had the freshness of youth no amount of nipping and tucking could replace, gliding along the aisle in first class smiling vacuously, checking seat belts were secure. Connie looked at the heat haze rising from the baked earth outside. In twelve hours and five minutes they'd be touching down at Heathrow. London and the house in East Heath Road would be cold and miserable; the thought made her shiver. Finding a flight at short notice had been a stroke of luck, though it meant leaving the hotel at the crack of bloody dawn to make the departure. Constance didn't do early morning and was tired and depressed. Florian's defection – to Rosamund Symington of all people – had left her feeling old. Once he'd confessed what was going on her priority had been to get away from the humiliation as far and as fast as she possibly could. Even another day would've been intolerable. And it wasn't just Florian – he wouldn't have been in the picture much longer – or even Rosamund, vindictive bitch that she was: it was the sad realisation that something good had come to an end. The annual winter trip had been such fun. But Connie wouldn't be back. Her beloved Mount Nelson, the scene of so many adventures and an oasis of civility and sophistication, would forever be a reminder of her rejection.

She closed her eyes, whispering to herself. 'Bloody, bloody, bloody.'

When she wakened, they were in the air. She pressed the overhead switch and the stewardess appeared, still smiling. Connie said, 'Can I have a gin and tonic, please? In fact, make it a large one.'

* * *

On his way to the off-licence with the money TT had tapped from his mother, Jet saw Mrs Timpson at her bedroom door. The blue dressing gown drowned her stick-thin frame. Over her shoulder, a wooden crucifix hung from the wall and candles flickered in the gloom. Her arms were folded across her body, one frail hand clutching rosary beads. Under the almost translucent skin the veins crawled like blue worms, the lips of her small mouth moving silently, and he realised she was praying. Seeing her reminded him of his father and made him uncomfortable. Jet hurried past. He knew the history; TT had told him: one lung had been cut away but the cancer had returned.

A more fragile faith might've faltered; hers had strengthened.

When he'd gone, she lit a cigarette from the one in her bony hand. 'You were late last night. I heard you come in.' She pointed an accusing finger at TT. 'Didn't bring a girl back here, did you? I won't allow fornication under this roof. If—'

'No, Mum, there was no girl. Jet's having problems at his house. You heard us gassing. Sorry if we disturbed you.'

'You didn't. I barely sleep. Scared to close my eyes in case I don't wake up again.'

He put his arm round her. 'The doctor said you had to give up the fags. You promised him you'd try.'

She snorted. 'I did. They tell everybody the same. Let's them pretend they've done their job. Even if I had, what difference would it make? Your old mum's done, Thomas. God will take me when he's ready.'

'Maybe you should speak to them.'

She stepped away to look at him and he saw her eyes, watery and empty, black holes sunk in her head. 'Whatever time I've left won't be spent getting prodded and poked by men in white coats filling their day until they can get back out on the golf course. No, thank you. There aren't many pleasures left in life. Not worth giving them up for an extra six months of misery.'

'Is it all right if Jethro stays for a couple of nights?'

'Hasn't he got a home of his own to go to?'

'Django's on a bender, better Jet stays clear until it's over. I said he could park it up here.'

'Django?'

'His father.'

'You didn't mention your friend was a Gypsy.'

'Didn't think you'd mind.'

'Do they believe in salvation through Our Lord Jesus Christ?'

'The first thing I asked. Wouldn't bring him near here if he didn't.'

She took his face lovingly in her skeletal hands. 'You're a good boy, Thomas. I'm proud of you. He can stay as long as he likes.'

Mrs Timpson's door was closed. Jet was glad he didn't have to look at her diseased frame and watch the mouth's whispered devotion to a God who'd abandoned her. TT's mother was dying. Slowly. Not like the man on the street outside the Admiral Collingwood. That had been quick; instant. The rush as the axe split his skull, splintering the bone, ending his existence with a single blow, had been thrilling. Killing him had been a buzz.

Awesome.

TT was lying on the bed in his room. Jet put the carrier bag down, pulled the metal ring on a can and handed him a lager.

'She says you can stay.'

'What if I don't want to?'

'Doesn't matter, you're staying. It's better. Safer.'

'Tell her thanks. What's the next move?'

TT drank from the can and belched. 'The guy we're dealing with – Felix – is a flunky. Glass is the boss. Supposed to be smart. Give him a day or two to figure out we're more trouble than we're worth. We'll make contact and carry on where we left off.'

Jet wasn't convinced. 'I don't know, TT. We fired the bookies and killed one of his men.'

TT sat up, suddenly angry. 'In case you've forgotten, Jethro, they started it when they stole what was ours. All we did was fight back.'

'Not how they'll see it.'

Timpson lost it. 'I couldn't give a flying fuck, it's the truth. Sure, they'll be out for blood, it's only natural, we'd be the same. That won't last. Sooner or later they'll be ready to talk. Now drink your drink and leave the thinking to me. By the way, if she asks, you believe in God, all right?'

'I do. Don't you?'

TT said, 'My old man ran off with the floozy he was shagging when I was three, my mother's got cancer, and I don't have a pot to piss in. What do you think?'

* * *

Henry had gone from a minor player, there on sufferance because Rafe had insisted on including him, to not even that. As much a prisoner as Nina. No one in the house spoke to him unless it couldn't be avoided. When this nightmare ended, he'd go his own way, pick up the pieces and never see his brother again – a prospect that would've appalled, even frightened him not long ago. Now, it couldn't come quickly enough: his hero had morphed into a madman, infatuated with a cocaine-snorting tart, devising more and more dangerous and elaborate games to play with a gangster. Across the hall, their hostage was forgotten as the drugs diminished their ability to think and took them deeper into a morass of their own making.

Footsteps on the stairs told him someone was coming. The door opened. Rafe stood in the frame, dressed in the three-piece herringbone suit he'd had made by Anderson & Sheppard on Clifford Street, paid for by one of the many performance bonuses from Sangster-Devlin when he and Julian were the blue-eyed boys. His blond hair was swept back above a white shirt and a cross-striped silk Crombie tie. Henry remembered the Crombie; he'd been with him the day he'd bought it.

Rafe came towards him, confident and assured, more handsome than Henry had ever seen him. He said, 'You and I shouldn't be estranged, we're brothers. I suggest we put the past behind us and start again.'

Henry said, 'Will you let Nina go?'

Rafe shook his head. 'That isn't an option, Henry. Maybe it never was. Maybe I should've let Julian kill her in Poland Street.' He sighed. 'But I didn't. Either way she was always going to die. Forget her, she isn't important. This is us. I'm offering to clean the slate – a truce, if you like. One way or another this will be over and it'll be you and me against the world, how it's always been. The alternative...' he paused '... isn't attractive. We both understand what that is. And, I'll tell you the truth, Henry, considering it even for a moment makes me want to be sick.'

He dropped the conciliatory tone. 'Nina Glass sealed her fate the moment she gave the old jeweller her business. That wasn't me, that was fate.'

'That's crap and you know it.'

Rafe pinched the corners of his eyes, suddenly weary of the conversation. 'Even if it were possible, I've no intention of spending twenty years behind bars.'

'What do you mean "even if it were possible"?'

Rafe sat on the bed. 'Face facts, brother. I'd be dead in a month. Filleted like a trout in the showers some morning, left to bleed out on the tiles. For Luke Glass, arranging that couldn't be easier. Except that wouldn't be the last thing they did. By the time they finished I'd be begging them to end it.'

He saw the shock on Henry's face and smiled. 'I'm not making it up.'

Henry answered quietly. 'I believe you.'

'Then, you'll agree, it can't happen. I won't let it.'

'You said it would be over soon.'

'Sooner or later.'

'When? How? And can we really go back to who we were?'

'No, no, of course not. Why would we? We'll have dared to do things other people couldn't dream of. Shucked off our comfortable, privileged, bored-out-of-our-skulls existences and stepped out onto the ledge. We'll have lived.'

Henry's mouth wouldn't work; he struggled to get the words to form. 'I saw how you behaved around Coco and was blaming her. But it isn't her, it's you. You're insane, Rafe. Completely off your rocker. To hell with your truce – I don't want it.'

Rafe blinked as though he'd been slapped. 'What you want doesn't matter. Imagine being gang-raped before they cut off your balls and stuff them in your mouth. Because that's exactly what Luke Glass will tell them to do. You're younger. Prime meat; they won't be in a hurry.'

'So, you'll stand by while Julian shoots her? What about me?'

'He says we can't trust you.'

'And what do you say?'

Rafe didn't answer. Julian wasn't alone – if Henry had been anybody else, he'd be dead already. He said, 'We're going out.'

'I'm not going anywhere.'

'Good, somebody has to stay. Nice of you to volunteer.'

'Why me? Why not Julian?'

'Because.'

'Because you know what he'd do if he's left with Nina, that's it, isn't it?'

'Get off your high horse. I'm giving you another chance, Henry. A chance you don't deserve, by the way. Screw it up and I can't save you even if I wanted to. But remember what I said. Dying will be a sweet release if Luke Glass catches us. I'm putting all our lives in your hands. Fuck us and I'll kill you myself, brother or no brother.'

* * *

In the beginning, they'd checked on her regularly. Not any more. Her failed attempts to escape had given them confidence. Except for the trips to the bathroom, Nina was invisible. If it hadn't been for Henry bringing her food, she'd have gone hungry. A muffled voice travelled across the landing, then it stopped. Downstairs she heard them laughing: something was happening.

Suddenly, the light went on and hurt her eyes, glancing like a thousand shooting stars off the fluted champagne glass Coco was holding as smoke trailed from the smouldering tip of the joint in her other hand. She smiled, pleased with herself. Nina understood why: the change was remarkable – with her hair teased out like a rock chick, she was beautiful. Coco pouted, turning slowly so Nina got the full effect of the off-the-shoulder dress split to the thigh, matching the high heels and the blood-red of her lips.

'Not bad, even if I say so myself. What do you think? Will it be enough to get Luke's attention?'

The question was intended to bring a reaction. It didn't. Behind Nina's blank expression her mind worked furiously processing what was in front of her. These people were idiots. They were actually going to LBC. Luke would see through them. Tonight, the nightmare would end for her and begin for them – unless he killed them before he found out where they were keeping her.

Coco spilled champagne on the carpet and apologised like a naughty little girl. 'Oops, sorry. I'm so excited. I'm finally going to meet the great Luke Glass. I can't believe it.'

She flashed the platinum membership card like a magician at the finale of a trick.

'He's so-o-o-o handsome. I keep imagining him... no need to paint a picture, I'm sure you understand. You must be kicking yourself you're his sister – or perhaps that doesn't stop you people. Anyway, I wanted you to see what he'll get if he's a good boy. Don't be too jealous. I'll be gentle with him.'

At the door Coco fired the barb she'd saved till last. 'Been scrolling through the text messages on your phone. Interesting. Just an old-fashioned girl at heart, aren't you, Nina? Who would've believed it? And I know who the bracelet was for.' She wrote in the air. '*"From N to M – all my love."* So sweet.' Her fingers ran the length of her thigh and disappeared inside the split in her dress. 'Maybe I'll pass on Luke and have Mark instead. Would that be all right?' She giggled. 'On second thoughts, perhaps I'll be greedy and have both of them.'

24

I'd liked Vincent – on another day I'd mourn him. The best respect we could pay his memory was to find the bastards who'd murdered him and make them wish they'd never been born. That went double for the fuckers who had my sister. Danny had been a monster. I'd watched him do things. Sickening, unspeakable things that were the work of a sadist. Now, I wasn't so certain. My brother's instincts weren't often wrong: he'd recognised there were always people waiting to take what we had away from us by any means possible. All that had stopped them was fear of what he'd do to them.

The club was the last place I wanted to be – the alternative, hour after hour of waiting for news that might not come, was worse. I hadn't heard from Oliver Stanford; all right by me. Though he wasn't aware of it, his race was run.

Every few yards somebody waved hello or spoke to me, no notion of what was going on behind the smiling mask. I remembered Shani and wished she was here. She'd promised she'd be back. I didn't believe her. Tonight, I didn't believe anybody.

Across the room Mark Douglas's features revealed what he was going through. He caught my eye and nodded imperceptibly. If I'd ever doubted his feelings for Nina, I didn't any more. Whoever had her better hope I found them before he did.

In a booth, a man, one of a group of four, imperiously clicked his thick fingers and said something out of the corner of his mouth that made his cohorts laugh. His fat face was flushed and sweating; he was drunk. The best kind of drunk – on free booze. I recognised two high-ranking Met officers who'd long come to consider partying on the house as their right. When LBC opened, I'd encouraged them and their greedy ilk – a distraction from what was going on at the back door.

But like Stanford, their time was up; they just hadn't got the memo. They'd served their purpose. LBC didn't need them. I didn't need them.

One night, very, very soon, they'd show up all set for a jolly and be turned away at the door. It wouldn't go down well and they'd make a noise, insist on speaking to the boss. The boss would blank them and keep blanking them until they got the message that the gravy train they'd been riding was pulling into the station; they'd reached the last stop.

They weren't alone. On any given evening, MPs, High Court judges, even the odd member of the cabinet could be found with their snouts in the trough. I despised all of them. They were the lucky bastards Danny had been on about.

The four ordered champagne and fell on it like jackals when it arrived, still grinning, so fucking pleased with themselves it wasn't real. A minute later, more clicking fingers were in the air. And that was the trouble with their kind. Enough was never enough. They had a nice little scene going but didn't appreciate they'd fallen on their feet and wouldn't be satisfied until they'd kicked the arse out of it.

Yet, difficult as it was to credit, they thought they were the good guys, on the side of law and order, when in fact they were thieving scum who hadn't the balls to actually steal.

Mark Douglas crossed the floor and stood beside me – he'd had his eye on them, too – and ran his hand through the designer stubble on his jaw. 'I'd like to drag them by the hair into the street.'

'Get in line, Mark.'

'Coppers on the take are the lowest of the low.'

Douglas had a short memory: not long ago he'd been kicked out of Police Scotland, fortunate not to be prosecuted. I thought he was joking. He wasn't; he was serious.

* * *

On the drive from Hampstead, traffic was light. Julian kept under the speed limit and tried to ignore Coco's grating laugh in the back seat. She was hyper. Rafe was taking a chance bringing her along to face down the gangster on his own territory. Outrageously stupid, much riskier than robbing the jeweller. The last thing they needed was a female coked out of her head. Nobody had asked Julian what he'd thought – the decision had been taken without him. If they had, he'd have told them they were fucking crazy.

When they were passing the zoo on Prince Albert Road, Coco snapped at Julian. 'Can't you go any bloody faster? Be quicker to get out and walk.'

He gritted his teeth. 'Better get a grip on your woman, Rafe, or this won't end well for any of us.'

Rafe heard the resentment in his voice. 'Concentrate on doing your own bit and leave Coco to me. She'll be fine.'

'Not if she does something silly. She's a reckless bitch on a good day and we both know it.'

Rafe spoke quietly, the suppressed anger unmistakable. 'Shut it,

Julian. Another word and I'll do what I should've done when you got us fired from Sangster-Devlin. You're hardly in a position to talk about reckless.'

Julian didn't have an answer and settled for muttering under his breath.

They crossed into Great Portland Street and drew in behind a dusk blue Hyundai. Rafe leaned across the passenger seat. 'Let's go over it one more time.'

'Not necessary, I know what to do.'

Rafe said, 'You really are an awkward bastard when you put your mind to it.'

Julian turned on him. 'Stop treating me like the junior partner or when you and your junkie girlfriend come out of the club, I won't be there.' He smiled, slow and sly. 'You hadn't considered that, had you? You just assumed that, as usual, Julian would be a good sport and do what he was told. Well, maybe he will and maybe he won't.' His fist hammered the dashboard. 'As for the plan, we're not even sure Glass will be there. If he is, you'll send me a text and I'll send him the video from Nina's phone. After that, I turn it off, remove the SIM card and get moving. When I get your call, I pick you up at the door. Not exactly rocket science, is it?'

'Just don't fuck it up.' Rafe put his arm round Julian. 'This is as good as it gets. Nobody will be expecting it. In an hour, we'll be on our way to Hampstead and a party. Now, let's do this thing.'

* * *

Connie walked unsteadily from Terminal 3 clutching her Prada handbag – her luggage, all five suitcases, would be delivered tomorrow. The flight had felt longer than usual, probably because of her mood. After two or three G & Ts she'd fallen asleep. When she'd woken up, the first thing she'd remembered was Florian and the strumpet he'd chosen over her and ordered more booze. It hadn't helped. Connie was drunk and sorry for herself and couldn't care less who knew it.

From a cloudless sky, stars shone pinpricks of hard winter light on the earth. Out on the terrace of the Mount Nelson overlooking the pool, they'd have finished dinner and be sipping Cointreau Blood Orange, clinking their glasses together, laughing at her. Later, they'd kick the bedclothes off and make love naked under the ceiling fan in Rosamund's suite.

Bastards!

The cold night air hit her like a blow. She threw a resentful look at the heavens and made her way past the waiting crowd to the first available taxi. Connie Greyland didn't do queues. The driver saw a sizeable tip coming towards him and hurried to open the door. She didn't thank him; it didn't occur to her. He slid behind the wheel and checked his elegant passenger out in the mirror – she'd been a looker once upon a time.

'Where to?'

Connie slurred, 'East Heath Road.'

'Hampstead?'

'No, Timbuk-fucking-tu.'

The man was a thirty-year veteran; stroppy people were all in a day's work – you couldn't let them get to you. He engaged the gears, slid away from the rank, and threw a cheery question over his shoulder. 'Been somewhere nice?'

Connie closed her eyes. In a day, two at most, the whole of Knightsbridge and Chelsea would have the juicy details and her humiliation would be complete. Remaining in London wasn't an option. Too degrading for words. And South Africa was out. Her annual pilgrimage to Cape Town had been spoiled forever. Where would she go?

She exhaled and wearily shook her head. 'Just drive, will you?'

* * *

Rafe let go of Coco's hand, flashed the platinum VIP visitor's card to the two men in black Giorgio Armani suits at the entrance and strode confidently past them into the club. The stewards saw fabulous-looking women every night of the week but couldn't stop themselves from staring at Coco. She felt their hot eyes on her, demurely lowered her head in a gesture of modesty at odds with the thigh-length split in her dress, and rested manicured fingers on Rafe's arm. A wave of cocaine paranoia washed over her and she fought the urge to run. He sensed her anxiety and lightly squeezed her hand to reassure her. They stopped to admire the alabaster sculpture of Fortuna, the goddess of chance in Roman religion. Slowly, deliberately, Rafe brushed Coco's hair away and kissed below her ear. She closed her eyes, offered him the tapered run of her neck, and purred her pleasure. One of the men gave the other an envious nudge and whispered. Rafe could guess what had been said. He slipped a protective arm round Coco's waist and led her inside.

Nobody challenged them. Rafe hadn't expected they would.

A hostess with flawless skin approached, smiling as though they were old friends she hadn't seen in ages. 'Welcome to LBC. Is this your first visit?'

Rafe said, 'Yes.'

'Then I'll have to get you to register.'

'How do we do that?'

'I'll do it for you, Mr...'

Rafe handed her the VIP card Coco had discovered in Nina's bag and answered with the name of the manager at Sangster-Devlin who'd fired him. 'Lennox. Toby Lennox.'

When she left Coco said, 'Toby Lennox? Where did that come from?'

Rafe smoothed his lapel. 'Settling an old score. Let's just say that's one Julian owes me.'

They found a seat in an elegant line of mirrored booths against the wall and sank into the plush upholstery. Music they didn't recognise drifted from the club downstairs. All around older men were deep in conversation with younger women who could've stepped off the cover of *Vogue*. Rafe said, 'Money buys almost anything, doesn't it?'

Coco said, 'They've spent a small fortune on this place. I love it.'

Rafe pointed at the ceiling. 'I'm guessing the chandelier alone cost more than some people's houses. Look at the size of it. Might even be an antique. Glass is a dragged-up thug but he recognises style when he writes a cheque for it.'

Coco anxiously dug her nails into the back of his hand. 'Rafe, at the end of the bar, that's him, isn't it? God, he's handsome... and when you realise what he does... what he's capable of...'

'Calm down. You're acting like a bitch in heat.'

She checked her make-up in the mirror and stood. 'I'm going to the ladies. Only be a minute.'

He grabbed her wrist and pulled her back, his fingers dry and firm matching his tone. 'No, you're not. You're staying here.'

'But, Rafe—'

'Don't be an idiot. Do you think you're invisible? That I can't see the change in you every time you're left on your own for five minutes?' He laughed softly to himself. 'You're making the same mistakes as Julian – thinking you're always the smartest person in the room, and that I'm a bloody fool. Wrong on both counts, my darling. If I opened your bag, what are the chances I'd find the coke you stole when nobody was around?'

His grip tightened. Coco cried out. 'You're hurting my arm!'

Rafe tossed his blond hair out of his eyes and spoke through gritted teeth. 'We need our wits about us. This is a game so long as we don't get caught. When it's over you can shove as much snow up your nose as you like. I won't stop you. Now, get it together and do what we came to do – let's introduce ourselves to Mr Glass.'

25

My jaw was numb from smiling at people I didn't know and didn't want to know. If just one more punter with a champagne glaze in his eyes clapped me on the back, I'd break his fucking arm.

Mark Douglas prowled the room like a leopard in the Serengeti, searching the crowd for God alone knew what. I recognised the signs. We were in the same boat, consumed by our powerlessness, impotently waiting for the kidnappers to make their next move.

Around midnight, despite my best efforts, the booze wasn't doing what it was supposed to do and I glanced anxiously at my phone for the hundredth time in an hour. Through the crowd, a couple picked their way between the tables. Instinctively, I knew they were heading for me and would've avoided them if I hadn't noticed the woman. Stylish females were often stick-thin with a sadness in their eyes that said they'd kill for pie and chips and a slug of HP sauce. Not this one – there was enough to hold onto. In a roomful of money vying for centre stage, it took a helluva lot to make an impression. The Egyptian lady, Shani, had managed it without trying. For Charley's hookers, it was essential, setting the bar higher than most girlfriends or wives – even rich men's wives –

would get close to, guaranteeing nobody would quibble with what they charged.

This one had it. Everything about her said she thought so, too. Wearing a scarlet dress cut to the thigh, her hair a wild Medusa tangle of curls and crimson streaks, she oozed sensuality from every perfect pore, forcing me to reassess the man she was with.

Her companion was middle-twenties and handsome. What struck me about him was his pleasant in-your-face attitude that only came from a private education. Confidence rolled off him. He offered a hand for me to shake and tossed his blond hair in an effete gesture at odds with the woman by his side. Inwardly, I prepared myself for losing ten minutes of my life I'd never get back, chatting to yet another star fucker who wanted to be able to tell friends he'd met the famous Luke Glass. And by the way, up close he hadn't seemed so tough.

If the guy had been by himself, I'd have found an excuse to nip the conversation in the bud before it started. The female got him an audience.

He said, 'Sorry to burst into your evening. I'm sure having to be nice to total strangers, night after night, is a monumental bore, but this is our first visit to the club and it wouldn't be right not to at least say hello.' He held out his hand. 'Toby Lennox. Very pleased to meet you, Mr Glass.'

'Luke, it's Luke.'

'Allow me to introduce my fiancée, Caroline.'

Attracting women had never been a problem. Holding onto them was something else. This one was special. She tilted her head, raised her chin and looked squarely into my eyes; hers were smoky and dark and I wanted to know more. Then, I noticed the dilated pupils and realised the frankness in her stare wasn't real. From there, it was a short journey to the hint of redness at the inside of her nose even make-up couldn't conceal. I'd seen it before – plenty of times – even with my sister. I took a half-step back and let her hand fall from mine. Instantly, the spell she'd woven broke and shattered in a thousand drugged-up pieces. Toby sensed the change in me. His fake smile tightened, he apologised and held up his phone. 'Excuse me, I really have to take this.'

My focus stayed with his woman, mentally peeling away the gloss money had bought. She sussed she was losing me and tried to recapture the moment. But it was gone. I saw her boyfriend tap a text message, then my mobile vibrated in my inside pocket and it was my turn to apologise.

Nina's strained face filled the screen and the vacuous world of rich men and their high-class problems faded: she was tied to a chair, arms snaking behind her, the dressing gown she was wearing ripped away exposing her pale breasts, an uneven line of dried blood on one of them. For days, I'd thought about my sister in every waking minute. Seeing her when I least expected it was almost too much. My heart leapt in my chest. My head swam. Momentarily, my vision clouded. When it cleared her lips were moving, but with the noise in the room, the words were lost.

The woman in front of me had to be wondering what was wrong. Her partner stood a respectful distance away, looking at me curiously. I didn't explain.

Mark Douglas was around somewhere: I needed to find him. Now!

Nina was alive. She was alive.

* * *

Constance was wakened by the jolt of the brakes as the car came to a stop outside her house on East Heath Road at the end of the fifty-minute drive from the airport. After the long flight, even in first class, she was stiff, her throat sore from the air con. One irate eye opened, then the other. She brushed herself down and wordlessly handed the driver a credit card.

He shook his head. 'Don't suppose you have cash, do you? The bloody machine, it's on the blink. Excuse my French.'

'You don't suppose right. Unless rand are any good to you?'

The man flicked on the overhead light, took the red fifty from her fingers and inspected it; the image of a young Nelson Mandela at the site of his capture near Howick stared up at him. Connie said, 'I've been out of England for weeks. That's all I have.'

He sighed, disappointed. 'I suppose it'll have to do. It's my own fault. How much is it worth?'

In the night sky clouds drifted across a yellow moon. She pushed the wrought-iron gate open, went inside and closed it before she answered. 'About two pounds fifty.'

* * *

Charley loved everything about LBC – the run-up to Christmas should've been special. Tonight, her heart wasn't in it. Her relationship with Nina had been difficult from the first day they'd met. As the only female in the family, Nina had behaved like a princess able to twist her brothers round her little finger and wasn't ready to accept she'd lost her crown. Somehow, the two women had found a way to co-exist. Although they weren't friends and probably never would be, Charley would give anything to hear a bitchy typically Nina comment aimed at her. It would mean things were back to normal.

The worst was knowing she'd contributed nothing to getting her back. Mark had managed to get a grip on himself and taken some of the responsibility off Luke. Liverpool Street Station had looked like an opportunity but it hadn't worked out and they were no further forward, chasing the game while the abductors toyed with them.

Luke was standing at the bar with a glamorous couple she didn't recognise, faking interest in what they had to say. Charley didn't envy him, though it was better than brooding at home. She moved between the tables, checking her girls working the room. At this level, hooking wasn't the worst job in town. If they were smart these women would retire well fixed, set up for the rest of their lives. Others would snare a rich husband and spend his money for him. Inevitably, that wasn't everybody's story – those who couldn't get off drugs found themselves on a downward spiral that would end in a fatal overdose or nightly humiliation up against a wall.

She retraced her steps until she was where she'd started. Luke was still at the bar, alone, staring at the phone in his hand, his expression twisted in horror. Something was wrong. Charley scanned the club for the couple he'd been talking to and saw them at the door. The female with the red streaks seemed reluctant to leave, looking longingly back at Luke. The man whispered in her ear and rolled a coin over his knuckles, fingers rising and falling like scissor blades as it travelled. With a final flick of his wrist, it disappeared into his palm.

He smiled across at her and Charley froze.

PART III

26

The stranger's cocky smile as he headed to the door extinguished any lingering doubt. They'd never met but Charley had seen a grainy image of him speaking into his phone on the concourse of Liverpool Street Station – for all the world just a guy talking to his girlfriend, when in reality he was twisting the knife. She wanted to shout, wanted to scream. Her lips moved but no sound came; her legs wouldn't respond. Luke's words echoed in her brain.

'One million. Two million. Ten fucking million! They can have it. Have it all. Except they still won't let her go.'

When she'd heard him tell the kidnapper to kill Nina, hatred had churned, sour and bitter inside her. Charley had waited her whole life to be part of this family and wasn't ready to accept she'd lost the only sister she'd ever have. Now she knew Luke was right, that whatever they did, whatever they paid, it wouldn't be enough. The people who had Nina would kill her – it was the only way for it to end.

Because it wasn't about money. It was about control.

The poor recording quality from the railway station CCTV had made it impossible to make out the man on the phone's face under the grey hoodie and difficult to be certain what he'd been doing with his other hand. Now, she knew: walking a coin, his party trick.

Charley looked frantically round the club. Luke was slumped like a zombie on a barstool, still staring at his mobile. Douglas was nowhere to be seen. She grabbed the arm of a waiter carrying champagne and glasses on a silver tray, sending the drinks sliding into space in slow-motion to shatter on the marble floor. Charley went down with them and landed on the broken glass, tearing one of her stockings as pain stabbed her palm. She scrabbled to her feet and fell a second time. All she could think of was the man. The waiter tried to help her up. She barked at him. 'Luke and Mark Douglas, tell them to get to the front door!'

'Are you sure—?'

'Do it!'

'You're bleeding.'

'Do it now!'

She ran to the stewards at the entrance. They'd see the blood and the ripped tights, put two and two together and come up with five. None of that was important – all that mattered was rescuing Nina.

She screamed at them. 'The man and woman who were here, where did they go? He's blond, she's wearing a red dress?'

'Oh, yeah, a car picked them up.'

'Which direction did they take?'

'West towards Cavendish Square Gardens but they could be going anywhere.'

'What kind of car?'

Both men shrugged; they hadn't noticed.

'What colour?' Charley lost her temper. 'For fuck's sake wake up!'

One of them said, 'You've hurt your arm.'

'Then, you're not completely blind. Good to know.'

* * *

Connie put the key in the lock. Immediately, the mean little smile on her lips from making a fool of the taxi driver died – the house was warm, the central heating was on, and there was a light at the top of the stairs. Surely, she hadn't flown six thousand miles away and forgotten to switch everything off? In the lounge, she stared horrified: cushions were on the floor, a newspaper lay discarded on the sofa, and there were ring-marks and dirty cups on the glass-topped coffee table. Connie didn't allow anyone to smoke inside – a vile enough habit without having it follow you around – yet she could smell it. The proof wasn't hard to find: a cold grey finger, all that remained of a cigarette that had burned itself out, balanced on the edge of an ashtray overflowing with butts. The place was a mess. Irritation gave way to fear. She'd had visitors; she'd been burgled and the intruders had made themselves at home. The question was, were they still here?

Calling the police was her first thought. A noise from the bedroom above startled her. She lifted the brass poker from the side of the fireplace, reassured by its weight in her hand. The property, built in the Victorian era, originally belonged to her great-grandfather. Connie had played here as a child and knew every inch of it. She climbed the stairs staying clear of the spots where the old wood groaned when someone stood on it. At the top, she stopped and listened, hearing a sound from the first bedroom on the right. Slowly, she pushed the door, her heartbeat racing, no idea what she expected to find. Through the window, a shaft of moonlight played on the far wall. Apart from that the room was in semi-darkness. As her vision adjusted her hand flew to her mouth: a woman was gagged and bound to a chair in the middle of the floor, eyes pleading, mumbling words it was impossible to make out.

Connie gasped and stepped back. 'Oh my God! Who are you? What's going on? I'm calling the police.'

She sensed something and turned. In the gloom, the boy wasn't more than eighteen or nineteen years old, fear etched on his fresh face. His hands went to her throat, digging into the soft flesh until she couldn't breathe. The instinct to survive gave her strength: she kneed him in the groin, hard enough to make him cry out, lose his grip and drop to the carpet. The woman in the chair screamed from behind the gag, fighting the bonds keeping her prisoner. Connie couldn't help her; she could only save herself. She stumbled from her teenage attacker, struggling to force air into her lungs, and was on the landing when his fingers closed round her ankle. For what seemed like an eternity her arms flailed, reaching for something to hold onto. Then she fell, crashing into the bannister, her head thudding off the wall and the steps in a crazy tumble of arms and legs all the way to the bottom.

Her broken body lay at an unnatural angle and Henry knew she was dead.

I'm giving you another chance, Henry

Fuck us and I'll kill you myself, brother or no brother

That wouldn't be happening. He'd become one of them – no different from Rafe and Coco and Julian. The realisation made him sick to his stomach.

Mark Douglas stood in the middle of the empty street, looking up and down. In the entrance to LBC, the stewards stayed in the background, studying the shine on their shoes. From their body language, I guessed it hadn't been their finest hour. If there was anything to deal with, I'd deal with it later. Charley dripped blood onto the floor; she was pale, her eyes watery – the energy that had been her trademark since the day she'd blown like a tornado into my life missing. For a second, I thought she was going to cry, then she pulled herself together and answered the question I hadn't had time to ask. 'He was doing the thing with his hand. That's how I knew it was him.'

She wasn't making sense. 'What thing? Who?'

'Him. The guy who took Nina – the couple you were talking to. Rolling a coin. Like he did at Liverpool Street. As soon as I saw it...' She tried to stem the blood coming from the cut on her arm. Douglas joined us inside the door, his features taut, face flushed with anger. She flashed a look at him and went back to what she was saying. 'Can't you see? It was planned, all of it, right down to the car picking them up as soon as they left. But why come here and deliberately seek you out? Only a fool would take that kind of chance.'

I could tell her. And the truth wouldn't do me any favours. I'd allowed myself to be distracted by the girl's provocative beauty, while the alcohol I'd thought wasn't working blinded me to what was really going on. The bastards had wanted to witness my pain. Watch me react to my sister, beaten and tied to a fucking chair. They were bold, I'd give them that, but by coming here they'd pushed their luck too far and screwed up – the CCTV footage would let us identify the car reg. That would give us the owner and an address.

Oliver Stanford wouldn't appreciate having whatever sweet dream he was in the middle of interrupted. Tough shit, Oli.

Charley and Douglas only knew some of what had gone on tonight; they were due an explanation. I wasn't looking forward to giving them one. My mobile was glued to my sweating palm. 'C'mon,' I said. 'There's something I need to show you.'

We made our way through the gaping crowd enjoying being on the fringe of something that had nothing to do with them. Other people's hassles were always exciting — they'd heard a commotion and were keen to be in on the act. I passed an overfed guy with a bad comb-over, a woman on his arm I hoped for his sake wasn't his wife: somebody had overdone it with the Botox giving her open mouth the look of a fish on a slab at Billingsgate market. In the morning, she'd be on the blower to her friends with the story, light on reality, heavy with gory descriptions of blood and gangsters and a danger that hadn't existed. At least, not for them. The truth wouldn't be allowed to get in the way of a good yarn. But it was an ill wind. Word would get around and the club would be busier than ever.

We didn't speak until we were downstairs. I let them go ahead and closed the door.

'You asked why these people would come to the club. It's simple. This whole thing hasn't felt right from the beginning. Because it isn't. They waited days before making contact. When they did, it wasn't with some extravagant demand. In fact, all they wanted to know was how much Nina was worth to me. Cutting the conversation short threw them off track. Until then, they'd been completely in control.' I spoke directly to Charley. 'I'd gladly trade places with Nina. Telling him to kill her was the hardest thing I've ever done. And I'd do it again. Mark said they were having a laugh. He was right. These clowns think they're invincible. They're about to realise that isn't the case.'

I held the mobile so they could both see and played the video. When Nina appeared, Douglas tensed. Charley's reaction was more obvious – her hand found mine. And in that moment, she was my sister and I loved her. The camera trembled. Nina gazed unblinking into the lens, the older version of the defiant little kid who'd told big bad Danny Glass to go fuck himself, fired her dinner at his head, and dared him to do something about it.

She was exhausted and she was angry but she didn't act as

though she was afraid. Whoever was in the room with her couldn't begin to guess the willpower needed to pull it off.

Nina's voice was strong and even. 'Luke, you know me better than I know myself. Always have. Imagine the words. Pretend they came from me. We both understand what they'd be so do what you have to do. Charley, you're a Glass. I'm glad you're my sister.' Her tone softened. 'And, Mark. Serves me right for keeping secrets from you, doesn't it? Lesson learned. It took a long time to find you, Mark Douglas, but you were worth waiting for. Thank you for teaching me it was okay to trust and that, more than anybody on earth, I could trust you. Whatever happens, I love you and always will. Don't—'

The video ended. Nina's face froze on the screen. Douglas spoke before anybody else, his voice cracking. 'If... I'll tear them apart. Tear their fucking heads off and pluck out their eyes.'

I put my hand on his shoulder. 'Just leave some for me.'

* * *

Julian bent over the steering wheel, guiding the car past the elegant semicircle of white stuccoed terraced houses of Park Crescent shining in the moonlight and into Marylebone Road. In the back seat, Rafe and Coco laughed hysterically.

Julian said, 'What's so funny?'

'You should've seen his face. The other sister spotted me as we were leaving.'

'Fuck! What did you do?'

'Smiled at her, what else?'

'You've got brass balls, I'll give you that, Rafe.'

A giggling Coco was already reaching into her bag for the white powder that had become a permanent fixture. Rafe didn't admonish her – not this time. They'd achieved what they set out to achieve the moment they realised who they'd brought with them from Poland Street. Tonight, they'd gone into the lion's den and were still shivering with the excitement of it. He kissed Coco on the lips. 'You were wonderful.'

'Not as wonderful as you.'

Julian said, 'So, what now?'

Rafe accepted the bump off Coco's painted nail. The drug hit him and he shook his head.

'Now, Julian, you can have a turn with Nina Glass. I won't stop you. Then we end it.'

'You mean...'

'I mean we end it.'

27

After the struggle, the silence was unnatural, covering the house like a cloak, and the chance – probably the last chance she'd ever have – had disappeared. Nina's head dropped to her chest; she pressed her eyes tight to stop the tears. For the briefest moment when the door had opened, she'd seen the unknown woman and the flickering embers of hope had sparked into flame. Suddenly, Henry had been behind her, in the half-light unrecognisable from the compassionate youth who'd stood up to his brother to protect her. That boy was gone. His hands had closed round the woman's throat, squeezing until she couldn't breathe. She'd fought him, her eyes bulging, tongue protruding between her teeth. The poker had fallen from her grasp but she hadn't given in, kicking him between the legs, forcing him to lose his grip.

What happened next, Nina could only imagine. They were on the landing, out of sight. A series of dull thuds meant one of them had fallen down the stairs – she prayed it was Henry.

* * *

In his long career in the service, Oliver Stanford had spent a lot of time waiting: for a suspect to break down and confess, an informant to bring the proof he needed to bring charges, or a jury to come back with a verdict. For a police officer, patience wasn't a virtue; it was a necessity. This was different. Sitting in his study in the dark wearing the awful green and white striped pyjamas Elise had bought him, pale moonlight falling on the lawn behind the house, the sweet, smoky saltiness of the ten-year-old Talisker in his hand, wasn't the comfort it should've been. Tonight, of all nights, it would take more than that.

Stanford had been lying in the dark, staring at the ceiling, listening to the gentle rise and fall of his wife's breathing when the mobile on the bedside cabinet rang. He'd reached out to answer it before it could disturb Elise. Given what was going on, the call wasn't a surprise. Difficult though it was to believe, some clowns had been foolish enough to abduct Nina Glass. Sooner or later her brother would expect him to earn the tidy sum that hit his secret bank account every month.

He'd whispered, 'Hold on,' and gone downstairs. The conversation that followed wasn't worthy of the name. The gangster had done the talking – laying out his demands and the consequences of failure in no uncertain terms. 'I've given you the car reg we got from our own CCTV. Now, I need a name and an address. If for any reason you don't or can't deliver, the arrangement we have will be over and prepare yourself for what happens next. You've got half an hour. Don't disappoint me or I can't be responsible for how this goes for you.'

Stanford had kept his voice low. 'Be reasonable, Glass, it's the middle of the fucking night. What you're asking—'

The reply chilled him. 'This is me being reasonable, copper.'

'I can't guarantee—'

The line had died. That had been twenty-five minutes, thirty-five seconds and two whiskies ago.

But who was counting?

* * *

Coco was eating the face off Rafe, fumbling inside his trousers. His hand cupped her exposed breast, squeezing the erect nipple between his thumb and forefinger, feeling it change from hard to harder as the drugs and the adrenaline pumping through their veins did their work.

Julian's hands tightened on the steering wheel, his eyes on the rear-view mirror; he was wishing it was him instead of Rafe. He took a right at York Gate, then left at Ulster Terrace, and settled back to enjoy the show. By the time they got to Swiss Cottage, they were both naked – Coco on her back, legs over Rafe's shoulders, her tiny knickers dangling round one ankle. He knelt, half on half off the seat, thrusting between her thighs and Julian adjusted the mirror to get a better look.

Rafe realised they were being watched and grinned. 'Want to join us, Julian? Don't think she'll turn you down this time.'

It ended in a cacophony of loud moans and frantic cries as they collapsed into each other and lay still. After a while, Coco asked in a little-girl voice, 'Are we there yet?' and they laughed.

* * *

Resentment dripped from Oliver Stanford's oily voice. I couldn't have cared less – the bastard owed me. He said, 'The car's registered to a Constance Greyland.'

'Where?'

'East Heath Road.'

He gave me the address and fell silent. If he was expecting me to thank him, he was sadly mistaken. Getting him to perform was like pulling teeth. The next words out of his mouth told me he saw it differently.

'You've absolutely no idea what I had to do to get info like that at this time of the night.'

He was correct, I didn't know and didn't want to know. Stanford was fine about the nice house in Hendon, the private education for his daughters and the trips abroad for him and Elise. When it came to carrying his share of the weight, he was a whole lot less enthusiastic.

I was tired of Danny's tame copper and he was tired of me.

He said, 'I couldn't use my usual people. When you do what you're going to do, it'll come out. Questions will be asked. Questions I don't have answers for. Threatening me is a waste of time. In the Curtis Green Building, more often than not, two and two makes four. All it'll take is some over-eager detective sergeant to use the brains God gave him and I'm finished.'

The speech sounded as though it had been put together while he was waiting for his contacts to come back to him. Stanford was pathetic. He'd confused me with somebody who gave a fuck.

I threw him a bone. 'Wait a couple of hours then call it in. Say a source you're sworn to protect put you onto something going on near the heath. Keep your head and you'll come up smelling of roses like you've done so often in the past. Wouldn't be surprised you get a commendation. The thing I'm not sure about is two plus two equalling four. In Scotland Yard? You're having a laugh, aren't you, Oli? Now, if you'll excuse me, I've got some bad bastards to sort out. You know, your old job.'

* * *

Rafe and Coco were still giggling when Julian drew up to the house. Rafe pulled her to him. 'Had enough excitement yet? Or do you want us to break into the Queen's bedroom?'

Coco's head fell back; he kissed her neck and she purred. 'There's no such thing as enough.'

'Enough for the moment. We've done what nobody else would dare to do. Taken it to the limit and beyond. It's time to tidy up the loose ends and move on.'

Julian overheard the last bit. 'By loose ends I hope you mean the Glass woman. I've been waiting to tidy her up from the start.'

'I do indeed and you've earned it, Julian. Can I watch? Fair's fair.'

Henry opened the front door before they got to it. His face was ashen and Rafe realised something was terribly wrong. 'What's happened? Don't tell me you've let her get away or so help me, brother, I'll—'

'It isn't that.'

'Then what?'

He pulled the door back to reveal the body at the bottom of the stairs, the eyes staring, seeing nothing. 'Fucking hell! Who is she?'

Julian pushed them aside. 'What have you done? That's Aunt Connie.'

Rafe said, 'She's supposed to be in South Africa.'

Julian fell to his knees beside the dead woman. 'Jesus Christ! Oh, Jesus Christ!'

28

Henry was in his room, traumatised, afraid Julian would go after him for what he'd done. The boy should never have been involved – he wasn't his brother; he didn't have the stuff for this. Julian sat in a chair by the wall, away from Rafe and his crazy chick. They were high, in party mood, snorting and drinking, loudly reliving their visit to the gangster's club. Rafe had changed out of his suit and was in his underpants; Coco had taken off the red dress and was swanning around in her bra and knickers, pretending not to notice the effect she was having. Julian had never liked the superior Rafe or the snooty Coco, but at that moment he hated them. Doing it in the back of the car was the bitch's way of making him jealous, reminding him of what he wanted and was never going to have.

Death didn't suit his aunt: she looked old. Her nephew's response to finding her at the bottom of the stairs with her neck broken wasn't about her. He didn't kid himself he'd suffered some great loss; they hadn't been close. Constance Greyland's biggest concern had always been herself, and her appetite for men – the younger the better – was an open secret. For a while, he'd sucked up to her hoping she'd include him in her will. It hadn't worked.

She didn't like him and hadn't hidden it. He'd spotted her once in Mayfair at a corner table in Le Gavroche having lunch with a man who could've been her son. Julian had been entertaining a Sangster-Devlin client and as Connie and her stud were leaving, had turned away so she didn't see him. He'd told Rafe she was in South Africa and had given him a key. A lie. The idea of Connie giving him or anybody else permission to come into her house whenever they chose was risible – he'd taken it from the hook on the kitchen wall on his last fruitless visit; a tiny vindictive act he hadn't understood at the time.

Across the lounge, Coco threw her head back. 'And his face, did you see it? Has anyone ever been more shocked? Not what I imagined. Maybe he's not a big bad gangster after all.'

Traces of white powder dusted Rafe's top lip. One hand held a glass of brandy, the other a stubby Gauloises. 'Yeah,' he said, 'lost a shilling and found a penny. We'll let him have his precious sister back, all right. What I'd give to be a fly on the wall.'

Coco seized on the possibility of more fun. 'You aren't thinking about doing something else, are you? Fantastic! If—'

'No, we've pushed our luck and got away with it. Let's settle for what we have. Unless...'

'Unless, what?'

* * *

Nina heard Rafe and Coco laughing their way up the stairs, giggling like naughty kids, and knew it didn't bode well: they were high. Growing up, Nina had tried every substance under the sun. She'd started smoking at eleven and had her first brandy-induced blackout twenty-four months later in a public park in Dulwich. From there, her progression had been sadly predictable – marijuana, moving on to stealing prescription painkillers, trying ecstasy, heroin and all stops in between. Danny had threatened to put her in rehab and keep her there unless she got a grip. Fortunately, she'd managed to straighten up, but the painful journey had left her with a keen appreciation of how drugs affected people in different ways. Rafe was a control freak; cocaine would heighten his self-confidence to the point of grandiosity, convincing him he'd accomplished great things when, in reality, he hadn't. Coco's innate cruelty would go unchecked. No knowing where that would lead or how it might end. Together, these two were a potentially fatal combination.

Coco stood in the centre of the room in her high heels, bra and knickers, bright eyes dancing in her head. Behind her, Rafe smiled a stiff superior smile, twirling a gun in his hand. Very obviously, their trip to LBC had gone well; they were euphoric. Acid, sour and bitter, rose in Nina's throat.

Coco pouted. 'We thought you might be lonely, didn't we, Rafe?' Her head tilted to the side like a child asking a hard question. 'Are you lonely, Nina?'

'I'll be all right if you give me a drag of whatever you've been smoking.'

Coco might not have heard. She said, 'We've come to play a game and cheer you up. I like games. We played one with your brother earlier. His reaction to your little video was priceless. He crumbled.'

Nina sneered at the lie. 'You must've been hallucinating. Luke doesn't break. Not for anything. All you've done is motivate him. Enjoy yourself because it'll be over faster than you think.' She faked a laugh. 'I won't feel a thing. Not how it'll finish for you.'

Rafe emptied the copper-coloured shells from the weapon into his palm, put one back in the chamber and spun the drum, making sure Nina saw him.

Coco sucked her thumb. 'You're going to love this. It's so-o-o-o exciting.'

'Then, why don't you go first? I don't mind.'

The bravado didn't come easily. None of it real. Russian roulette was for reckless fools and desperate losers who'd reached the end of the line. People with a death wish. She was young. She had Mark and everything to live for. With or without their drug of choice, they neither knew nor cared if their 'game' ended in her death.

The maths was simple: one in six – an approximately 17 per cent chance of dying, 83 per cent of coming out alive. With the barrel against her temple, the odds of surviving seemed a lot less.

Coco's enthusiasm revealed the depths of her depravity. 'Come on, Rafe. We haven't got all night.' She giggled again. 'Oh, sorry, my mistake, we *do* have all night.'

Rafe spun the cylinder a second time and put the gun to Nina's forehead. Coco studied her face, searching for the slightest flicker of fear, eager to savour it. Nina closed her eyes tight and thought of Mark. Please don't let it be him who found her body; that would be too hard to bear.

Time had no meaning. Her heart thumped in her chest as she waited for the hammer to fall. When it did, the 'click' of metal against metal was like a peel of thunder in the silence and Nina thought she was going to be sick.

Coco whooped and clapped her hands. 'Fabulous! Again! Do it again!'

Nina heard the muted whir of the drum, felt the cool of the revolver on her skin, and almost fainted.

Rafe pressed the trigger.

Another click; louder than before.

The bedroom filled with the sound of Coco screaming her delight. 'Yes! Yes!'

Surviving came at a cost – the psychological damage was

immense. Nina slumped into the chair. Coco, wrapped up in the moment, didn't notice and squealed like an immature girl. 'Let me try! Let me have a try! I want to do it!'

Rafe gave her the gun and shrugged an apology at the helpless Nina. 'Well, it is her turn, after all.'

Coco straddled Nina's legs, stroking her hair like a lover. 'As Rafe says, it's my turn.'

She traced a line with the gun through the sweat on her victim's breasts, panting like a bitch in heat, choosing where to place the shot. 'Here, maybe?'

The barrel followed the soft sweep of Nina's neck, forcing its way past her clenched teeth and into her mouth, 'Or, here?'

Coco laughed. 'This is better than sex'. Suddenly, without warning, she stuck the gun in Nina's right ear and fired. It didn't go off. Disappointment overwhelmed her. She fired again and again and would've kept firing if Rafe hadn't snatched the revolver out of her hand.

'When the Gods speak, Coco, a wise man listens. They don't want Nina Glass dead just yet.'

29

To a south London boy like me, north of the river was a foreign country. Since opening LBC, I'd seen more of it than I'd wanted. And here I was again, driving through the shuttered city – me, Mark Douglas and Charley in the first car, George Ritchie, Felix and three of George's men in the second, their shoes resting on the battering ram and the three-feet-long Halligan bar on the floor at their feet. Oliver Stanford was a gutless, self-serving coward but he'd come through with the address and I knew exactly where we were going. What I didn't know was what was waiting for us when we got there.

At Swiss Cottage Tube station, we pulled up to a set of traffic lights and waited for them to change. Whatever we were thinking we kept to ourselves. Douglas gripped the wheel with both hands, his expression a mask in the moonlight. I understood better than anybody what was behind it and didn't envy the fools we were on our way to meet. Charley had insisted on coming. I hadn't tried to stop her – she was family, her stake in this was as valid as mine. Sister No. 2 was a woman who never looked less than fantastic, no matter the circumstances. Even now, sitting alone in the back seat, that was true, but her fidgeting fingers gave away her anxiety.

On the other side of the road, near the flickering neon sign of a Lebanese restaurant, a bearded man in a heavy black coat scavenged a bin, scooping his dirty paws deep into it, peering at his haul, slowly sifting it and letting it fall through his fingers like a panhandler in the Klondike in the last days of the gold rush.

There were thousands of homeless in London, dossing, trying to survive another merciless winter's night in one of the richest countries on earth. There was a moral in there somewhere. Tonight wasn't the night to search for it.

I got out of the car and crossed the street. The man had his back to me, too engrossed in his fight to survive to notice. When he did, he froze and stepped away, ready to run, eyes darting in his head. He didn't trust me – experience had taught him there was no reason he should. The beard, thick and matted, made it impossible to guess his age and up close the coat wasn't a coat – it was two coats, one on top of the other. We both had our reasons for being on the street at this time in the morning. His was very different from mine. Except, in our own way, we were doing what had to be done. I put my hand in my pocket and took out the best part of what was probably a couple of hundred quid. His eyes flitted greedily between me and the money and back again, wary and confused. He licked his cracked lips, wiped the palms of his filthy mitts on himself, struggling to fathom what was going on. In his world, random acts of kindness didn't happen very often. When they did, they came with conditions – a bed in exchange for a sober night and a pledge to get off the drink; a bowl of soup for sitting still long enough to listen to a lecture about a carpenter's son from Nazareth.

With me there was no catch.

I leaned forward to encourage him to take the cash. At first it seemed his fear had won, then a grubby hand fired like a rat from under his coats, grabbed it from my hand and he ran up Finchley Road.

Mark Douglas hit the horn to let me know the lights had changed. In the car, he said, 'What was that about?'

I didn't answer. Unwisely, he went on. 'He'll pour whatever you gave him down his throat.'

My reply summed up exactly how I felt. 'And that would be his business. Shut the fuck up and drive.'

At the beginning of Hampstead village, the cars parted company. Ritchie's peeled off and we carried on up the hill to where East Heath Road ended and West Heath Road began. Douglas took a right and drove down the incline. Fifty yards from a red-brick Victorian house set back from the street, he killed the engine and we rolled to a stop. The vehicle carrying George and Felix was facing us, already in position.

A light shone in a downstairs window. My mobile rang. Ritchie's Newcastle twang came down the line. 'They're at home. What do you want to do?'

Every atom in my body ached to get the bastards who'd taken my sister. I said, 'Let's wait a minute or two to see if anything occurs.'

'Okay, and then what?'

'We go in the front door.'

'They've got guns and aren't shy about using them.'

He was thinking about the jeweller and the bodyguard in Poland Street.

'We shoot if we have to, but dead's too easy. I want them alive, George.'

'Understood. We're ready when you are. Just say the word. They'll have Nina in the basement or upstairs.' He could've added if she's still breathing, but didn't. 'The first thing we do is take their toys away from them.'

I was George Ritchie's boss. We were friendly without being friends, yet at times he was more like the father I'd never had – a man I could depend on to point me in the right direction. If I fell, George would be there to catch me.

The air was cold, three or four degrees above freezing. By now, the homeless man would have the money counted and discovered that God liked him after all. Dealers didn't keep office hours and he might already have invested some of it in release from the pain of his existence. What I'd given him wouldn't change his life but tomorrow would look better than it had an hour ago. The same couldn't be said of the scum inside the house – for them there would be no tomorrow.

I called George. 'Okay, let's go.'

Telling Charley to stay in the car was a waste of breath, so I didn't bother. Felix lifted the latch of the wrought-iron gate, pushed it open, and we crouched our way to the front door. Behind us the moon bathed the heath in gold. I signalled to Ritchie; he nodded to Felix. Two of the men lifted the ram ready to let it go. The third hefted the Halligan bar with its machine-sharpened claws at one end, duckbill incline at the other.

From inside, the drone of male voices drifted to us and a woman laughed. I fought a feeling inside me I hadn't experienced since the final manic days of Danny. These bastards thought they'd got away with it. But they were about to get the surprise of their lives.

George tapped his guy on the shoulder. The ram swung back and crashed into the panel; the second impact made a hole the size of a fist; the third fractured the lock and the laughter stopped.

I imagined them scrambling for their guns. Weapons wouldn't do them any good.

They could die here or die somewhere else.

Their choice.

* * *

Mark Douglas had suffered more than anybody: my love was a brother's love, his feelings for Nina went deeper. On the video, she'd been hurt but alive. There was no way to know if she still was. I was watching him when the ram battered into the door, splintering the wood. Once. Twice. Three times. He hadn't so much as blinked. His lips were tight and dry, his breathing steady, eyes cold and empty. Eight days earlier in Poland Street, the people on the other side of the door had had no idea the hell they were bringing down on their heads.

They were about to find out.

Douglas was first in, followed by me. Instinctively, he dived up the stairs to search for Nina. Charley went with him. Ritchie grabbed hold of my arm and pulled me back. His gun was in his hand. 'Let me do my job, Luke. You shouldn't be part of this.'

I shrugged him away. 'You're a good guy, George, but your timing's shit. You need to work on it.'

The exchange was academic – Felix made the decision for us. He fired a bullet into the lounge door and kicked it open. I'd called them amateurs, fools, clowns, and they were all of that. Tonight, in north London, they'd proved it – convinced they'd got away with entering the lion's den and living to tell the tale, they hadn't bothered to keep their weapons handy.

It was party time.

He'd introduced himself as Toby Lennox – I doubted that was his real name – exuding an almost unnatural confidence that had set me on edge. His upper-crust accent was like scratchy chalk on a blackboard. We were from different worlds. In mine, you started with nothing and ended with nothing unless you were prepared to get down in the dirt and scrap for it. These fuckers had been given everything, brought up to believe they were special, entitled; better than the rest of us.

The words were inadequate; they were all I had.

Amateurs. Fools. Clowns.

One of them was a new face but I'd seen the man and woman before, scrubbed up and shiny-bright in LBC, going into their sadistic routine, savouring the hurt they were causing. Now, the shoe was on the other foot, they were out of their heads, terrified I'd tell Felix to shoot them.

An hour from now they'd be begging him to.

Felix Corrigan kept his gun on them and stepped aside to let me pass. On a glass-topped coffee table the platinum VIP card they'd used to blag their way into the club lay beside lines of flaky white powder that had once been the lush green leaves of the coca plant.

I overturned it; the glass top smashed, a cocaine cloud rose in the air, then lazily fell to the floor. Panic that had nothing to do with the gun pointed at her shadowed the woman's eyes. Unless she was ready to shove the carpet up her nose, her precious drug was gone.

Ritchie quietly ordered two of his men upstairs and came to stand beside me. I sensed his presence and spoke to him out of the side of my mouth. 'Is she all right? Is Nina okay?'

'We'll know in a minute when they bring her down.'

In LBC, the woman had been a stunner. Half naked and bombed, she had all the allure of a junkie hooker. Her rock-chick hair had lost its wild glory, her eyes were bloodshot and her nose was raw. Going low, going slow hadn't been for her. She blurted an explanation as far removed from helping her case as it was possible to get.

'It was a game, just a game.'

Her boyfriend shouted, 'For fuck's sake, Coco, shut up!' shifting from one foot to the other like somebody who needed to go to the bathroom and couldn't wait much longer.

His attempt to talk their way out of a painful death was no better than hers. 'She's all right. Your sister's all right.' His eyes flashed to the man by the wall. 'I made sure she wasn't abused.'

As a plea for mercy it was a long way short of the mark.

The question I asked had been in my head from the start. 'Who are you people?'

Whatever they said would be the wrong answer. They were smart enough to suss it. Before he could reply the sounds of a struggle drew me into the hall. A young guy was being dragged, crying and whimpering, onto the landing in a fight he couldn't win.

George spoke to the last of his heavies. 'Check if there are any more skulking around.'

Nina stood unsteadily between Mark Douglas and Charley, thinner than the last time I'd seen her, leaning on them for support, her knuckles white, closed tightly over his as though she'd never let go. Douglas had removed his jacket and draped it round her. When they got to the bottom of the stairs, I took her in my arms and held her. Words wouldn't form; a storm raged in my brain. After a few moments I gently passed her back to her lover and prepared to unleash its fury on the fuckers who'd broken her. Before I could, Ritchie's guy whispered in his ear and George tugged at my sleeve. 'Sorry to interrupt but there's something you need to see.'

'Just tell me.'

'There's a dead woman in the basement.'

It should've been a surprise. Somehow it wasn't.

'Any idea who she is?'

He shook his head and I spoke to Nina. 'You're safe. It's over. The nightmare's over.'

She lifted her chin defiantly, like I'd seen her do as a kid going up against Danny. Half of London was terrified of Danny Glass. My sister hadn't been one of them. And it never ended well for him. Nina focused on the people who'd abducted and abused her.

'Over? You can't be serious.' She pulled free from Douglas and Charley and lunged past me at the female they'd called Coco, screaming her loathing. After so long tied to a chair, her legs wouldn't hold and she fell to her knees. Coco smirked at her distress – in her situation, unwise. Very unwise. Douglas rushed forward and cradled Nina in his arms until she stopped struggling, tears of frustration running in rivulets down her cheeks.

If anyone still doubted it was Glass blood flowing in my American sister's veins, what happened next would convince them. More than any of us, Charley understood what her sister needed: she dived across the room, dragged the female by the hair, and crashed her pretty face against the wall, breaking her nose in a sickening thud. Blood joined the cocaine cloud on the carpet but Charley wasn't done. Coco was scrambling on her hands and knees, begging the other two losers to help her, when Charley hauled her back and forced the ruined face to look at Nina. 'Say you're sorry. Tell my sister you're sorry, you bitch.'

It had taken longer than it should've but, finally, she realised the seriousness of her situation and whimpered. 'I'm... sorry.'

Charley brought a knee up hard into the terrified Coco's jaw and dropped her like a discarded doll, then turned on her cowering accomplices, anger and adrenaline pumping through her.

'Okay, you bastards, does anybody else want some?'

30

Ritchie watched me as the number rang out. Nobody answered. I'd started reluctantly to reassess my options when he picked up. The voice was thick with booze, the words slurred and mangled, and I remembered the cot at the other side of the Portakabin. He was ill, most likely dying. Tonight and any night, the only friend he'd have in the world to keep him company in the wee small hours when the fear of his approaching end crawled like a serpent in his diseased gut was the cheap cider I'd smelled on his breath, bought by the case because a bottle – even a large bottle – wouldn't do the job. I sensed the smile spreading over his ugly drunken face at the other end of the line when he heard we were on our way.

Scrap Hughie was a vile creature beyond redemption, but I needed him.

I was driving the lead car, Charley beside me in the passenger seat, Mark Douglas and Nina in the back. The gang were split between the other car and their own vehicle. As the drugs wore off their minds would be racing, thinking about escape, calculating the odds and concluding it was a non-starter. In their position, knowing what I knew, I'd have taken my chances and made a run for it.

Mark had his arm round Nina, whispering things no one else was meant to hear, heads lowered and close together, her leaning into him with his jacket still over her shoulders. I would've preferred to take care of this without my sisters. With what I'd seen from both of them, even hinting at it was more hassle than it was worth.

The moon followed our progress from Hampstead across north London, a baleful yellow eye judging us in the hours before dawn as we motored past the St Pancras and Islington cemetery, where Cora Henrietta Crippen, wife and victim of the notorious Dr Crippen, lay buried, and Muswell Hill, close to the birthplace of Ray Davies the founder of the Kinks, Danny's favourite group.

The atmosphere was a mix of relief Nina hadn't been seriously harmed, and rage at the bastards who'd abducted her. It was too early for the psychological damage to show itself. When it did, she wouldn't be alone on a cot in a Portakabin with a bottle of super-strength Frosty Jack's on the floor beside her: she'd be with her family.

We skirted Tottenham, crossed the dark smudge of the River Lea, and headed south. From start to finish the journey lasted forty-four minutes – the longest forty-four minutes the kidnappers would ever know.

The derelict industrial estate was eerie and bleak, reminiscent of the abandoned set of a post-apocalypse movie. I hadn't expected to see it or the red-brick railway bridge so soon. Behind me, Ritchie's headlights dipped and dived with every rut in the road. George knew where we were going, the others didn't, and as the high fence and hills of metal materialised through the trees, no inkling of what was coming would register with the doomed misguided fools.

Nothing could prepare them for what was on the other side.

We drew up at the padlocked gate and Charley said, 'What is this place?'

I didn't reply. 'It's better you two stay in the car.'

Nina sat forward. 'Better for who?'

'Both of you. Stay in the car. You don't want to see this, believe me.'

It was the wrong thing to say and I knew it the moment the words were out of my mouth. Nina seized on them. 'Danny was our flesh and blood. Do you really think anything could shock me after what he did?'

I reached for her hand but she drew it away. 'I'm trying to save you, Nina.'

Her reply stung me to the bone. 'You're nine fucking days too late, brother.'

Mark Douglas kept his mouth shut, smart enough not to put himself in the middle of an argument he'd no hope of winning. Neither had I; their minds were made up.

'Okay, if that's how you want it.'

Nina grabbed my arm, nails digging into me, willing me to understand. 'You've no idea what it was like, sitting in the dark night after night, expecting to be violated. If it hadn't been for Henry...'

'Which one's Henry?'

'The young one. Let him go, Luke, he doesn't deserve this.'

'I'll think about it.'

She softened and I realised how much the ordeal had taken from her. 'My faith in you never wavered. But no matter what you said, no matter what you did, they always intended to kill me, like the old jeweller and his bodyguard in Soho. I was just part of a game they were playing. Words can't describe how I feel so, whatever you do to them, don't worry about me. I'll be loving every fucking minute of it. Just leave Henry alone.'

There was no more to say.

We got out and walked the last few yards to the gate in the moonlight and waited for Hughie to make an appearance. In the distance, the Portakabin was where it had been and Coco shivered in her underwear in the near-zero temperatures; a couple of minutes from now the cold would be the least of her problems. Ritchie's guys flanked the three men, stone-faced, guns drawn – the prisoners didn't raise their heads. Henry, the boy Nina had made a plea for, was the exception, sobbing quietly next to his brother, and I got where she was coming from.

But if you lie down with dogs, you get up with fleas.

Peering through the steel mesh, knowing what lived here, was weird. Hughie's non-appearance wasn't an accident. This was how the scrap man got his jollies, letting the victims sweat before releasing the horror.

I'd called Danny a sadist; it seemed he wasn't the only one.

Rafe screwed up his courage. 'You're going to kill us, aren't you?'

In LBC, he'd been an over-confident upper-class nob hiding behind a phoney name, smiling too much and feeding me bullshit until the video of Nina on my phone gave them a front-row view of my hurt. On the return to Hampstead it would've been fun times. And why not? They'd made an idiot of Luke Glass in his own back-yard, validating every assumption about their superiority.

Except, it hadn't been true and they were going to die for it.

The third guy was different – no tears or questions from him. He said, 'What if we give you the stones?'

The gems they'd stolen in Poland Street; I'd forgotten about them.

'You give me them and I let you go?'

'Why not?'

I let him wait. 'How much are we talking about?'

'A lot. The jeweller said he only worked with the best.'

I had to stop from laughing out loud. Even with all that had gone on – kidnapping my sister and holding her for nine days, playing silly buggers with queries about how much she was worth to me, brassing it at the club and all the moronic rest of it – this tosser had the nerve to try to do a deal.

Some people.

'Where are they?'

'Somewhere safe.'

George shot a knowing look at me and was immediately on the phone to his guys cleaning the house in Hampstead – this guy's deal was a bust. He had nothing to bargain with; the stones were already ours. Clearly, he thought we were retarded. He said, 'You'll never find them.'

Now he was really getting on my tits. I said, 'What's your name?'

'Julian.'

'And what's your part in this... Julian?'

He hesitated, undecided on which lie to tell, finally going with a statement that had nothing to do with anything. 'The dead woman was my aunt, the house belonged to her.'

'So how come she's in the basement?'

He filled in the blanks. 'She was supposed to be in South Africa. For some reason, I don't know why, she came home early and Henry killed her.'

'Henry doesn't look up to killing anybody. Where were you?'

Julian sussed where the conversation was headed and didn't answer. It wasn't necessary. I could guess. 'You were outside in the car waiting for the others, weren't you? Yeah, you were. So okay, I'll do a deal with you, and it's this: tell me where the stones are hidden and I'll cut your fucking head off. But I'll make it quick. How does that sound?'

Before he could reply, George Ritchie said, 'Luke, he's here.'

Scrap Hughie emerged from the metal canyons dressed in the

clothes he'd had on the last time I'd seen him, and came towards the gate, his shadow following his bent frame like a question mark written on the ground. From somewhere deep in the depths of the yard, a dog bayed at the moon, fitting the mood to perfection. Hughie surveyed the scene through one bloodshot eye, travelling slowly over the people who'd been stupid enough to cross a Glass.

I said, 'Are your friends ready?'

'My friends are always ready.'

Ritchie said, 'Where's Freddie?'

Hughie chuckled and gobbed on the ground. 'Don't worry, George, he knows you're around; he can smell you. So this is the mob that took your sister.' The scrap man laughed a throaty laugh. 'Not so fucking cocky on it now, are they? Worth spending a few bob to square the account.'

I repeated my question. He ignored it and ran his single eye over the gang. 'You didn't mention you were bringing four.'

'Is that a problem?'

'Not for Freddie. But it'll cost you.'

'I'm good for it, Hughie.'

Through the mesh he grinned a yellow-toothed grin. 'That's what they all say.'

'Except, with me it's the truth.' The money wasn't important and I wasn't in the mood to haggle. 'How much more?'

'Double. And there's something I want you to do. Call it a favour for services rendered.'

'Pushing it a bit, aren't you?'

He spat again. 'Take it or fucking leave it. Up to you. Except make your mind up, it's bloody freezing.'

'I'll take it. How's this going to work?'

Hughie was a born marketeer who understood some 'customers' had requirements that weren't negotiable. 'Any way you want it to work. You're the boss, boss.'

It wasn't meant as a compliment.

'I'm asking how, Hughie. All together or one at a time?'

The oblique conversation was more than Rafe could stand. He broke down. 'What are you going to do to us?'

Hughie's lip curled contemptuously. 'A bit early with the tears, isn't he?'

'You're the expert, what do you suggest?'

He stroked his grizzled chin with a filthy mitt and looked up at me. 'Depends.'

'On what?'

'Just how much a spectacle you want to make it. I prefer the VIP version myself.'

He paused to let the terror build in the victims.

'Which is?'

'All of them at once. Lets you see a man's true character.'

I didn't disagree. 'What's the favour?'

'My dogs love me. When I die, Freddie won't do well. Give me your word you'll shoot him. Not George Ritchie. Not somebody else. You. Do it yourself.'

The lie, like all the best lies, came easily. 'All right.'

Hughie pulled a key from his pocket and unlocked the gate. Nina stood in front of the boy, arms out, protecting him. 'The others, yes, not Henry. You said—'

'I say a lot of stuff, Nina.'

'It's important to me, Luke. Henry isn't like them.'

'Tell that to the dead woman in the basement.'

Her lip quivered and I touched her cheek. My sister had been through enough. Adding to it would've been wrong. The boy fell to his knees at her feet and she stroked his hair. At the eleventh hour, Henry had been reprieved. The rest wouldn't be so lucky.

Nina went down the line, eyes locking on each of them in turn.

Rafe said, 'It wasn't personal.'

She answered, 'Well, it is now.'

When she came to Julian her hand closed round his crotch and squeezed hard. He moaned and doubled over. With Coco she leaned in close. 'I'm so-o-o-o going to enjoy watching you die, BITCH!'

Ritchie's guys hauled the whimpering woman and the two terrified men inside the gate, struggling and wailing. Coco's arrogance was a thing of the past; she cried and pleaded, pounding the heavies with her slender fists. 'Please! Please! We wouldn't have harmed her! It was a game! Just a game!'

She didn't get it, did she? They'd made us look weak. That couldn't be allowed to stand or every tuppenny villain who fancied his chances would have a pop. I'd told George Scrap Hughie heard things. That wasn't the whole story – it also worked in reverse. Those who needed to would get the message and know how it ended for anybody stupid enough to fuck with the Glass family.

Hughie locked the gate and walked his crippled walk to the Portakabin. When he got to the door, he closed it behind him. An eerie quiet settled over the yard. Coco was sitting on the ground, pulling at her hair, talking to herself like a madwoman. Her companions stood close together, hands clenched at their sides, eyes darting right and left.

Moonlight glanced off the twisted-metal towers, making them glow. In the silence, I heard my own laboured breathing, and, in spite of the temperature, I was sweating. Felix's fingers strayed to the gun in the waistband of his trousers, a necessary reflex for a guy in his profession. Ritchie's men were hard bastards who'd seen it all and done things even they were ashamed of. They edged away, putting distance between them and whatever was coming. Off to the side, Mark Douglas held Nina, still wearing his jacket, gently caressing her shoulder, tension written in dark lines on his face.

After a shaky start he'd come good, it had to be said, and I was glad he was here.

The exception was Charley, ramrod straight, mouth set tight, coldly watching the people through the fence who'd dared to harm her family.

The only ones in the know were George Ritchie and me. He'd seen me on my mobile in the house. I hadn't told him who I'd spoken to or what was arranged. But when I'd pointed the convoy in the direction of Hampstead Garden Suburb instead of south London, he'd have sussed it.

George was Danny without the insanity – capable of sanctioning what others couldn't and, afterwards, sleeping like a baby. With Ritchie, if it didn't make sense, he turned it down and went with what did. The difference tonight was that, like me, he'd seen the monster in action – albeit a controlled demonstration staged by Scrap Hughie to impress us.

It had certainly done that.

A wayward cloud passed across the sky, momentarily plunging Walthamstow into darkness. When it moved on, light returned and the animal was staring at us from the bottom of the yard. Even from this distance it was enormous. Coco's cry died in her throat; the people with me gave a collective gasp and took an involuntary step back. I joined them.

The dog padded forward, muscular shoulders rolling under its thick coat with every step, sniffing the air like a big cat sensing a wounded gazelle in the African veldt.

Then, the beast started running towards us.

31

Even with the fence, it was a terrifying sight. Without a barrier between us I could only imagine how I'd feel. Hughie's philosophical observation about character in adversity came true immediately. Rafe pulled Coco to her feet and pushed her into the path of the giant dog, her once-beautiful face contorted in fear. She stumbled, and it was on her, bowling her over like a toy, knocking her to the ground, burying its snapping jaws in the folds of her throat, lifting her in the air and shaking her like a rag doll. The beast bit a lump of flesh the size of my hand out of her thigh and circled the body, growling softly, licking its bloodied snout. Then – the most chilling thing I'd ever seen – the monster stood its front paws on her chest, raised its mighty head, and howled.

I hated this woman for what she'd done to my sister but, for her sake, I hoped she was dead.

Mark Douglas held Nina to him and tried to shield her eyes; she pulled his hand aside and kept watching. Henry turned away – it was supposed to have been a laugh; none of this was in the plan. Charley didn't flinch; she was calm, and in the light her skin had the alabaster glow of the goddess Fortuna at the entrance to LBC.

One of Ritchie's hardmen had his hands on his knees, loudly retching over his shoes at the side of the gate. Felix wasn't caressing his gun now; it was out and ready. George gazed on the slaughter, unmoved, although in ten seconds he seemed to have aged ten years.

Rafe hadn't waited to witness his girlfriend's demise, using the precious minutes sacrificing her had given him to race to the safety of the Portakabin. Julian, his partner in crimes against my family, chose the moment before the powerful animal crashed into the half-naked Coco to take off to the right. I could've told him he was wasting his time. Finding an escape route behind the rusting mountains wasn't on – the yard was completely enclosed. It had to be. And not to keep anybody out.

The 'VIP version' the scrap man talked about hadn't materialised. Nobody was complaining: what we were getting was more than enough. A series of hellish screams told me Hughie had delivered on his vision – the 'puppies' weren't in Freddie's division, not even close, but with three of them they'd tear Julian apart. He wouldn't be cutting that deal after all.

In front of us, the aberration of nature hauled what was left of Coco in a circle, stopping to sniff the mutilated body. Coco's head fell towards me and I saw her face: the mouth was open, the tongue hanging out, eyes wide and staring.

Suddenly, she blinked. Christ Almighty! She was still alive!

I signalled Felix to put her out of her agony. He raised his gun and aimed. Before he could fire, Nina broke from Douglas and knocked the weapon out of his hand, furious with me. And the message was clear: this was my sister's show. She'd decide when it ended.

Rafe was at the Portakabin, hammering the door, shouting for Scrap Hughie to let him in, offering everything he was heir to in exchange for his life.

The commotion reminded the dog he wasn't finished. His huge ears pricked up and he padded across the yard, gathering speed as he got nearer. Rafe saw him and hammered harder. A net curtain drew aside. Behind the glass Scrap Hughie had the grandstand view he'd promised us. Rafe's offers missed their mark – Hughie was a grasping, tight-arsed bastard but a dying man had no need of money.

Finally, Rafe accepted it was hopeless, pressed himself against the frame, and faced it. The killer leapt, teeth bared, and we held our breath at the savagery on display in a neglected part of north-east London. There were stars in the sky and it was bitterly cold. One of those nights where sounds travelled. His skull cracked under the pressure of the enormous jaws clamped to it, the weight of the beast alone enough to snap his spine.

For what felt like an age, impossibly, Rafe stayed on his feet, then slid slowly down the door with the dog tearing at what was left of him.

* * *

George Ritchie's men weren't sorry to leave – it had been harrowing, even for them. Nina watched them go and came to me, leaning heavily on Douglas, as angry as I'd ever known her, which was saying something. She'd been lucky. We'd been lucky. Tomorrow or the next day, maybe, she'd appreciate it. Right now, that wasn't where she was. Her eyes were hollow, sunk in her head. Talking was an effort but she had something to say and was determined to say it.

'Now, it's over.'

I didn't react; she was right.

Mark and Charley led her away. What Nina needed was time; didn't we all? She stopped to speak to a distraught Henry and threw a look back at me – she owed him and was making sure I hadn't forgotten. Through the gate, Scrap Hughie waited for me. The smell of cider was on him again and I guessed he'd been celebrating – the light in his eye had nothing to do with the moon.

'He's something, isn't he? Freddie's really something.'

Said with pride.

Hughie nodded towards the boy. 'What happens to him? You're letting him go, aren't you? You're going to let him go.'

We all need our moment in the sun – even a loathsome toad like this. He said, 'Remember what you promised. Yourself, nobody else.' He wiped his mouth on his sleeve. 'I'm thinking you'll want the word out about what happened here, am I right?'

'That's the point of it, Hughie, and stick around, you're not done.'

He gobbed through the wire and glared at me with his one eye.

Henry was still upset – with what he'd seen I didn't hold it against him and put a hand on his shoulder. 'Here's how it is. Nina wants me to let you go. Insists on it, actually. If it was up to me, you'd be in the yard with your arms and legs torn off.' I spoke to Ritchie. 'How much money have you got on you, George?'

'Sixty, seventy, why?'

'What about you, Felix?'

'I'm not sure, something like a hundred and fifty.'

I clicked my fingers. 'Give it to me. All of it.'

Henry was confused: I laid it out for him. 'Felix is taking you to Euston. Get on the first train, keep going and don't come back. Ever. Do you understand? One more thing. Mention this to anybody and I'll find you. Wherever you are, I'll find you.' I prised his palm open, pressed George and Felix's money in it, and closed my fist over his fingers hard enough to hurt. 'Have a nice life, Henry.'

Nina's car pulled away. Ritchie waited until it was out of sight before he spoke. 'No offence, Luke, you've made a mistake there.

The boy's lost his brother. On a good day he wouldn't be able to keep that to himself.'

Ritchie and I were roughly the same height though he could give me twenty years. I trusted his judgement and had come to depend on it, except there were times when he edged closer to the line than was wise. I took him aside. 'It's been a tough few hours all round, George, so I'm going to pretend I didn't hear what you just said. But if I want your opinion, I'll fucking ask for it. Are we clear?'

I left him and went back to Henry. 'The station opens around four-thirty. My advice: get yourself a coffee from a machine and hide behind an old newspaper until the trains start running. Do yourself a favour. With that accent, give Glasgow, Liverpool, Birmingham and Newcastle a miss. You won't fit in.'

Henry looked at the cash. 'What do I do when this runs out?'

Behind him, Felix raised his gun.

This what I know: three people can keep a secret if two of them are dead. And there's a lot to be said for a bullet in the brain. Especially if you don't know it's coming.

32

CHRISTMAS DAY

Dawn broke over Denmark Hill, black fading to grey, heralding the arrival of morning and the end of a night that had seemed to go on forever. Day after day tied to a chair in Hampstead expecting the bullet that would end her life had changed Nina. Mark held her in his arms as she fought the already familiar battle against her demons, twisting and turning under the covers, crying and kicking against them as they dragged her down to a dark place. The gang were gone. He'd watched them die horribly without feeling a scintilla of compassion for their pain. What they'd done lived on – the ordeal had affected Nina more profoundly than anyone could realise. She was listless and distracted, her mood swinging – one minute laughing, the next in tears, or snapping at him over trivialities – and rather than a grand reunion after their forced separation the lovers had avoided sex and kept their distance. All Mark could do was be there and trust the power of love to bring her back to him.

He slipped out of bed and stood at the window, no longer torn between his commitment to Nina Glass and his mission of exposing her brother's corrupt connections. Somebody inside the Met leaking the operation's existence had almost cost him his life, and if there had been an internal inquiry into the security breach, nobody had told him. Given what he was risking, what was at stake, it wasn't unreasonable to expect his handler to take better care of him. Clearly, he hadn't, and the rot had set in.

Looking back, that was the turning point, the moment Operation Clean Sweep lost its insider. Falling in love with the gangster's sister had taken him down another road; her kidnappers had done the rest. All water under the bridge.

On the other side of the window snowflakes drifted to the ground from a heavy sky. Douglas saw Nina's unlined face resting on the pillow and quietly picked up his clothes: he'd made his decision.

* * *

Mark Douglas wasn't the only one who'd had a bad night. Officers had broken down the door of a house in NW3, found traces of cocaine in the lounge and the body of a woman in the basement. A more extensive search unearthed a velvet purse containing one diamond and one sapphire thought to have been part of a robbery of a jeweller in Soho. The police had acted on a tip from one of Superintendent Stanford's sources. The senior officer had been unaware of the full implication of what they'd discover: Glass had found his sister and left him out of the loop. Bad news. Very bad news. It meant his relationship with the family was nearing the end.

Stanford wasn't sorry. At the start it had been only about money, but the longer the policeman carried the past around with him, the heavier it became. Elise was talking about next year being his last in uniform. It would be sooner than that. His daughters were home from uni for Christmas and their mother was like a cat with two tails, fussing over them as though they were honoured guests.

Soon, they would be all she had.

It was time, for their sakes, to put his affairs in order.

* * *

The conversation with DCI John Carlisle had been short and one-sided and ended with the detective angrily hanging up after Douglas told him to be at The Blue Bridge in St James's Park at eleven o'clock. Douglas hadn't forgotten the copper's reaction in a wintery Victoria Tower Gardens, when he'd asked for his help to find Nina: he hadn't given a damn. Or bothered to hide it, either.

'Copper'. He was starting to sound like Luke Glass and George Ritchie.

Since their last unsatisfactory meeting on the banks of the Thames there had been no contact. Not unusual, given the clandestine nature of an anti-police-corruption operation like Clean Sweep where, for obvious reasons, communication was kept to a minimum. Douglas's brief had reflected the singular focus of the mission: unmask bent police officers in the pay of criminals. In six months plus working for Luke Glass he'd come across exactly none, although he wasn't foolish enough to believe that meant there wasn't someone under the radar.

St James's Park in the heart of the city was as good a spot as any to break the bad news. The visitors who would laze on the grass in the summer sunshine wearing I LOVE LONDON T-shirts and drinking beer from the bottle were still a long way off. Douglas rubbed his hands together and waited.

The irony of The Blue Bridge brought a grim smile to his face. Because MI5 operatives were said to use it for secret assignations, the low-arched concrete crossing was known as The Bridge of

Spies. Douglas walked to the middle, leaned on the ugly metal railing and drank in the stunning views: to the west, Buckingham Palace looming like an alien craft through the chilly mist; in the east, a collage of Whitehall turrets and roofs, Horse Guards Parade, Big Ben and the London Eye, reminding him he was a long way from his native Glasgow.

Carlisle hadn't agreed to come. But even if he showed up, the decision had already been taken. The copper had had his chance. It was too late. Telling him to his face was the cleaner option. Whether he appeared or stayed at home would alter nothing.

On the other side of the frozen lake, a mallard with its distinctive dark-green head and white collar round the neck searched the water's edge for a break in the ice. Tomorrow, in the bowels of the Curtis Green Building, they'd start crafting an elaborate backstory for his replacement and the deadly game would go on.

When Carlisle headhunted him in Scotland, the senior officer had struck him as a straight shooter. Appearances had been deceptive; he wasn't – no stone should've been left unturned until whoever was responsible for the leak was discovered and charged with perverting the course of justice.

It hadn't happened. And he was glad. It gave him the excuse he needed to jump ship and set in motion a chain of events that might very well lead to Luke Glass killing him.

But for a future with Nina, it was a chance he had to take.

* * *

Carlisle barrelled towards him through the park, his body language telling him he'd left the Christmas cheer at home; the hostility on the phone was still there. His cheeks were flushed and he breathed through his open mouth, psyched up and ready to launch into the speech he'd put together in the car. He leaned his elbows on the railing beside Douglas and stared into the lake. 'Right, tell me, why am I here? And you better have a bloody good reason or—'

Douglas interrupted the threat from the man who was supposed to have his back. 'I'm out.'

The DCI's reaction was exactly as he'd anticipated: disbelief and anger. 'Out? What the hell're you talking about?'

'I'm done. Finished. Call it whatever you want.'

Carlisle's lips moved on his ruddy face, scrambling for an argument. 'Has something happened?'

These people lived in a world of their own.

'Does Glass—?'

'I said it before, Carlisle, your intel's old. I'm not prepared to put myself in danger for duff info. Did Danny Glass have a contact inside the Met? Be surprised if he didn't, wouldn't you? But he's out of the picture and I've seen nothing to make me think that connection is live. So, I'm walking away.'

'You can't do that. We've put too much into it to—'

Douglas's laugh was bitter with resentment. 'I don't give a damn what you've done. It isn't your arse on the line. While you're with your family, spooning cranberry sauce onto your turkey, I'll be looking over my shoulder like I do all day every day.'

The DCI stood. 'That's the job, you knew that when you took it on. In Glasgow, you couldn't wait to get your teeth into it, as I recall. You didn't need to think about it.'

'That was then, John, when I mistook you for one of the good guys and not a toadying snool. This is now. And now I'm pulling the plug.'

Carlisle changed his approach. 'Let's look at this calmly, Mark. Because you haven't seen anything doesn't mean the information isn't solid. Give it another six months.'

'No chance. Your intel's old and I'm out.'

'Three.'

'Not even one. When I walk off this bridge, I'm gone.'

'You're leaving the service?'

'Yes.'

'The service, the pension, a lot to turn your back on.'

'No offence... copper... stick them up your arse.' Further along the lake a pelican came in to land, flapped its wings and slid on the ice near Duck Island. Douglas said, 'And by the by, we found Nina, thanks for asking.'

Carlisle had forgotten about the Glass sister, then the words registered and he got it.

'*We?* You said... we.'

'I did, yeah. We found her.'

* * *

The Bayswater Arms on the corner of Queensway and Moscow Road wasn't George Ritchie's normal haunt – it was too close to where he lived and, in fact, he'd never been inside. Drinking at lunchtime wasn't his thing but at Christmas his basement flat had felt oppressive. Vincent Finnegan's funeral the previous day had been an eye-opener, even for a hardened campaigner like him. Finnegan had made widows out of wives, orphans out of children, cripples out of able-bodied men, fighting for The Cause.

Those left behind had shed tears.

There had been nobody to weep for Vincent.

They'd stood at the edge of the hole cut from the frozen earth of Putney Vale Cemetery as the coffin was lowered into the grave. Just the five of them – him, Luke, Felix, Mark Douglas and a kindred spirit of Finnegan's from another battle: Bridie O'Shea, taking time away from playing cards and drinking port and lemon in Kilburn and making more money than most of the outfits in London put together.

Not much to show for a life. Ritchie's own funeral would be no better. Luke had invited him to dinner with the family in the evening at the club. He'd told him he'd try to get along; they both knew he wouldn't. Ritchie scanned the pub looking for a face he recognised – ghosts from the past stalking him. God knew there were enough of them – and saw none.

Old habits died hard, right enough.

The thought reminded him of Felix's unresolved problem in the East End and George hoped Thomas Timpson's mother was enjoying her last Christmas with her son, because tomorrow it would be his turn.

* * *

TT sat at the head of the table holding a knife in one hand, a fork in the other, waiting for his mother to bring the food from the kitchen. Jet said, 'Shouldn't you offer to help her?'

Helping hadn't occurred to him and he dismissed the suggestion. 'She likes doing it, makes her feel useful. You help her if you feel bad about it. I won't stop you.'

He put down the fork and fingered the notes in his pocket – his Christmas present. 'When we eat this, I'm back to bed for an hour so I'll be fresh for tonight.'

Jet said, 'I'm going home tomorrow. Can't be here forever.'

'True, but you've made a bloody good stab at it, haven't you?' He smiled. 'We'll get a few down our necks tonight and you can say ta-ta to my old mum in the morning. I won't lie, not hearing you snore half the night isn't something I'll miss. Never outstay a welcome, mate, know what I mean?'

'When will we contact Glass?'

'Soon, Jethro, very soon.'

33

Dinner in the club on Christmas night should've been an opportunity for us to behave like a 'normal' family instead of individuals
thrown together by a regrettable genetic accident we'd spent our
lives trying to escape. Easier said. Charley saw a chance to sweep in
like the final day of the Henley Regatta and light the place up.
George Ritchie's response to the invite had been typically low-key,
thanking me for including him, although we both knew he
wouldn't be there. Ritchie was a loner who rarely showed up to any
social occasions. He'd broken whatever rule he had to attend
Vincent Finnegan's funeral, swelling the number of mourners to a
pitiful five.

I'd gone to Nina's house in Denmark Hill the day after the
hellish scene in Walthamstow. It hadn't exactly been a success: I
wasn't welcome. She was my sister, keeping secrets from her was
almost impossible, and she'd known what I'd do to the boy the
moment her car was out of sight.

I'd expected her to be in bed recuperating but this was Nina – as
tough as old boots and twice as loud. She was in an armchair by the
fire, drinking amber from a glass. I went to her. Silently, she turned

away from me. Mark Douglas understood we needed space and made himself scarce.

When he left, I knelt beside her and took her hand, ready to put a positive spin on the whole sorry mess. The flames of the fire danced in her eyes as she cut through my bullshit before I got started. 'He's dead, isn't he? Henry's dead.'

Denying it would've risked losing her.

'Yes.'

'Why? He wasn't one of them. He was good.'

My defence was doomed but it was all I had. 'He knew too much, Nina. He could've brought us down.'

She wasn't listening. 'I asked you to leave him alone.'

'It had to be done.'

Her fingers went to her injured breast. 'Since I was a kid, I've told myself you weren't Danny, that you were different. It's not true. You're the same. So am I. We're all the same and I hate it. I hate this family.'

'Nina—'

'Don't. Just don't. I could've taken him with me. I could've saved him and I didn't. That boy didn't deserve to die. You killed him anyway.'

'To protect you.'

'Liar, you were protecting yourself!'

'You're wrong.'

Her mocking laughter stung. 'Some upper-class idiots out of their heads on coke have the nerve to abduct Luke Glass' sister and almost get away with it. Imagine what it would do to your reputation.'

'That isn't—'

She rolled over me and kept going. 'Except, you did imagine it, didn't you? And a boy died to keep it from happening. Get out of my house! Get out and don't come back!'

At that moment she despised me for what I'd allowed in Walthamstow. But she was making a mistake, the same mistake I'd made with Danny: judging without appreciating what it meant to be head of the Glass family. And yeah, there might have been another way to deal with Henry. I hadn't reached for it.

Given the chance, I still wouldn't. Because this is what I know: reputations are hard won and easily lost. Without the fear of brutal retribution every ambitious ne'er-do-well would try their luck. We'd be fighting them off all over London. I couldn't have that and if Nina was standing in my shoes, neither would she.

What she felt for me was beyond anger. Trying to convince her was a waste of time. 'Pray you never have to make that kind of decision, because you'd understand how fucking hard it is to order a hit on a man who doesn't deserve it.'

She sneered. 'As usual, you're missing the point, brother. If it was as hard as you make out, you'd be hurting. You aren't. You're absolutely okay with it.'

I hadn't expected her to roll out the red carpet for saving her life, though the intensity of her bitterness shocked me and I defended myself. 'Listen, you liked the boy, he's gone, you're upset. I get it. Henry sealed his fate the minute he got involved with his brother and the other two. Everything after that was inevitable. I'm "okay with it" because it was necessary.'

She tried to interrupt. I didn't let her.

'Danny was a crazy bastard. We agree on that much. Doesn't mean he was always wrong, Nina. Anybody or anything that threatens us can't be allowed to exist. The first principle is to protect the family. Always. Danny understood that. So do I. And if you tell yourself the truth, so do you.'

I slipped the gun out of my pocket – a Walther PPK I'd had George Ritchie source – small, easy to carry, perfect. A famous firearm well capable of getting the job done: James Bond used one;

Elvis Presley had a silver-finish PPK with the inscription 'TCB' – taking care of business; less well known is that Adolf Hitler killed himself in the bunker in Berlin with his. Nina could rant and rave and order me out of her house. Some things weren't negotiable and whether she liked it or not she was joining the list of illustrious owners.

If it kept her alive, I'd be satisfied. I held it out until she reluctantly took it.

'From now on, where you go it goes. Are we clear?'

She started to object and changed her mind. Good decision, sister.

If I'd been a betting man, I'd have lost my money because at five minutes to ten, Nina arrived on Douglas's arm, dressed to the nines. I suspected he'd had more than a little to do with getting her to come. Charley saw them and ran to her. They threw their arms round each other and embraced. They'd been rivals rather than sisters and I hoped they'd turned that page. Physically, Nina seemed better than when she'd thrown me out of her house, recovered enough to hug everybody, except me. Forgiving and forgetting wasn't a Glass trait. Whatever else had changed, how she felt about me hadn't. But for better or worse we were together at Christmas and I'd settle for it.

TT was drunker than Jet had ever known him, spouting arrogant booze-fuelled talk. 'We've kept our heads down long enough, Jethro, it's time to pay Luke Glass a visit. Find out what he's saying to it.'

Jet wasn't convinced that was a goer. 'It's risky, TT. I mean, we torched his shop and killed his guy. He's hardly going to welcome us with open arms, is he?'

TT disagreed. 'What we did was retaliate, showed the bastard we weren't prepared to be shoved around. Spoke to Glass in the language he understands. He'll respect that.'

Jet humoured him. 'Maybe, but if you're wrong—'

'I'm not wrong. He's king of the castle now, that wasn't where he started. I heard him and his brother were a couple of young dickheads who started their careers stealing fags from shops. I'm guessing he'll look at us and see a younger version of himself. But, if it's too rich for your blood and you want out, it's okay. Just don't come back expecting to get in when it's sorted. I won't lie. Boz was better than you. Take him any day of the week. You've always been a bit out of your depth for this lark. I reckon reading the tea leaves in some old dear's cup is nearer your level. Prove me wrong.'

Insults dropped from TT's mouth like spit. This time he'd gone over the line. Jet finished his drink and stood. 'Tell your mother thanks for giving me a bed.'

'Where're you going?'

'Where I should've gone days ago – home, TT. I'm going home. Can't be worse than listening to you. Do what you like about Glass, just do it without me. I've had enough.'

Timpson sneered. 'You're scared. You're fucking terrified of him.'

Jet had been saving up his reply. 'I wouldn't go there. You're forgetting I was at the hospital when Boz was in. You were like a frightened little kid, or don't you remember? Doesn't matter, because I do. Maybe I'll put it about that the smell of disinfectant made the great Thomas Timpson wet his pants.' He pushed the empty pint measure away and got up. At the door of the snug he stopped. Jet wasn't done. He said, 'You bought the uniform – all those crazy tattoos and the Satanic shit – because you want to frighten people. Make them think you're a tough guy. The goat face does that, all right. Luke Glass is the real deal. Nobody needs tea leaves to predict your future, TT, you haven't got one.'

* * *

The food was standard Christmas fare, expensive and not particularly good. Dozens of places did it cheaper and better. If we were paying money for it, I'd be having a word with the manager. As it was, I made a mental note to speak to the chef after the holiday. In just a year, LBC had become one of the most exclusive nightclubs in London. We needed to be offering better than this.

Nina was all loved up with Douglas, playing with the beard he'd grown, ignoring me. From where I was at the other end of the table, she seemed to be back to her usual self, except the concern in Mark Douglas's eyes when she wasn't aware he was looking at her told me it was a brave attempt to put what had happened in Hampstead behind her and move on. I'd done my part – the people who'd hurt her were in the ground. Now it was Douglas's turn to make it right.

Charley had brought a guy, some dark-eyed Latin type called Bartolo or Battista. I'd forgotten his name and wouldn't push myself to remember it. If form was anything to go by, he wouldn't be around long enough for it to be important. She was supposed to be off but kept disappearing to check on her girls. It was a night for tipping big and all the hookers were working.

As predicted, George Ritchie was nothing if not consistent: he hadn't come. At Vincent Finnegan's funeral he'd hardly said a word and I'd understood what was going through his mind. We'd tossed dirt into the grave and were leaving the cemetery when Bridie O'Shea had fallen in step with me. I'd spoken to the old IRA firebrand a couple of times on the phone though we hadn't met face to face in a while. There was no need. What we had in common was making each other money and that was trucking along just fine.

She'd spoken in her accent that somehow managed to make every sentence sound like the melody of a song. 'I'm assuming you know who killed Vincent.'

'You assume right, Bridie.'

'And they're still breathing?'

'Not for much longer.'

She'd lit a cigarette and inhaled down to her boots. 'Anything I can do to help, just shout.'

'Appreciated. It'll be sorted.'

'Soon, I hope. A shipment of cash is scheduled to arrive at the club for washing on New Year's Eve. Wouldn't want your eye off the ball, now, would we?'

'Is my eye ever off the ball, Bridie?'

'No, but there's a first time for everything.'

The suggestion had irritated me and I'd spoken more harshly than I'd intended. 'For you, maybe, not me. And as for Vincent... we take care of our own. Always have, always will.'

She'd let my outburst pass. 'Walthamstow. That anything to do with you?'

Without leaving the backroom of her pub this old woman was up on just about everything that went on in London. Her question wasn't a question: Hughie had come good on the second part of the deal. I'd played along and hadn't given her the satisfaction. 'What've you heard?'

Bridie had gazed across the lines of tombstones, cigarette smoke swirling around her head. 'You're a helluva man, Luke Glass, and that's the God's truth. I wouldn't want to be falling out with you.'

'Then don't.'

At the rusted-iron gates she'd said, 'I didn't like your brother and made no bones about it. Danny was an animal, no offence.

But I like you. That's why I'll tell you something and hope the day doesn't come when you discover it for yourself.' Bridie had held up a hand to emphasise her point. 'While there are other people in the picture – friends, lovers... sisters – you'll always be weak. Until you only have you to look out for, you're vulnerable. Accepting it as a fact is the only way. That or a life not worth living.'

'Any more words of wisdom, or is that it?'

She'd smiled. 'If you're too bull-headed to learn, for myself I've found a glass or two of twelve-year-old Irish whiskey works nearly as well. Now, give my best to your sister.'

'Which one?'

She'd walked to the waiting car that would take her back to the pub in Kilburn and her beloved cards. Over her shoulder she'd said, 'Whichever one needs it. You'll know that better than me, I'm thinking.'

* * *

A little after one o'clock in the morning, Nina and Mark Douglas slipped away without saying goodbye. I saw them leave, hand in hand, and guessed the evening had been good for them. Charley was canoodling with Mr Italy, smiling, oblivious to everything but the words he whispered in her ear. My sisters were happy and I was glad. Tomorrow, or rather today, it would be business as usual for the Glass family.

A waiter touched my shoulder. 'There's a woman in a taxi at the door asking for you.'

On another night I would've been interested. Now wasn't the time. I said, 'Tell her I'm busy, tell her you can't find me, tell her any bloody thing.'

He caught my mood and hesitated, wondering if it was worth

pushing it, deciding it was. 'I think you'll want to see this one. I really do.'

At the pavement the black cab purred a thin stream of blue smoke into the cold air. Behind the wheel the driver stared ahead, unconcerned with how long he had to wait; the clock was ticking on triple-time. I opened the back door and held my breath. The distinctive beige, white and gold markings of the lynx fur coat she was wearing caught the highlights in her hair as she smiled and held out her hand. 'Merry Christmas, Luke. I'm not too late, am I?'

I didn't answer. It was the most ridiculous question I'd ever heard.

* * *

We kissed and didn't stop kissing until we got to Marble Arch, when we came up for air and I managed to get out a breathless, 'I thought you were in Cairo. What're you doing here?'

'I wanted to surprise you.'

She'd certainly done that.

I said, 'Can I assume the driver knows where he's going?'

'Yes, my place, now shut up and kiss me again.'

Her place turned out to be a fourth-floor apartment overlooking Holland Park. We fell through the door, locked at the lips. Shani broke away to turn on the lights and let me see how the other half lived. For a south London lad from a broken home on a council estate, I hadn't exactly done badly. In fact, I was doing very well, all things considered. But 'doing very well' was relative. What I was looking at was genuine wealth.

She stood in the middle of the floor, smiling at me as though she had a secret and hadn't decided whether to tell it. Her arms dropped to her sides and the coat fell away. Underneath, she was naked and I gasped a second time. Shani gently mocked me, repeating what I'd said in the taxi.

'Can I assume the driver knows where he's going?'

* * *

In books, people having sex are always perfect for each other. Everybody knows their role. Nobody fluffs their lines. They fit, it works, and the reader is treated to a choreographed display of desire they can't hope to emulate. In the bedroom, I took her erect nipple in my mouth while my fingers traced the smooth, hollow contours of her thighs. Shani moaned and moved to meet them and we lay teasing and toying with each other in an unhurried journey of discovery that accelerated when she coiled her legs behind my back, crossed her slender ankles making us one, and matched me stroke for stroke. One minute she was on top, riding me, biting her lip, eyes hard; then she was kneeling with me shafting her from behind.

Eventually we fell apart, exhausted, hot sweat glistening on our sated bodies. Her explanation was unnecessary; she volunteered it anyway. 'I couldn't stop thinking about you.'

My reply was selfish and sincere. 'Please tell me you aren't going back too soon. You only just got here.'

Her expression was set and serious, like a child who'd been asked a difficult question and was determined to find the answer. 'I must. I have no choice. I'm the only one left.' She kissed me again and I sensed the sadness pass from her as quickly as it had arrived. Shani said, 'So why are we wasting time talking?'

* * *

Nina was pale. Mark saw she was tired and checked his watch. He leaned in close and gently kissed the graze on her temple skilfully concealed with make-up. 'I'm about ready to go, how about you?'

She smiled a weary half-smile. 'Your place or mine?'

Douglas reached for her and covered her fingers with his. 'Isn't it about time we had *our* place?'

An inner light brightened Nina's eyes. 'Mark... are you sure? I mean, things aren't—'

He stopped her. 'Things are fine. We're fine. Now answer the question.'

'Which question is that?'

'Nina Glass, will you marry me?'

She shook her head. 'No, I like you too much.'

'Pretend you don't. Pretend you hate me. Does that make it easier?'

The throaty laugh was classic Nina and Mark was glad he'd picked now to ask. 'It's a big decision. Think about it.'

She took his face in her hands. 'Mrs Nina Douglas. There's nothing to think about.'

'So, is that a yes?'

'That's an absolute yes.'

Mark knew what Nina was thinking and put a finger to her lips, unwilling to lose the moment to regret. In the darkness they'd found each other again, their lovemaking tender and selfless though still with the fire that had been there from the beginning. He whispered, 'Forgive him, Nina,' and felt her tense beside him on the bed.

'I can't. I just can't.'

'You have to.'

'No, you don't understand. That boy, Henry—'

'Was a threat. To all of us. He wasn't to blame – it wasn't his fault – but sooner or later he'd get caught. And what they'd done... what we'd done to them... would come out.'

Nina turned onto her side and faced him. 'Would you have done it? Would you have killed him? I need to know.'

Mark stroked her cheek. 'Yes. Yes, I would.'

'Even if I begged you to let him go?'

'Even then. Your brother did the right thing. You have to do the same. Holding it against him will drive a wedge between you. I won't stand by and watch that happen. Luke isn't like us, he's the head of the family. That brings huge responsibility and, honestly, he was the one who saved you, not some boy you hardly knew.'

The truth, spoken gently, hit home and Nina fell quiet. After a while, she said, 'I don't trust him. He's my brother but I don't. How can I? He lied to me.'

'What choice did he have?'

'There's always a choice. I could've handled the truth.'

Douglas didn't argue. He said, 'It's easy to think so now. When it was happening... when the dog was tearing them apart... The boy didn't die like that.'

He didn't tell her that alone in the middle of the night he saw the monstrous beast tearing them apart and heard their agonising screams. She pressed her head against his chest, listening to his heart beating while Mark ran his fingers through her hair.

'I love you, Nina. From now on, whatever happens, remember that.'

She sighed and closed her eyes. 'I will.'

34

At six-thirty in the morning every light in the block of flats was out. Dawn in December wouldn't fully break for another ninety-three minutes. When it did it would reveal an overcast sky heavy with sleet. The men crept along the outside landing on the third floor, heads down. Felix spoke into the mobile to the leader. 'It's Timpson we're here for. Don't touch the mother. She isn't part of this. It's not her fault her son's a piece of shit.' He held the phone away from his mouth and made a face at George Ritchie in the passenger seat. 'His pal left the pub last night and went home to his own drum. We'll deal with him later. I almost feel sorry for him. His life's over – he just doesn't know it yet.'

'He'll skip.' Ritchie watched the men take up position on either side of the door. 'Before you get sentimental, Felix, don't forget what they did to Vincent.'

'Sentimental? About this guy? No chance, he's going to Fulton Street and he's not coming back. Let's do it.'

* * *

Somehow, TT had managed to undress. Finding his way under the covers had been too big an ask and he'd collapsed on top of the bed. His mouth hung open, pallid thighs – the only part of his body that hadn't been defaced – parted obscenely. The crash of the front door caving in didn't reach him; he was still drunk. Rough hands closed round his ankles and dragged him to the floor. His tattooed arms were tied behind his back and a hood pulled over his head. And for the first time since the hospital on Whitechapel Road, Thomas Timpson was afraid.

In the room across the hall, his mother heard the forced entry and was instantly awake. Footsteps running in the hall brought her to the bedroom door in time to see them haul her semi-conscious boy away. Her frail fingers gripped the rosary beads that never left her hand, her lips moving as she prayed. The widow's faith in a merciful God was unshakeable but it stopped short of believing *He* would intercede. Whatever Thomas had done made no difference to how the woman who'd given birth to him felt about her only child. Her church taught her to hate the sin, love the sinner. She closed the bedroom door and knelt down by the side of her bed, made the sign of the cross and whispered the familiar introduction to her prayer.

'In the name of the Father, and of the Son, and of the Holy Ghost.'

* * *

Mark Douglas lay on his back and stared at the ceiling. Beside him, Nina breathed softly, deep in sleep for the first time since they'd freed her. It wouldn't last, and when the truth came out it would be worse than anything she could've imagined. What he'd done was madness. Asking her to marry him before he'd come clean with her brother about who he was and what he'd been doing was unforgivable. What it would do to an already fragile Nina he couldn't think about without hating himself even more than he already did. Luke Glass had treated him well, he enjoyed working for him but, as he'd seen with the dog at the yard in Walthamstow, underneath the businessman façade was an uncompromising killer.

35

In its time the derelict building in Fulton Street had been many things: originally, stables for the master's horses, then a laundry in one era, a fireworks factory in another. For a while it was a brewery, the malt kept in bins as large as a three-storey house, while a standing army of cats kept the rats in check. Under its roof, Victorian children as young as eight had dipped matches into a dangerous chemical called phosphorous and contracted 'phossy jaw'. Danny Glass had bought it as an investment – one day it would be demolished and the land sold for a shedload of money. Until that happened, he'd found another use for it.

George Ritchie got out of the car and squeezed through the rusted metal door hanging off its hinges. He'd heard the rumours about the private abattoir and the horrors that went on there when he'd worked with Albert Anderson. The unimaginable cruelty this place had witnessed seemed to have seeped into the bricks. Ritchie smelled something rank, without a name, and shuddered in the gloom. The sound of wings fluttering made him look up to see stars, light years away, blinking through the gaping hole in the rafters.

Behind him, Felix watched his men bring in their unresisting prisoner, sobbing and moaning underneath the hood. In the back of the car they'd beaten him with the butts of their guns and removed the tattoo on his chest with a cigarette lighter, brushing the flame against the skin until it blistered and blackened, leaving charred flesh where the eagle with the snake in its beak had been.

For Thomas Timpson it was only the beginning.

Two more men arrived in a white van and rolled a gleaming Thunder Black Pearl Indian Chieftain motorcycle down a wooden ramp to the pavement, like grooms leading the odds-on favourite for the Cheltenham Gold Cup into the Winner's Enclosure; they pulled back the broken door panel and wheeled the powerful machine inside. Ritchie saw its streamlined profile, driven by an impressive 1890cc engine, and immediately understood. 'Nice one, Felix. Very creative.'

'Thought you'd approve, George.'

'I do. I do.'

'This bastard deserves a right royal send-off for what he did to Vincent and that's what he's getting.'

'Absolutely. But Luke's the boss, so not till I've spoken to him.'

* * *

I was making love to a beautiful woman, lost in her, dizzy with her scents and sighs, when the mobile rang on the bedside cabinet. As I reached to answer it I realised I wasn't alone: Shani was asleep beside me, her dark hair on the pillow framing her lovely face. And I knew it hadn't been a dream – last night had really happened. Whoever was calling could fuck right off.

George Ritchie might've been reading next week's weather forecast from the London *Evening Standard* for all the emotion he put into it. He spared me the details and got straight to the point.

'We've got one of them.'

In his typically economical way, he was asking if I wanted to be there. In any other circumstances, my reply would be yes. Vincent Finnegan had been in my life for decades; when I was still a boy, he'd already been a man. The people who murdered him didn't deserve mercy and wouldn't get any, with or without me. Watching them die would be a pleasure.

That wasn't always how I'd felt. Seven years in prison changes a man, and it had changed me. I'd wanted out. Out of the business and everything connected with it. Danny's 'Team Glass' bollocks and his emotional blackmail, milking the fact that he'd brought me and Nina up, had drawn me back in against my will. Shani had been in my life five minutes – maybe she wasn't the one – but unless I finally did what I'd promised myself during the lonely nights in Wandsworth, I'd never know.

This could be the beginning. The beginning of the end of it. Instead of just another gory episode to add to a very long list.

George said, 'No need to tell you what I think.'

He was correct about that.

'There isn't but tell me anyway.'

'When something nasty's going down it's my job to make sure you're a hundred miles away with two dozen witnesses prepared to swear on a stack of bibles they were standing next to you. I'm saying allow me to do that job. We've got this, Luke. It doesn't need you. Felix is up for it. So am I. And I can promise it won't be quick.'

Shani stirred. Her arm snaking round my waist pulled me closer and I felt the delicious warmth of her body against me. If I'd needed an excuse, I had one. I spoke quietly. 'You missed your vocation, George, should've been a politician or a priest. I'll take your advice. One more thing. Make a noise about it so it doesn't happen again.'

'Understood. They'll hear it in Highgate Cemetery.'

* * *

TT's goat face was hidden under the black bag. Felix saw what his guys had done to him and didn't disapprove. They'd worked with Vincent Finnegan – this was their revenge. It was their due. George was thirty yards away across the factory, on the phone with Luke. Felix waited for him to finish his call and reassessed the raid on the East End flat; they'd captured the main man but his mate had slipped through the net. So, not a complete success. These people had jumped Vincent outside the Admiral Collingwood pub and left an axe in his brain. The Irishman had been worth ten of them – anything short of absolute retribution wasn't worth celebrating.

Ritchie closed his mobile and came over to Felix. 'What's the word, George? Is he coming?'

'No, he's leaving it to us.' He eyed the bike. 'Is it yours?'

'Yeah. I saw it on the forecourt of a dealers near Bexleyheath the day after Luke put me in charge of Jonas Small's old territory and decided to give myself a present. Sweet, isn't it?'

Ritchie nodded at Timpson. 'Not sure that's how he'll see it. Wake him up. Be a shame if he missed the big finale.'

They tore the bag off TT's head and slapped his cheeks, laughing among themselves at his self-inflicted ugliness. Timpson's chest was raw and weeping and looked unbelievably painful, though not for much longer. His eyes fluttered open in his goat face and he groaned and vomited on the ground. The men faked disgust; one of them kicked him in the groin. Felix hunkered down, casually drawing a line with his finger through the scorched skin.

TT screamed. His teeth chattered. 'Please, please...'

Felix removed the medallion and weighed it in his hand. 'We'll need this to identify you.' He pursed his lips. 'And it's too late for please, old son. Way too late. Forgetting our limitations is always a mistake. You got a result with Jonas Small and let it go to your napper.'

Timpson trembled and Ritchie wished Felix would get on with it before the bastard died of shock. Felix said, 'Setting fire to the bookies was fair enough. I didn't appreciate it, but I got where you were coming from. You'd lost your nice little number and you were disappointed. One of your guys got a hiding for the blaze. That was when you should've taken a reality check and left it. Except, you didn't. And now this is where we are. They say the Devil looks after his own. Apparently, like so much of what "they" say, it's just another load of cobblers.'

He stepped away and let his men do their work: the steel wire rope, manufactured in Singapore, was 5 m long, 8 mm in diameter with a load capacity of 240 kg and hard eye thimble loops at both ends. In the first shafts of pre-dawn light as they attached one end to the Chieftain, the other round Timpson's ankles, it writhed like a silver snake on the factory's concrete floor. Felix straddled the bike's black frame, turned on the ignition and drowned out Thomas Timpson's screams.

Somebody handed him a crash helmet. Felix smiled and put it on. 'It pays to take safety seriously. Can't be too careful with a baby like this.'

He revved the engine and pulled away.

36

Losing sleep had become the norm for Mark Douglas; the previous night was no exception. He'd asked the woman he loved to marry him and she'd said yes – he should've been the happiest man in the world. And he'd seen the light his proposal had brought to the darkness surrounding her. For that, alone, he ought to have been grateful. Douglas had been falling in love with Nina from the first moment they'd met and was sure she felt the same. She'd told him that throughout the ordeal in Hampstead knowing he was out there had given her the strength to survive. His betrayal might tip her over the edge. Yet she had to know because, until she understood who Mark Douglas really was, they'd be living a lie. Quitting Operation Clean Sweep, quitting the police, wasn't enough. Nina deserved the truth. What happened after that was in the lap of the gods. He left her and went through to the lounge, picked up his phone and called Luke. The number rang out. He wasn't answering.

* * *

We were in a cool little java joint in Neal's Yard with only ten seats, toying with cups of Colombian double-roasted, relaxing after a morning trawling the sales. An early lunch of vegetable pakora and chickpea curry in a restaurant in Great Queen Street had mellowed us and we were chilling. My first mistake was opening my mobile to discover five missed calls – one from George Ritchie, four from Mark Douglas. Across the table, Shani was sensational, wearing a black turtleneck, an open-fronted red-and-grey poncho, and jeans. Her eyes stayed on me as I lifted the phone, no doubt wondering what women wonder when the man with them reverts to type and puts business before pleasure. She needn't have been concerned. It was ten past three in the afternoon with a blanket of cloud low enough to touch in the sky above Covent Garden, a whole thirteen hours since she'd burst into my life unannounced; neglecting her was the furthest thing from my mind.

I said, 'Let me answer these, it will only take a minute.'

Famous last words and my second mistake.

Ritchie's legendary brevity came down the line. 'It's done. Want the details?'

'Tell me when I see you.'

He hung up and I moved on. Douglas's repeated attempts at contacting me sparked fear something had happened to Nina. Physically, she'd looked well but I knew she was mentally and emotionally fragile. I'd seen them leaving LBC, loved up and happy, and I'd relaxed, certain my sister was in good hands. But in my world, things had a habit of going bad fast.

He'd borrowed a leaf from George Ritchie's book. 'We need to meet.'

'Why? What's wrong, Mark?'

His reply wasn't an answer, it was an order. 'Fulton Street in an hour.'

* * *

DCI John Carlisle shuffled papers in the folder in front of him and ignored the stone faces staring at him from round the table. Calling a meeting during the holiday was never going to be popular. Some of these officers were old school, fiercely protective of the service, wilfully blind to its shortcomings. Not all of them were ready to recognise corruption existed, let alone eradicate it. A few short hours ago they'd been kicking back, planning to watch old movies on TV while the Christmas Day hangover moved on, assisted by a hair of the dog. Naturally, they weren't happy. If he'd left it till January to bring them up to speed, there would've been hell to pay.

A Deputy Assistant Commissioner who usually spent the festive season on a beach in Barbados spoke quietly, barely concealing his irritation. 'I hope you have a bloody good reason for this, Carlisle. Our families see little enough of us as it is. Not appreciated, I assure you.'

Even Assistant Commissioner of Specialist Operations William Telfer – the legendary Billy T, the copper's copper – seemed short on patience. He said, 'This better be important, John.'

'It is, sir. Very important.'

'All right, let's hear it.'

Carlisle had spent most of the previous night mulling over how to break the news, in the end deciding it didn't matter: any way you looked at it, it was a disaster. He breathed deeply. 'We've lost him.'

The DAC leaned forward. 'We've lost who? Who've we lost?'

'Our insider in the Glass organisation. He's quit.'

'Quit? He can't. After the bloody resources we've poured into this? Why?'

Carlisle had an answer for him. 'Because we let him down and he knows it. Somebody blabbed about his existence and we did sod all to find out who because the leak came from one of us. Had to be.' His eyes travelled over each of them. 'Operation Clean Sweep was supposed to be the best-kept secret in the service. I gave our man my word he'd be protected. On that basis, he went into the belly of the beast knowing all it would take was one slip, one wrong word, and his bloated body would wash up under Tower Bridge.'

It would've been prudent to leave it there. Carlisle wasn't done. 'It won't be the first time we've given less than our best to rooting out institutional corruption in the Met. Our history isn't exactly covered in glory, is it?'

In the bowels of the Curtis Green Building, surrounded by dust sheets and stacked chairs, heating pipes draped in spiders' webs and a pile of forgotten traffic cones, the reference to Countryman, an infamous investigation into police corruption marred by blatant attempts at obstruction from the very top, charged the atmosphere in the storeroom. None of them were keen to be reminded of the stain on the Met's reputation.

Telfer felt the temperature rise and said, 'Careful, John, careful. This isn't the nineteen seventies. We appreciate you're upset but stick to the facts, eh?'

Billy T was reining him in before he said more than was wise. Carlisle heeded the warning and dropped the accusation from his tone. 'We met yesterday morning in St James's Park. Before I got there, I had a bad feeling about it – the relationship had soured – and I wasn't wrong.'

Telfer said, 'Soured how?'

Carlisle remembered the bitterly cold morning on the embankment, when Douglas had told him Nina Glass was missing and asked him to help find her. He also remembered his off-hand response.

let her brother sort it

'Douglas was angry that we'd sold him short, convinced we only wanted to root out the bad guys that were expendable.'

'That's rubbish!'

'Is it? He doesn't think so.'

The DAC was an idiot; he pressed on. 'Are you saying he was scared?'

Carlisle had to force himself to look at him. 'Of course, he was scared. Who wouldn't be? He'd believed in the mission. Now, he doesn't. So why risk his life for it? Simple as that.'

'Didn't you try to talk him down?'

The Deputy Assistant Commissioner's question revealed how far removed he was from reality. Carlisle replied honestly. 'I spoke to him, of course. His mind was made up. He thinks we abandoned him and I couldn't disagree. He also doubts our information. Everything pointed to Danny Glass having at least one bent copper on his payroll. Our man hasn't come across him. Which means either Luke Glass is onto him and has kept him in the dark, or the connection – if it ever existed – disappeared with Danny.'

He paused to let them catch up and continued. 'The flaw in that particular theory is obvious. Luke Glass is ruthless, in his own way every bit as vicious as his brother. If he suspected anything, anything at all, our man would be dead. Which leaves only one option. And you aren't going to like it.' The unblinking eyes round the table told the DCI he was right. He said, 'Accept we've been barking up the wrong tree from day one. Finding nothing because there's nothing to find.'

Carlisle counted the bowed heads and heard the whispered 'Christ Almighty's.

Telfer said, 'When are we bringing him in?'

This was the most damning part. 'We aren't, sir.'

'I'm not following.'

'He's leaving us, leaving the Met. Out all the way.'

Billy T had earned his reputation as a good guy. He said, 'I'm sorry to hear that, I really am. We've sickened a fine officer. What exactly does that mean for us?'

John Carlisle opened the file in front of him and passed round profiles of three people the group hadn't seen before. He said, 'The Glass family aren't the only criminal enterprise in London, and Douglas isn't the only brave man in the service.'

'Who are we targeting?'

'That's what we're here to decide. Bridie O'Shea has West London sewn up. Rumour has it the old soak is getting help from our side. A hard nut to crack. God knows, we've tried. Her career started with the IRA when she was in her early twenties. Soon after she married a known Provisional bombmaker called Wolf Kavanagh who somehow managed not to get caught. Wolf's gone to a better place and we've been trying to get something concrete on her for decades. They talk about the luck of the Irish, don't they? Maybe it's time Bridie's ran out. Alternatively, the Bishops are a possibility. Colin Bishop's dead and Kenny's retired, whatever that means. Kenny's nephew Calum's running the show. Intel suggests the first thing he did when he took over was grease a few palms.'

The DAC was like a dog with a bone. 'And what about Glass?'

False hope was the last thing this guy deserved. Carlisle wasn't about to give it to him. 'We blew it and lost an exceptional officer in the process. We move on. Let's have a look at these officers, see what we think, and maybe do a better job of taking care of whoever draws the short straw.'

* * *

When Nina woke, she wasn't certain if it had been real or just a beautiful dream. Then, the memories arrived: kissing in the taxi on the way to her place, and making love for the first time since her abduction, and Mark's unexpected proposal. A sudden need to be with him forced her out of bed; she tiptoed to the lounge. He was on the sofa, sitting forward with his back to her, talking to someone on the phone. He said, 'Fulton Street in an hour,' and closed the mobile.

Nina rounded on him, anger already flushing her neck and cheeks. 'Why're you calling Luke?'

Douglas looked startled and hesitated a second too long. 'I...'

'Is it about me? Didn't I make it clear how I feel about Luke Glass? After what he did to Henry, I've nothing to say to him and probably never will.'

'Nina, I—'

'And in spite of that, you're *actually* going to ask him if you can marry me? Jesus Christ, Mark!'

'You don't understand.'

'Unfortunately, I do. Playing happy families at Christmas was the last thing I wanted. I let you persuade me to go to the club because you promised there would be no contact with him. None. Now you're treating me as though I'm one of his possessions, a silly girl who needs her brother's permission to be with the man she loves. I don't believe it. Let me know what the two of you decide.'

She stormed back to the bedroom and slammed the door.

37

On the drive through the afternoon traffic to Holland Park, Shani didn't speak, disappointed and obviously unhappy our day had come so abruptly to an end. She'd travelled a long way to surprise me and was due an explanation, at the very least an apology. I offered neither. Douglas had avoided giving a name to why he had to see me so urgently. Whatever it was, it wasn't good. As Shani was getting out, I made a stab at repairing the damage.

'I'll call you later when I sort this.'

Her response was short and not very sweet. 'If we were together is this how it would be? Aren't there people in your organisation who take care of things, or does it always have to be you?'

My mind went to George Ritchie and Felix Corrigan and the 'things' they'd taken care of in the early hours of the morning. One more secret to add to the list.

'It's been a bit crazy recently, Shani. The honest answer is that when it's me the business needs, it's me the business gets. And, yes, that isn't likely to change.'

Her expression said it wasn't what she wanted to hear. Her family were well off – I'd seen inside the flat – and she was drop-dead good-looking. This lady could have anybody. Why would she settle for less?

'If it's any consolation last night was the best night of my life. I wasn't in a great place till you showed up. Let me do what I have to do and hook up later. It can't end like this.'

She didn't say we would but she didn't say we wouldn't.

I could hope.

* * *

From the other side of the street the building that had witnessed so many unspeakable acts of cruelty cast a stark silhouette against the sky. At the gates of Putney Vale Cemetery, Bridie O'Shea had called my brother an animal, a damning indictment from a woman who was no stranger to violence. I hadn't disagreed. But the carnage at the scrapyard in Walthamstow had been inhuman, a low to rival any Danny had authored. Being with Shani, even for a few hours, had reminded me of my better angels and the vows I'd made to myself during those long years in Wandsworth to quit this life. Promises too easily forgotten as I morphed into the very thing I'd claimed to detest.

Maybe the time had come to part company with Fulton Street, Danny's private killing ground, walk away from the past and into a future with the lady from Cairo.

Douglas had insisted we meet without telling me why. His car was parked outside and, for reasons I couldn't explain, a flicker of unease ran through me. The very ordinariness of the metal door complaining on its hinges when I opened it calmed my nerves and I went inside. The first thing I noticed was the smell of burning diesel oil in the air, then shapes materialised like spectres: the rusted-iron pillars supporting what was left of the roof; the lime-washed brick walls surrounding me; and puddles of water gathered in shallow pools on the uneven concrete floor.

It hadn't rained.

Instinctively, I realised it had come from the hose they'd used to wash away the blood of the guy who'd murdered Vincent.

To my left, something moved and I tensed. Mark Douglas stepped into the light; he was completely naked, hands clasped behind his head, his muscular frame taut and toned under bone-white skin.

He said, 'Thanks for coming, Luke. Sorry it has to be like this.'

And suddenly, I didn't want to hear what he had to say.

* * *

He turned slowly, his eyes on me, and the flicker of unease inside me became a wave. His next words rocked my world to its foundations and the past rushed in. 'No bugs. No wire. I'm clean.'

Around the same time Charley had landed on the scene from nowhere claiming to be my sister, Oliver Stanford had warned me the organisation had been infiltrated. He didn't have a name; it had seemed too much of a coincidence. I'd put two and two together and come up with five because Charley hadn't been the mole.

In the beginning, I'd had George Ritchie, always suspicious, in my ear reminding me Douglas was an ex-copper who might not be who he claimed. It was a fair point. I'd listened to him and taken it carefully. As the man from Glasgow proved himself over and over again, I'd started to believe. What an actor. And what a performance he'd given, pretending to be my strong right hand, while plotting to destroy me. It deserved an award. Only a special kind of bastard would have the nerve to pull off something so audacious.

Mark Douglas was special.

Mark Douglas was the insider.

I threw myself at him and knocked him to the ground, screaming, 'You fucker! You fucker! I almost shot my own sister because of you.'

There was a crack as his nose broke; blood poured into his mouth and down his chin. I hit him again and again and dragged him onto his knees. He took it without trying to defend himself. I pressed my gun against his temple, so hard the barrel bit a red circle on the pale skin, raging at his betrayal and the memory of the unimaginable wrong he'd almost made me do.

'What happens now, Mark? Let me guess. Flashing blue lights and uniforms, is that it? Is that what you're sorry about? Because you won't see the first one that comes through the door. And that's a promise.'

He raised his head and looked at me. 'There's nobody coming. It's just you and me.'

I drew my arm back, ready to do him again, and stopped.

None of this was right. None of it made sense.

I said, 'If the police aren't on their way, why are we here?'

He spat a broken tooth on the ground and wiped his lips. 'I'm not one of them. I was. Not any more.'

'Then, I don't understand. You can't really think you're walking out of here alive?'

Sweat filmed his forehead and mingled with blood on his belly and thighs. He was risking his life and was afraid, yet here he was. Few people had the balls to do what he was doing. For once, I'd called it right: he *was* a special kind of man, but it wouldn't save him. The gun's black barrel dug underneath his jaw, forcing his head back. I said, 'Maybe I'm getting slow in my old age. I don't get this. One way or another, even if you've had a Paul-on-the-road-to-Damascus conversion, you're a fucking dead man. Explain it to me. Tell me what this is about.'

'I've asked Nina to marry me. We love each other. I'm done with who I was. Finished with it. I want in.'

His answer stunned me and for a moment, I couldn't speak. When my voice returned, the insanity of what he was saying roared in my head. 'After what you tried to do to the family? Are you crazy?'

'We were on opposite sides of the fence. I was part of an undercover operation. Doing my job, Luke, just like you were doing yours.'

'What's the op called?'

'Clean Sweep.'

'What's its focus?'

'Police corruption. Dirty cops.'

Stanford.

I cocked the trigger and he blinked. 'What've they got? What do they know? The truth, you bastard, or, so help me, I'll finish you right now.'

'Intel reported your brother had connections inside the Met. Deep inside. Not beat coppers. Higher. Much higher. I've convinced them the information is old. About Danny Glass, okay, maybe there had been a link. With Luke Glass, they're wrong, there's nothing. Why would I do that?'

'I've no idea why you would do anything, Mark.'

He was making his case, pleading for his life. I let him. 'I could've blown the whistle a dozen times. Two dozen. I didn't. You can kill me and dump my body somewhere. Nobody will be looking for it. Don't you think I knew that when I asked you to meet me? Whatever you do won't change the fact that I love Nina. To have a future it has to be built on something real. Something honest.'

'You're saying... what?'

'I want to keep going the way we are. No lies. No deception. Part of the organisation, and, when I marry Nina, part of the family. It's your call.'

My laugh was bitter. 'It always was.'

Douglas squared his shoulders and waited for my answer. While the bizarre conversation was going on darkness had fallen around us and as he knelt helplessly on the cold concrete in front of me my mind returned to that first night when he'd put himself in the firing line in the lane at the side of the club and single-handedly avoided a massacre. Since then, Douglas had delivered on everything demanded of him. His temporary collapse when Nina was abducted showed how committed he was to my sister. Positives and plenty of them. But enough to earn him a stay of execution?

I shook my head. 'In another life it might've been different.'

'We'd be friends.'

I didn't share his confidence.

'Except it isn't, it's this life. After what you've done, what you've been... I'd always be looking over my shoulder, questioning every word out of your mouth.'

'That's not how—'

The gun felt cold and heavy in my hand. 'What you don't understand is that in this family, as well as the business, trust is the most important thing. Once that's lost there's no way back for any of us.'

The shot echoed in the confined space like an explosion. Wings beat in the aftermath high above as birds in the rafters took flight. Douglas teetered for a second or two, pitched forward and rolled over, blood pooling around him from the wound in his chest. For a second, I thought I'd pulled the trigger. Then heels clacked on the concrete and Nina walked past me like an apparition, staring straight ahead. I hadn't heard her come in and didn't know she was there. She stood over Douglas, looking down at him, her pale face expressionless. He was still breathing but the light was fading in his eyes. His fingers trembled, crimson bubbled at a corner of his lips and he whispered, 'I love you, Nina.'

She raised the Walther I'd insisted on giving her and pointed the short silver barrel at his bleeding body, smiling a sad smile, her grip steady. 'And I love you, Mark. But what does that matter if I can't trust you?'

Nina emptied the magazine into him from a range of no more than three feet. Hard to miss, especially with five bullets. One would've been enough. I supposed she needed to be sure.

EPILOGUE

The barman rang the bell and shouted the same unfunny lines he'd used every night for the last twenty years. 'All right, ladies and gents, do your talking walking. Some of us have homes to go to even if you don't. And if you have a car, don't forget to take it with you.'

He covered the pumps with a tea towel and turned his attention to cashing up. The stranger on a stool at the end of the bar finished his drink, slipped a gold medallion embossed with the Satanic symbol of an inverted pentacle from his pocket, dropped it quietly on the counter, and left. The staff would recognise it and, tomorrow, the word would be out.

* * *

For weeks I'd been dealing with circumstances beyond my control. Chasing the play. Always on the back foot. But the end was in sight. It had to be. Driving through north London at ten to six in the morning on what had become a familiar path gave me plenty of time to think. The weather forecast promised a bright chilly day of blue skies and cold sun. I rolled the window down, letting the cool air clear my head, and reluctantly started to accept – maybe for the first time – that my role as head of the family had been preordained. In Fulton Street, the shots from Nina's gun had roared like an avalanche in my ears, and as each bullet ripped into Douglas's body the chance of ever escaping the life I was trapped in disappeared. There was no point in calling the lady from Cairo. I'd never be able to give her what she needed.

My sister's reaction to her lover's deception had been brutal and final. Thirty-eight hours later, according to Charley, who was looking after her, she still hadn't spoken more than half a dozen words. The happiest I'd ever seen her had been with Mark Douglas, but though I might have been prepared to take him back, she wasn't. Nina had trusted him completely. He'd broken that trust and she might never get over it. She was hurting, hiding her feelings behind drugs and drink; dealing with Douglas's deception the same way she'd dealt with being abandoned by her mother.

Another betrayal.

She needed time. Maybe even that wouldn't be enough. Nobody was better placed to help her through it than her sister. Charley understood her pain. I was glad she was around.

They say what doesn't kill you makes you stronger. What a load of fucking bollocks.

The people responsible for her abduction had paid with their lives. No consolation. The same could be said for the losers who'd put Vincent Finnegan in the ground before his time. George Ritchie still hadn't volunteered the details. I wouldn't be chasing him for them.

What was done was done.

I'd found my mind returning to Douglas more often than I wanted. His doomed confession had brought a long-running issue to a head: Oliver Stanford, a carry-over from Danny – pompous, arrogant, and increasingly not worth a fuck. When I'd been frantic with worry and needed his help to find Nina's car, he couldn't have cared less. He'd enjoyed it.

Except, an insider in my organisation was as serious as it got and threw his contribution into serious doubt. Once again, a question of trust. Maybe he'd known about the mole and kept it to himself. His little game. Or it was his connection, originally with Danny, that had sparked the unwanted attention of his peers. That made him a dangerous liability.

We'd agreed to meet on Parliament Hill, Hampstead Heath. When I arrived, he was already there, standing with his back to me, hands thrust into the pockets of his coat, taking in the view.

Stanford heard me approach and spoke without turning. 'Marvellous, isn't it? I must have been here thirty times over the years and it's still a fantastic sight.' He pointed to the cityscape brightening in the morning light. 'Look at it: St Paul's Cathedral, the Palace of Westminster, the Shard – bloody monstrosity that it is.'

Usually, he was a tight-lipped bastard who preferred to stay on the sidelines and criticise. Hearing him so effusive jarred, until I saw his hand shaking and realised he was afraid.

'They say Guy Fawkes planned to watch parliament blow up from just about where you are now, Oliver. That's why it's called Traitors Hill.'

He blinked his blue eyes and didn't rise to it. After a while, he said, 'I'm trusting you to look after Elise and the girls. Can I do that?'

Trust was in big demand.

'Don't worry about them, they'll be taken care of.'

He nodded, satisfied with my answer. I slipped an envelope to him and handed him a pen. Stanford signed the typed note inside, barely glancing at it, and put it in his pocket. He breathed deeply and let it out as though a weight he'd carried around for too long had been lifted. His features relaxed and I caught a glimpse of his younger self, perhaps the man he'd wanted to be before money and what it could buy got in the way.

'And Elise will be all right?'

'Like I said, you have my word.'

He scanned the London skyline for the last time in his life. 'You know, I hated your brother. Detested him, actually. Danny Glass was the scum of the earth.' Stanford smiled his smug smile; he wasn't afraid any more. He said, 'But I liked him a lot fucking better than you.'

There's a lot to be said for a bullet in the brain, *even* if you're expecting it.

POSTSCRIPT

The body of Superintendent Oliver Stanford was found on Parliament Hill, Hampstead, four miles from his home, by a woman walking her dog. A note to his family apologising for what he'd done was in his hand. On the witness stand his wife, Elise, disputed her husband would ever take his own life, claiming, without proof, he'd been murdered by criminals from the London underworld. The inquest lasted two days and heard evidence that, in the months before his death, the senior officer had been drinking heavily and was depressed about his approaching retirement.

The coroner returned a verdict of suicide.

* * *

The house on East Heath Road became the centre of a murder hunt following the discovery of former socialite Constance Greyland's corpse in the basement. Ms Greyland was a regular visitor to South Africa and had only recently returned. In a dawn raid on the property in Hampstead following a tip-off, a team of Met officers seized gems believed to be part of a larger haul from a robbery in Poland

Street, Soho, drug paraphernalia, and a quantity of cocaine. Warrants have been issued for Rafe and Henry Purefoy, Charlotte Boothby-Bell, also known as Coco, and the victim's nephew, Julian Greyland.

As yet, the bulk of the stolen stones has not been recovered.

* * *

The Operation Clean Sweep file on the Glass family has been closed but the search for corruption in the Metropolitan Police Service continues.

ACKNOWLEDGMENTS

I always say a book is not the product of just one person. For what you are holding in your hand to exist, a host of people had to add their particular skills and talents to it. They did and I applaud them. The list of contributors is too long to mention everyone by name, but at the top must be the tremendous team that is Boldwood Books: Amanda, Nia, Claire, Megan and, of course, Sarah, who understood what I was trying to do from the start. I am grateful to all of you for your professionalism, your never-flagging belief, and the sheer energy each of you brings to the process. It's a real joy to work with you.

My editors, Sue Smith and David Boxell, deserve a special thanks for making me seem much better than I am. Sometimes when I'm writing I can almost hear you groan as I abuse and misuse the English language in pursuit of giving a character the voice in my head.

And last – why is this woman always last? – my wife, Christine, who puts up with me and carries on dredging one great idea after another from the bottomless well of her immense imagination. I'm a lucky guy.

Owen Mullen
Glasgow, November 2021

MORE FROM OWEN MULLEN

We hope you enjoyed reading *Hustle*. If you did, please leave a review.

If you'd like to gift a copy, this book is also available as an ebook, digital audio download and audiobook CD.

Sign up to Owen Mullen's mailing list for news, competitions, updates and receive an exclusive free short story from Owen Mullen.

https://bit.ly/OwenMullenNewsletter

ALSO BY OWEN MULLEN

ABOUT THE AUTHOR

Owen Mullen is a highly regarded crime author who splits his time between Scotland and the island of Crete. In his earlier life he lived in London and worked as a musician and session singer. He has now written seven books and *Family* was his first gangland thriller for Boldwood.

Follow Owen on social media:

 twitter.com/OwenMullen6

 bookbub.com/authors/owen-mullen

 facebook.com/OwenMullenAuthor

ABOUT BOLDWOOD BOOKS

Boldwood Books is a fiction publishing company seeking out the best stories from around the world.

Find out more at www.boldwoodbooks.com

Sign up to the Book and Tonic newsletter for news, offers and competitions from Boldwood Books!

http://www.bit.ly/bookandtonic

We'd love to hear from you, follow us on social media:

facebook.com/BookandTonic

twitter.com/BoldwoodBooks

instagram.com/BookandTonic

Printed in Great Britain
by Amazon